THE CURATE'S AWAKENING

BETHANY HOUSE PUBLISHERS

Minneapolis, Minnesota 55438

The Novels of George MacDonald Edited for Today's Reader

Edited Title	Original Title

The two-volume story of Malcolm:

| *The Fisherman's Lady* | *Malcolm* |
| *The Marquis' Secret* | *The Marquis of Lossie* |

Companion stories of Gibbie and his friend Donal:

| *The Baronet's Song* | *Sir Gibbie* |
| *The Shepherd's Castle* | *Donal Grant* |

Companion stories of Hugh Sutherland and Robert Falconer:

The Tutor's First Love	*David Elginbrod*
The Musician's Quest	*Robert Falconer*
The Maiden's Bequest	*Alec Forbes of Howglen*

Companion stories of Thomas Wingfold:

The Curate's Awakening	*Thomas Wingfold*
The Lady's Confession	*Paul Faber*
The Baron's Apprenticeship	*There and Back*

Stories that stand alone:

A Daughter's Devotion	*Mary Marston*
The Gentlewoman's Choice	*Weighed and Wanting*
The Highlander's Last Song	*What's Mine's Mine*
The Laird's Inheritance	*Warlock O'Glenwarlock*
The Landlady's Master	*The Elect Lady*
The Minister's Restoration	*Salted with Fire*
The Peasant Girl's Dream	*Heather and Snow*
The Poet's Homecoming	*Home Again*

MacDonald Classics Edited for Young Readers

Wee Sir Gibbie of the Highlands
Alec Forbes and His Friend Annie
At the Back of the North Wind
The Adventures of Ranald Bannerman

———

George MacDonald: Scotland's Beloved Storyteller by Michael Phillips
Discovering the Character of God by George MacDonald
Knowing the Heart of God by George MacDonald
A Time to Grow by George MacDonald
A Time to Harvest by George MacDonald

HAMPSHIRE BOOKS
™

THE CURATE'S AWAKENING

George MacDonald

BETHANY HOUSE PUBLISHERS
MINNEAPOLIS, MINNESOTA 55438

The Curate's Awakening
George Macdonald

Originally published as *Thomas Wingfold, Curate* in 1876 by Hurst
and Blackett Publishers, London.

Library of Congress Catalog Card Number 93–72038

ISBN 0-87123-838-1 (trade paper edition)
ISBN 1-55661-372-5 (Hampshire Books edition)

Copyright © 1985
Michael R. Phillips
All Rights Reserved
Hampshire Books edition published in 1993

Hampshire Books™ is a trademark of Bethany House Publishers

Published by Bethany House Publishers
A Ministry of Bethany Fellowship, Inc.
11300 Hampshire Avenue South
Minneapolis, Minnesota 55438

Printed in the United States of America

Contents

Introduction 7
Map 14
1. The Diners 15
2. A Staggering Question 21
3. The Cousins 27
4. The Curate 38
5. A Most Disturbing Letter 44
6. Polwarth's Plan 49
7. A Strange Sermon 62
8. Leopold 66
9. The Refuge 72
10. Leopold's Story 80
11. Sisterhood 84
12. The Curate Makes a Discovery 88
13. The Ride 94
14. A Dream 99
15. Another Sermon 104
16. The Linendraper 107
17. Rachel and Mr. Drew 114
18. The Sheath 121
19. A Sermon to Helen 125
20. Reactions 130
21. A Meeting 136
22. A Haunted Soul 142
23. In Confidence 150

24. Divine Service 158
25. Polwarth and Lingard 165
26. Wingfold and Helen 171
27. Who Is the Sinner? 179
28. The Confession 184
29. The Curate and the Doctor 191
30. A Visit 200
31. The Lawn 206
32. The Meadow 211
33. The Bloodhound 218
34. The Bedside 228
35. New Friends 235
36. The Curate's Resolve 244
37. Helen Awake 247
38. The Abbey 251

Introduction

George MacDonald (1824–1905) was not the sort of writer who in our generation would be "critically acclaimed" by the secular press or the Pulitzer committee. This is no reflection on his writing but simply on his priorities as an author. He was trying to accomplish something which runs counter to the values of our secular society. His message was essentially a spiritual one, and it is only in that context that he can be understood and his work fully appreciated. In each of his books, different facets of his vision of God's character emerge. Through no single one do we obtain the complete scope of MacDonald's perception of God, yet each contributes to the total picture. In *Thomas Wingfold, Curate*, here *The Curate's Awakening*, MacDonald penned one of his strongest novels from a spiritual vantage point—one which adds a forceful and radiant brushstroke to the image of Christ he sought to present to the world.

George MacDonald often seemed to poke fun at organized religion. Christianity in England and Scotland during the late nineteenth century was, despite pockets of revival and great fervency, locked for the most part into the constricting doctrines of Calvinism carried to the extreme. God's wrath was severe and greatly to be feared, and woe to him who had not been born one of the "chosen elect."

In the midst of this legalism, MacDonald emerged with a warm view of a God of love and compassion. From the pulpit and the printed page, MacDonald proclaimed that God's essence was love.

It was not, according to the outspoken Scotsman, God's will that *any* should perish, that any should be so far removed that He could not reach down and pour His love into him. MacDonald's writings portrayed an entirely contrasting picture of God—a tender and compassionate Father. Much of today's awareness of God's loving fatherhood has sprung from evangelical pioneers like MacDonald—men who dared stand against the tide of the commonly held views of God's character.

People flocked to MacDonald and devoured his writings because of the deeper sense of truth they found in them. However, MacDonald was scorned by official churchdom. He had rebelled against the established order and refused to relax his attacks upon the Phariseeism within the church in which he had been raised and in which he had unsuccessfully sought to become a leader. Trying to influence the system from within, he had been ousted because of his strong views. Thus he took his case directly to the public. And their response to his books affirmed the truths he believed in his heart.

In 1876, at the height of his popularity, MacDonald released a novel which departed from his usual mode. In the story of Thomas Wingfold, MacDonald reveals his true heart toward the church—it was not the *men* themselves in positions of church leadership which he disdained, but rather the narrowness of their mindset. In fact, we observe all the more clearly the great love MacDonald had for the church. For in his new novel MacDonald chose as his principal character a member of the clergy. Thomas was a shallow man with no personal faith, a man who plagiarized his sermons, a man with little personality, unequipped to occupy the pulpit and still less to lead even the humblest of his parishioners.

And yet in spite of all this, Thomas Wingfold quickly endears himself to us, and we immediately sense MacDonald's own love for him. For Wingfold possessed the one quality which MacDonald revered above nearly all others—*openness*. His ears were not plugged with self-satisfaction and tradition but were ready to listen, ready to look for truth outside the usual boundaries, ready to learn from any quarter.

With this openness came an honest heart, one willing to take a thorough look at whatever new presented itself. Might there indeed be truth present? In the character of Wingfold we see a host of qualities which accompany openness—humility, a willingness to admit oneself ignorant, a lack of airs, an absence of defenses. Thomas had no walls standing between his true self and the outside world, no predisposition to argue or justify or defend or show where another was in the wrong. And intrinsic to the open mind and heart, MacDonald clarifies the vital and necessary role of doubt. The open mind, he insists, has the courage to voice uncertainties and to seek logical and reasonable and scriptural answers—answers compatible with God's character. In *The Curate's Awakening* we encounter one of MacDonald's most contemplative, spiritual books which directly confronts the most basic of questions: Is Christianity true? Does it make sense? Are its precepts to be believed? Or is it a hoax?

To MacDonald, the attributes lived out by his title character comprise the essence of spirituality. It is not how much a person knows, but how willing one is to learn; not where one stands, but in which direction he is progressing; not what doubts he harbors, but into what truth such doubts eventually lead; not how spiritual one may appear in men's eyes, but how much truth that one is seeking in the quietness of his own heart. In such views MacDonald's forerunning influence on C. S. Lewis and Francis Schaeffer and other contemporary writers can clearly be seen. For like these men, MacDonald stood strongly for a Christian faith which was reasonable and consistent. He firmly believed in the practice of that faith as the key to substantiating God's existence.

Hence, in Thomas Wingfold we are presented with an unusual MacDonaldian hero—a non-man, a personality totally asleep, but (and most important of all) a man who is willing to listen and whose dormant heart loves the truth. Therefore, when he is confronted by an atheist with the question, "Tell me honestly, do you really believe one word of all that?" (a reference to what he preaches in church from Sunday to Sunday), the curate's complacency is dealt a lethal blow. Thus begins Wingfold's awakening and his moving journey into spiritual vitality.

But this is not the story of merely one waking, but of two. Alongside the story of the curate runs the parallel account of Helen, another personality sound asleep. A shocking catastrophe sud-

denly intrudes into her life, after which she can never be the same
again. Like a splash of icy water in a sleepy face, her brother's
alarming troubles serve to rouse Helen's deeper nature into wake-
fulness, as does unbelieving Bascombe's badgering of Wingfold's
shaky faith. Even Bascombe himself plays a significant role by il-
lustrating graphically the very antithesis of openness. His smug,
unquestioning self-satisfaction is typical of all MacDonald rejected.

Wingfold and Helen as well as fellow pilgrim Mr. Drew are
helped by an unlikely deformed dwarf by the name of Polwarth, a
vintage MacDonald saint who finds very little to feed him in the
local church, but whose heart daily grows more in love with his
Lord by the humble service he renders to those who cross his
path.

However, this is not merely a story about openness and
growth, but about the very nature of the God-man relationship,
the sin that separates man from his Maker, and God's response.
In the story of Thomas Wingfold, we have another example of
MacDonald's confrontation with a knotty issue, one without sim-
plistic answers. In recounting the trials concerning the integrity
of a preacher trying to live truth consistently in his own life, the
hero runs headlong into a dilemma of integrity in another. But the
new difficulty is no "small" sin in the world's eyes, such as reading
someone else's sermons, but it is the very worst of all possible
sins—murder. Suddenly we are face-to-face with the contrast between a horrible sin and a seemingly trifling one. And the question
is: What is to be man's response? And what is God's response?

As we work our way through the drama and the formidable
questions raised, MacDonald's point becomes clear—sin is sin, and
God is sufficient to deliver man from *all* of it—from the tiniest
to the most gruesome. God is the God of all men, and all men are
sinners alike—though the degrees vary tremendously. *The Curate's Awakening* can be viewed as a parable of the heart of man
and God's loving response. No matter how small or how ugly the
sin, God in His compassion seeks our deliverance, healing, and re-
birth. Repentance and recompense are man's response to the conviction of the Holy Spirit, and then God's forgiveness washes clean
the evil heart of man.

It can be easy to discuss spiritual themes in the comfortable surroundings of our "normal" lives. But when murder breaks through the door, are our theories sufficient to the task? Is God's grace big enough to cover even that?

MacDonald here is not offering any commentary on social justice. Many of his contemporaries did that very thing, and through their writings much of the corruption of the nineteenth century was changed. But MacDonald was making no attempt to say what ought to have been the response toward the authorities had Leopold lived a full and normal life. He was offering no solutions on the physical plane, but on the spiritual. He was making the point that, yes, God's love *is* great enough and far-reaching enough to cover all sins and all men who come before Him for forgiveness.

Thomas Wingfold, along with the characters in MacDonald's other books, represents for us another facet of that "ideal" character which can serve as a model as we progress through life's journey. In his portrayals, MacDonald was painting a portrait of Christ—a portion of the Ideal Man here, another quality there. In Gibbie we see the eyes of love, in Robert Falconer the hands of service, in Annie the radiance of humility, in Hugh and Alec the prodigal's search and return, in Malcolm the authority which comes from simplicity. Every character reveals a different stroke of the brush, which all taken together illumine MacDonald's lifetime masterpiece: the portrait of the Christ he loved and served. The story of Thomas Wingfold adds one of the most vital ingredients of all to the sacred image—the picture of the Christlike heart. In Wingfold we are shown the response of the open heart when confronted with truth—however unpleasant that confrontation at first may be. It is a response of openness and humility, which leads to growth and eventual oneness with Christ.

This edition of *Thomas Wingfold, Curate*, retitled *The Curate's Awakening* and edited for the Bethany House series, is the first of a trilogy involving the title character. The different books by George MacDonald which I already have edited form a unity, each contributing, as I have said, its own unique brushstroke to the whole. It is my hope that you will enjoy and be spiritually nurtured not only by this book, but that you will gain truth and gather strength from the whole series, both those which have come before and those which will follow.

11

For years my personal vision has been to work toward a revitalization of interest in MacDonald and a republication of his classics. At this point I would like to publicly express my appreciation to those who have contributed to the renewal of interest in his works. I am particularly grateful to Carol and Gary Johnson of Bethany House who took a chance with this series of edited MacDonald novels at a time when few other publishers had shown any interest in resurrecting the works of this obscure writer of a century past. Since that time the entire Bethany House staff has worked to achieve excellence in this continuing series, both editorially and in terms of design and production, and I thank them all for their diligence. Though MacDonald is now becoming more widely recognized and published, it is Bethany's groundbreaking work which has paved the way. For their courage in making this publishing commitment, all of us who love MacDonald owe them a debt of gratitude. I am so grateful to all these people for their part in making this vision a reality, and to the hundreds of you who have written to both myself and the publisher, confirming that MacDonald's work is indeed of interest and importance in our own day.

Michael Phillips
One Way Book Shop
1707 E Street
Eureka, CA 95501

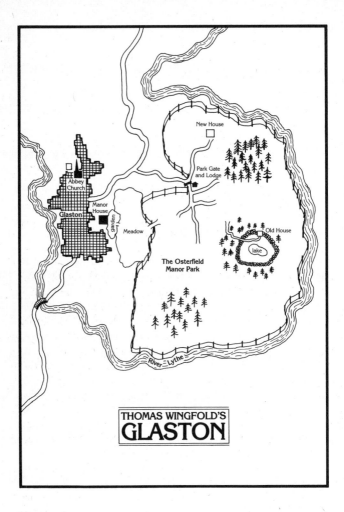

THOMAS WINGFOLD'S
GLASTON

1   The Diners

A swift, gray November wind had taken every chimney of the house for an organ pipe and was roaring in them all at once. Helen Lingard had not ventured out all day. Having spent the morning writing a long letter to her brother Leopold at Cambridge, she had put off her walk in the neighboring park till after lunch. In the meantime, the wind had risen and brought clouds that threatened rain. She was in admirable health and was hardly more afraid of getting wet than a young farmer. Actually, she *enjoyed* the wind, especially when she was on horseback. Yet as she stood looking from her window, she did not feel inclined to go out. The weather always made an impression upon her senses; when the sun shone she felt more lighthearted than when it rained. In consequence, she turned away from the window with the sense that the fireplace in her own room was on this day even more attractive because of the unfriendly look of things outside. Happily, the roar in the chimney was not accompanied by a change in the current of the smoke.

An hour and a half later Helen was still sitting before the fire, gazing into it with something of a blank stare. She had just finished reading a novel and was not altogether satisfied with the ending. The heroine, after much sorrow and patient endurance, had married a man whom she could not help knowing to be unworthy of the choice. Indeed, Helen's dissatisfaction went so far that, although the fire kept burning away in perfect contentment before her, she yet came nearer to truly thinking than she had ever in her life. Now thinking, especially to one who tries it for the first time, is seldom a comfortable operation, and hence Helen was very close to becoming actually uncomfortable. She was on the border of making the unpleasant discovery that the chief business of life is to discover, after which there is little more comfort to enjoy of the sort with which Helen had up to then been familiar.

I do not mean to imply that Helen was dull in her mental capacities, or that she contributed nothing to the bubbling of the intellectual pool in the social gatherings of Glaston—far from it. Helen had supposed she could think because the thoughts of other people had passed through her quite regularly, leaving many a phantom conclusion behind. But this had been *their* thinking, not hers.

The social matrix which up to this time had contributed to her development had some rapport with society, but scanty association indeed with the universe. So her present condition was like that of the common bees: Nature fits everyone for a queen, but its nurses prevent it from growing into one by providing for it a cell too narrow for the unrolling of royalty, and supplying it with food not potent enough for the nurturing of the ideal. As a result, the cramped and stinted thing which comes out is a working bee. And Helen, who might be both, was, as yet, neither. She was the daughter of an army officer who, after his wife died, had committed her to the care of a widowed aunt. He then left almost immediately for India, where he rose to high rank. Somehow or other he amassed a considerable fortune, partly through his marriage with a Hindu lady, by whom he had one child, a boy some three years younger than Helen. When their father died, he left his fortune equally divided between the two children.

Helen was now twenty-three and in charge of herself. Her appearance suggested Norwegian blood, for she was tall, blue-eyed, fair-skinned, and dark-haired. She had long remained a girl, lingering longer than usual on the indistinct borderland between girlhood and womanhood. Her drawing instructor, a man of some insight, used to say that Miss Lingard would "wake up somewhere about forty."

The cause of her so nearly touching the borders of thought this afternoon was that she suddenly became aware of a restless boredom. It could not be the weather, for the weather had never affected her to this extent before. Nor could it be lack of society, for George Bascombe was to dine with them today. So was the curate, but he did not count for much.

Whatever its cause, Helen was dimly aware that to be bored was to be out of harmony with something or other, and was thus almost on the verge of thinking. But she escaped falling directly into it by falling fast asleep instead. In fact, she did not wake until her maid brought her a cup of tea some while before dinner.

———

The morning which had given birth to this stormy afternoon had been a fine one, and the curate had gone out for a walk. Not that he was a great walker; his strolls were leisurely and comprised of many stops. He was not in bad health and was not lazy. Yet he had little impulse for much activity of any sort. The springs in his well of life did not seem to flow quite fast enough.

He sauntered through Osterfield Park and down the descent to the river. There he seated himself upon a large stone on the bank. He knew that he was there and that he answered to "Thomas Wingfold"; but *why* he was there, and why he was not called something else, he did not know. On each side of the stream rose a steeply sloping bank on which grew many fern bushes, now half-withered. The sunlight upon them this November morning seemed as cold as the wind that blew about their golden and green fronds. Over a rocky bottom the stream skipped down the valley toward the town, where it seemed to linger a moment to embrace the old abbey church before setting out on its leisurely slide through the low level to the sea.

Thomas felt cold, but the cold was of the sort that comes from the look rather than the feel of things. With his stick he kept knocking pebbles into the water and listlessly watching them splash. The wind blew, the sun shone, the water ran, the ferns waved, the clouds went drifting over his head—but he never looked up or took any notice of the doings of Mother Nature busy with her housework.

His life had not been particularly interesting, although early times in it had been painful. He had done fairly well at Oxford; it had been expected of him and he had answered expectation. But he had not distinguished himself, nor had he cared to do so. He had known from the first that he was intended for the church, and had not objected but accepted it as his destiny. Yet he had taken no great interest in the matter.

The church was to him an ancient institution of approved respectability. He had entered her service; she was his mistress, and in return for the narrow shelter, humble fare, and not quite shabby garments she allotted him, he would perform her observances. Now twenty-six years of age, he had never dreamed of marriage, nor even been troubled with a thought of its seemingly unattainable remoteness.

Thomas did not philosophize much about life, nor his position in it. Instead, he took everything with an unemotional kind of acceptance and laid no claim to courage or devotion. He had a certain dull prejudice in favor of honesty, would not have told a lie even to be made Archbishop of Canterbury, and yet was completely uninstructed in the things that constitute practical honesty. He liked reading the prayers in church, for he had a somewhat musical voice. He visited the sick—with some repugnance, it is true, but without delay—and spoke to them such religious commonplaces as occurred to him. He never thought about being a gentleman but always behaved like one.

He did not read much, browsing over his newspaper at breakfast with a polite curiosity sufficient to season the loneliness of his slice of fried bacon, taking more interest in some of the naval intelligence than in anything else. Indeed, it would have been difficult to say in what he did take much interest. Occasionally he would read the poets, but paid more attention to the rhythm than the meaning.

After a few more splashing stones, Wingfold rose and climbed the bank away from the river, wading through mingled sun and wind and ferns, careless of their shivering beauty and heedless of the world's preparation for winter.

Mrs. Ramshorn, Helen's aunt, was past the middle age of woman. She had once been beautiful and pleasing, but had long since ceased to be either. Only now had she begun, but sparingly, to recognize the fact, and thus felt aggrieved. Hence her mouth had gathered a certain peevish look about it from her discontent, making her more unattractive than the severest operation of the laws of mortal decay could ever have done. As it was, her face wronged her heart, which was still womanly and capable of much emotion—though seldom exercised. Her husband had been Dean of Halystone, and a man of sufficient weight of character to have the right influence in the formation of his wife's. He had left her tolerably well off, but childless. She loved Helen, whose even-tempered serenity had gained such a power over her that Helen was really mistress in the house with neither of them knowing it.

Naturally desirous of keeping Helen's fortune in the family, Mrs. Ramshorn did not have far to look to find a cousin capable of making himself acceptable to the heiress. He was the son of her younger sister who was married, like herself, to a dignitary of the church. This youth, George Bascombe by name, whose visible calling at present was to eat his way to the bar, Helen's aunt often invited to Glaston. And on this particular Friday afternoon, he was on his way from London to spend Saturday and Sunday with the two ladies.

The cousins liked each other, had not enjoyed more of each other's society than was favorable to their aunt's designs, and stood in as suitable a position for falling in love with each other as Mrs. Ramshorn could well have desired. Her chief uneasiness arose from the all-too-evident fact that Helen Lingard was not a girl of the sort to fall readily in love. But that was of little consequence, provided it did not come in the way of her marrying her cousin. Her aunt felt confident he was better fitted to rouse Helen's dormant affections than any other youth she had ever met.

Upon this occasion she had asked Thomas Wingfold to dinner as well with two purposes behind the invitation. By contrast, she hoped he would show off her nephew's advantage in Helen's eyes. She also desired to do her duty to the church, to which she felt herself a member in some undefined professional capacity by virtue of her departed husband, the dean. Wingfold was new to the parish. As he was merely the curate, she had not been in any hurry to invite him. On the other hand, due to the absence of the miserable nonresident rector, Wingfold was the only clergyman officiating in the grand old abbey church.*

The curate presented himself at the dinner hour in Mrs. Ramshorn's drawing room, looking like any other gentleman, reflecting nothing of the professional either in dress, manner, or tone. Helen was seeing him for the first time away from the pulpit and, as she had expected, saw nothing remarkable. He looked about thirty, was a little above average in height, and was well enough constructed as men go. He could just as well have been a lawyer as a clergyman. But Helen's eyes seldom did more than slip over the faces presented to her. Besides, who could be expected to pay much regard to Thomas Wingfold when George Bascombe was present?

There, by the mantel, stood a man indeed! Tall and handsome and strong, dressed in the latest fashion, self-satisfied but not offensive, good-natured, ready to smile, clean in conscience. Everyone who knew George Bascombe counted him a genuine good fellow. George himself knew little to the contrary, while Helen knew nothing.

While in her own room Helen seemed somewhat dull and inanimate; but in the drawing room living eyes and presences served to stir up what waking life *was* in her. When she spoke, her face dawned with a clear, although not warm light, and her smiles were genuine. Although there was much that was stiff, there was nothing artificial about Helen. Neither was there much of the artificial about her cousin; his good nature and his smile, and whatever else appeared upon him, were all genuine enough. The only thing not

---

*Smaller parishes unable to maintain a full-time *vicar*, or priest, were presided over by a *curate*—a clergyman who was appointed to preach and perform the duties and services of the priest but who did not hold that office himself. The *rector* held responsibility for overseeing the business of the parish on behalf of the Church of England.

quite satisfactory about him was his manufactured, well-bred, dignified tone of speaking.

Beside Bascombe's authoritative voice, his easy posture, his broad chest, and his towering height, Thomas Wingfold dwindled away and looked almost a nobody. And besides his inferiority in size and self-presentment, he had a slight hesitation of manner which seemed to anticipate, if not to court, the subordinate position which most men—and most women too—were ready to assign him. He said, "Don't you think?" far oftener than "I think." He was always ready to fix his attention upon the strong points of an opponent's argument rather than reassert his own in slightly altered phrase. Hence—self-assertion being the strength of the ordinary man—how could the curate appear any other than defenseless and, therefore, weak?

Bascombe and Wingfold bowed in response to their introduction with proper indifference. After a moment's solemn pause, they exchanged a sentence or two which resembled an exercise in the proper use of a foreign language. Then they gave what attention Englishmen are capable of before dinner to the two ladies.

At length the butler appeared. The curate escorted Mrs. Ramshorn, and the cousins followed—making, in the judgment of the butler as he stood in the hall and the housekeeper as she peered from the door that led to the stillroom, as handsome a couple as mortal eyes need wish to see. They looked nearly of the same age, the lady the more stately, the gentleman the more elegant of the two.

2   A Staggering Question

During dinner Bascombe had the talk mostly to himself and rattled on well. Occasionally his aunt chided him for some remark which might appear objectionable to a clergyman. After dinner the men withdrew, but little passed between them over their wine. As neither of them cared for more than a couple of glasses, they soon rejoined the ladies in the drawing room.

Mrs. Ramshorn was taking her usual forty winks in her arm-chair and their entrance did not disturb her. Helen was looking over some music; presently she sat down at the piano. Her timing was perfect and she never blundered a note. She played well but woodenly. The music she chose was good of its kind, but this had more to do with the instrument than feelings and was more dependent upon execution than expression. Bascombe yawned behind his handkerchief, and Wingfold gazed at the profile of the player. *With such fine features and complexion, how can her face be so far short of interesting?* he wondered. It seemed to be a face that held no story.

The time came for the curate to take his leave, and Bascombe stepped outside with him to have a last cigar. The wind had fallen and the moon was shining. As Wingfold stepped onto the pavement from the threshold of the wrought-iron gates, he turned and looked back at the house. It stood firmly in its red brick facade, and aloft over its ridge a pale moon floated in the softest, loveliest blue, with just a cloud here and there to accent how blue it was. At the end of the street rose the great square tower of the church, looming larger than in the daylight. There was something in it all that made the curate feel there ought to be more—as if the night knew something he did not.

His companion carefully lighted his cigar, took it from his mouth, regarding its glowing end with a smile of satisfaction, and burst into a laugh. It was not a scornful laugh, neither was it a merry or humorous laugh. It reflected satisfaction and amusement.

"Let me have a share in the fun," requested the curate.

"You do have it," replied his companion—rudely, indeed, but not quite offensively, and put his cigar in his mouth again.

Wingfold was not one to take offense easily. He was not important enough in his own eyes for that, and he decided to let the matter drop.

"It's a fine old church," he remarked, pointing to the dark mass invading the blue—so solid, yet so clear in outline.

"I'm glad the masonry is to your liking," returned Bascombe.

"It must be some satisfaction, perhaps consolation, to you," a little scorn creeping into his tone.

"You make some allusion which I do not quite understand," returned the curate.

"Now, I am going to be honest with you," replied Bascombe abruptly, taking the cigar from his mouth. He stopped and turned toward his companion. "I like you," Bascombe went on, "for you seem reasonable. And besides, a man ought to speak out what he thinks. So here goes! Tell me honestly, do you really believe one word of all that?"

And as he spoke he pointed in the direction of the great tower.

The curate was taken by surprise and made no answer. It was as if he had received a sudden blow in the face. Recovering himself presently, however, he sought room to pass the question without direct encounter.

"How did the thing come to be there?" Wingfold countered pointing to the church tower.

"By faith, no doubt," answered Bascombe, laughing, "—but not *your* faith. No, nor the faith of any of the last few generations."

"How can you say there is no faith in these recent generations? There are more churches built now, ten times over, than in any former period of our history," protested Thomas.

"*Churches*, yes," replied Bascombe. "But *faith*—I'm not so sure. Just because there's a church standing somewhere doesn't necessarily mean there's faith inside its walls. And what sort of churches are they you refer to? All imitations. You are indebted to your forefathers for your would-be belief, as well as for whatever may be genuine in your churches. You hardly know what your belief is. Take my aunt—as good a specimen as I know of what you call a Christian! Yet she thinks and speaks no differently than those you would refer to as heathens."

"Pardon me, but I think you are wrong there."

"What! Did you never notice how these Christian people, who profess to believe that their great man has conquered death, and all that rubbish—did you never observe the way they talk about death, or the eternity they say they expect beyond it? They talk about it in the abstract at one moment, but when it comes down to real life, in their hearts they have no hope, and in their minds they have no courage to face the facts of existence. They haven't the pluck of the old fellows who looked death right in the face without dismay. You see, their so-called religion does them no good. They don't really believe everything they say, or what they hear from the pulpit. They fill up the churches every Sunday, but as I said before, there's no faith."

"But your aunt would never consent to such an interpretation of her opinions. Nor do I allow that it is fair."

"My dear sir, if there is one thing I pride myself upon, it is fair play, and I agree with you there at once—she certainly would not. But I am speaking not of creeds, but of beliefs. And I assert that the form of Christianity commonly practiced, not only by my aunt but by most of the rest of your congregation, comes nearer the views of the heathen poet Horace than those of your saint, the old Jew, Saul of Tarsus."

It did not occur to Wingfold that possibly Mrs. Ramshorn was not the best personification of the ideal Christian, even in his noncommittal congregation. In fact, nothing came into his mind with which to counter what Bascombe had said—the real force of which he could not help feeling. His companion followed his apparent yielding with renewed pressure.

"In truth," he continued, "I do not believe that even *you* believe more than an atom here and there of what you profess. I am confident you have a great deal more good sense than to believe it."

"I am sorry to find that you place good sense above good faith, Mr. Bascombe. I thank you for your good opinion, which, if I read it correctly, must amount to this—that I am one of the greatest humbugs you have had the misfortune to be acquainted with."

"Ha! ha! ha! No, no—I don't say that. I can make allowance for prejudices a man has inherited from foolish ancestors and which have been instilled into him his whole life long. But, come now—did you not come to the church and become a clergyman merely as a profession, as a means to earn your bread?"

Wingfold did not answer. This was precisely the reason he had signed the articles and sought holy orders. He had never entertained a single question as to the truth or reality in either act.

"Your silence reveals honesty, Mr. Wingfold, and I honor you for it," said Bascombe. "It is an easy thing for a man in another profession to speak his mind, but silence such as yours, casting a shadow backward over your past, requires courage." As he spoke, he laid his hand on Wingfold's shoulder with the grasp of an athlete.

"I must not allow you to mistake my silence, Mr. Bascombe," Thomas answered. "It is not easy to reply to such questions all at once. It is not easy to say in times like these, and at a moment's notice, what or how much a man believes. But whatever my answer might be had I time to consider it, my silence must not be interpreted to mean that I do *not* believe as my profession indicates."

"Then am I to understand, Mr. Wingfold, that you neither believe nor disbelieve the tenets of the church whose bread you eat?" asked Bascombe, with the shocked air of a reprover of sin.

"I decline to place myself between the horns of any such dilemma," returned Wingfold, who was gradually becoming more than a little annoyed at Bascombe's persistence.

"It is but one more proof to convince me that the whole Christian system is a lie—a lie of the worst sort, seeing it even can lead an otherwise honest and direct man into self-deception. Goodnight, Mr. Wingfold," he concluded with a superior tone.

With lifted hats, but no handshaking, the men parted.

While Bascombe sauntered back to his aunt's with his cigar, Wingfold walked slowly away, his eyes on the ground as it glided from under his footsteps. It was only nine o'clock, but this the oldest part of the town seemed already asleep. Wingfold had not met a single person on his way and hardly had seen a lighted window. But he was unwilling to go home. At first he attributed this strange inner restlessness to his having drunk a little more wine than was appropriate for him. In the churchyard, on the other side of which lay his home, he turned from the flagstone walk into the graveyard, where he sat down upon a gravestone. He was hardly seated before he began to discover that something other than the wine had made him feel so uncomfortable.

What an objectionable young fellow that Bascombe is!—presuming and arrogant. His good-natured satisfaction with himself made it all the worse. And yet—and yet, Thomas' thoughts churned on, *is there not something in what he said?* Whatever Bascombe's character, it remained undeniable that when the very existence of the church was denounced as humbug, he himself had been unable to speak a word in her behalf!

Something must be wrong somewhere. Was it in him or in the church?

Whether in her or not, certainly there was something wrong in him. Had he not been unable to utter the simple assertion that he did in fact believe the things which, as the mouthpiece of the church, he had been speaking in the name of truth every Sunday—and would again speak the day after tomorrow?

Why could he not say he believed them? He had never consciously questioned them before. He did not question them now. And yet when a forward, overbearing young infidel of a lawyer put it to him as if he were on the witness stand, a strange obstruction rose in his throat, making him incapable of speaking out like a man.

Wingfold found himself filled with contempt, but the next moment was not sure whether this Bascombe or one Wingfold were the more legitimate object of it. One thing was undeniable—his friends *had* put him into the priest's office, and he had yielded simply as a means to earn a living. He had no love for it except occasionally when the beauty of an anthem awoke a faint admiration within him. Indeed, had he not sometimes despised himself for earning his bread by work which any pious old woman could do better than he? True, he attended faithfully to his duties. All the same, it remained a fact that if barrister Bascombe were to stand up and assert before the entire congregation that there was no God anywhere in the universe, the Rev. Thomas Wingfold could not prove to anybody that there was. Indeed, so certain would he be of discomfort that he would not even dare advance a single argument on his side of the question.

Was it even *his* side of the question? Could he in all honesty say he believed there was a God? Or was this not all he really knew—that there was a Church of England which paid him for reading public prayers to a God in whom the congregation was assumed to believe?

These were not pleasant reflections, especially with Sunday drawing near. There were hundreds, even thousands of books which could triumphantly settle every question his poor brain might suggest, but what could that matter? How could he possibly begin appropriating the contents of those thousands of volumes in order to convince himself, for bare honesty's sake, while all the time Sunday came in upon Sunday like waves on a shore? On each one he must stand up and preach that which he did not now know if he truly believed. Sunday after Sunday of dishonesty and sham. To begin now, and under such circumstances, to study the evidences of Christianity was about as reasonable as sending a man whose children were crying for their dinner off to China to make his fortune!

He laughed the idea to scorn, and discovered that a gravestone in a November midnight was a cold chair for study. So he rose, stretched himself disconsolately, looked again at the dark outline of the church, then turned and walked away. At the farther gate he glanced back again and gazed one more moment at the tower. Toward the sky it towered, and led his gaze upward. The quiet night was still there, with its delicate heaps of cloud, its cool-glowing moon, its steely stars, and something he did not understand. He went home a little quieter of heart, as if he had heard from afar something sweet and strange.

3   The Cousins

It is often very hard for a tolerably honest man, as we have just seen in the case of Wingfold, to express what he believes. And it ought to be yet harder to say what another man does not believe. And in that George Bascombe was something of a peculiar man. Therefore, I shall presume no further concerning him than to say that the thing he *seemed* most to believe was that it was his mission to destroy the beliefs of everybody else.

Where this mission had come from he would not have thought a reasonable question. Perhaps it had come from his lawyer's training to pick apart the opinions of others. He would have answered that if any man knew any truth or understood any truth or could present any truth more clearly than another, then that truth was open to debate and must be defended by the one claiming to understand it. But the question never occurred to him whether his own presumed commission was verily truth or not. And it must be admitted that a good deal turns upon that.

According to some men who thought they knew him, Bascombe was rather careless of the distinction between a fact, or law, and truth. They said he attacked the beliefs of other people without ever having seen more than a distorted shadow of those beliefs—some of them he was not capable of seeing, they said—only capable of denying. Now while he would have been perfectly justified, they said, in asserting that he saw no truth in the things he denied, was he justified in concluding that his not seeing a thing was proof of its nonexistence? Was he justified in denouncing every man who said he believed something which Bascombe did not believe? But he himself never bothered with such questions; there was sham in the world and his duty was to expose it.

It may seem strange that the son of a clergyman, which Bascombe was, should take such a part in the world's affairs, especially against the views of the church in which he had been raised. But one who observes will quickly discover that, at college at least, clergymen's sons little reflect the behavior prescribed by the doctrines their fathers teach. The cause of this is matter for the consideration of those fathers.

Bascombe had persuaded himself, and without much difficulty, that he was one of the prophets of a new order of things. At Cambridge he had been lauded by a few as a mighty foe to imposters and humbug—and in some true measure he deserved the praise. Since then he had found a larger circle, including a few of London's editorial offices. But all I have to do with now is the fact that he had grown desirous to add his cousin, Helen Lingard, to the number of those who believed in him, and over whom, therefore, he exercised a prophet's influence—though he would not have appreciated the religious connotation of that description.

No doubt, the fact that the hunt was on the home grounds of such a proprietress as Helen—a beautiful, gifted, and ladylike young woman—added much to the attractiveness of the intellectual game. To do Bascombe justice, that she was an heiress had very little weight in the matter. If he had ever thought of marrying her, that thought was not consciously present when he first wished to convert her to his views of life. But although he was not in love with her, he admired her and believed he saw in her one resembling himself.

As to Helen, some of my readers may find it difficult to believe that she could have come to her years without giving serious thought to any questions or aspirations, or without forming any definite opinions that could rightly be called her own. She had always had good health and her intellectual faculties had been well trained. She had studied music thoroughly and was quite talented. She could draw in pen and ink with great perspective. She was at home in mathematics and literature. Ten thousand things she knew without wondering at one of them. Any attempt to rouse her admiration she invariably received with quiet intelligence but no response. Yet her drawing master was convinced there lay a large soul asleep somewhere below the calm gray morning of that wideawake yet reposeful intelligence. As for any influence from the direction of religion, a contented soul may glide through all his life long, unstruck to the last, buoyant and evasive as a bee in a hailstorm. And now her cousin, unsolicited, was about to assume, if she should permit him, the unspiritual direction of her being, so that she need never be troubled by the quarter of the unknown.

Mrs. Ramshorn's house had formerly been the manor house. Although it now stood in an old street, with only a few yards of ground between it and the road, it had a large and ancient garden behind it. A large garden of any sort is valuable, but an ancient garden is invaluable, and this one retained a very antique loveliness. The quaint memorials of its history lived on into the new, changed, and unsympathetic time, and stood aged, modest, and unabashed. Its preservation was owing merely to the fact that their gardener was blessed with a wholesome stupidity incapable of unlearning what his father, who had been gardener there before him, had had marvelous difficulty teaching him. We do not half appreciate the benefits to the race that spring from honest dullness. The clever people are often the ruin of everything.

Into this garden Bascombe walked the next morning after breakfast. Helen saw him from her balcony, also the roof of the veranda, where she was trimming the few remaining chrysanthemums that stood outside the window of her room. She ran down the little wooden stair that led into the garden. Nothing at that moment could have been more to his mind.

"Have a cigar, Helen?" George offered.

"No, thank you," she answered.

"I don't see why ladies shouldn't enjoy strong things as well as men."

"You can't enjoy everything—I mean one can't have the strong and the delicate both at once. I doubt you could have the same pleasure in smelling a rose that I have."

"Isn't it a pity we can never compare sensations?"

"I don't think it matters much," answered Helen. "We would have to keep our own in the end."

"That's good, Helen! If a man ever tries to humbug you, he will find himself wholly unable. If only there were enough like you left in this miserable old hulk of a creation!"

It was odd how Bascombe would frequently speak of the cosmos as a *creation*, though he would heartily disavow any assent to the notions of a *creator*. He was unaware himself of this curious fact.

"You seem to have a standing quarrel with the creation, George. Yet you have little ground for complaining of your lot in it," remarked Helen.

"Well, you know, I don't complain for myself. I don't pretend to think I have been ill-used. But I am not everybody. And there are so many born fools in it."

"If they are born fools, they can't help it."

"That may be. Only it makes it none the more pleasant for other people. But unfortunately, they are not the worst sort of fools. For one born fool there are a thousand who choose to be so. For one man who will honestly face an honest argument, there are ten thousand who will dishonestly shirk it. There's that curate fellow, for example—Wingfold I think Aunt called him—take him, now!"

"I can't see much in him to rouse indignation," returned Helen. "He seems to be a very inoffensive man."

"I don't call it inoffensive when a man sells himself to the keeping up of a system that—"

Bascombe checked himself, remembering that a sudden attack upon a time-honored system might rouse a woman's prejudices. Helen had already listened to a large amount of his undermining remarks without perceiving the direction of his tunnels. Bascombe had had prior experiences as the prophet-pioneer of glad tidings to the nations, and had seen others whom he regarded as promising pupils turn away in a storm of disgust. He did not want to make the same mistake by going too far too soon with Helen.

Leaving the general line of attack he had begun to make, George turned instead toward a particular doctrine, hoping to subtly sway Helen toward his views. "What a folly it is," he resumed, "to try to make people good by promises and threats—promises of a heaven that would bore the dullest among them, and threats of a hell which would be enough to paralyze every nerve of action in the human system."

"All nations have believed in a future state, either of reward or punishment," objected Helen.

"Mere ghosts of their own approval or disapproval of themselves. And where has it brought the race?"

"What then would you substitute for it, George?"

"Why substitute anything? Shouldn't men be good to one another simply because we are all made up of each other? Do you and I need threats and promises to make us kind? And what right have we to judge others worse than ourselves?" He blew out a huge mouthful of smoke and then swelled his big chest with a huge lungful of air.

Tall, stately, comfortable Helen walked on composedly at his side, thinking what a splendid lawyer her cousin would make. Perhaps to her his views sounded more refined than they were, for the tone of unselfishness and the aroma of self-devotion floating about his words pleased and attracted her. Here was a youth in the prime of being and the dawn of success, handsome, and smoking the oldest of Havanas, who was concerned about the welfare of less-favored mortals. And how fine he looked as he spoke, his head so erect.

To a Darwin reader, they must have looked like a fine instance of natural selection as they walked among the ancient cedars and clipped yews of the garden. And now in truth for the first time did the thought of Helen as a wife occur to Bascombe. She listened so well, was so ready to take what he presented to her, and was evidently so willing to become a pupil, that he began to say to himself that here was the very woman made for him. No, not made, for that implied a maker. But the very woman for him at least. That is, if ever he should bring himself to limit his freedom by marriage—the freedom to which man, the blossom of an accidentally evolving nature, was either predestined or doomed, without will in himself or beyond himself, from an eternity of unthinking matter, ever producing what was better than itself, in the prolific darkness of non-intent.

At the end of Mrs. Ramshorn's garden was a deep sunk fence and on the other side, a large meadow—a fragment of what had once been the manor park. In the sunk fence was a door with a little tunnel by which they could pass from the garden under the high dyke of earth into the meadow. On the other side of the meadow, surrounded by another fence with a small door in it, was the park. The day being wonderfully fine, Bascombe proposed to his cousin a walk in the park. They fetched both keys from the house, and in a few minutes had gone through the tunnel, walked across the meadow, through the gate, and thus into the park. The ground was dry, the air was still. Although the woods were very silent and looked mournfully bare, the grass grew nearer to the roots of the trees, and the sunshine filled them with streaks of gold, blending in a lovely way with the bright green of the moss that patched the older stems. Neither horses nor dogs say to themselves, I suppose, that the sunshine makes them glad, yet both are happier on a bright day according to the rules of their existence. Neither Helen nor George could have understood a poem of Keats or Wordsworth, and yet the soul of nature did not fail to have an influence on them.

"I wonder what the birds do with themselves all the winter," murmured Helen.

"Eat berries and make the best of it," answered George.

"I mean what becomes of them all? We see so few of them."

"About as many as you see in summer. Because you hear them you imagine you see them."

"But there is so little to hide them in winter. They must have a hard time of it in the frost and snow."

"Oh, I don't know," returned George. "They enjoy life on the whole, I believe. It's not such a bad sort of world. Nature is cruel enough in some of her arrangements though. She has no scruples in carrying out her plans. It is nothing to her to sacrifice millions of tiny fish for the life of one great monster. But still, barring her own necessities and the consequences of man's foolhardiness, she is on the whole rather a good-natured old woman and scatters a tolerable amount of enjoyment around her."

"One would think the birds must be happy in summer at least, to hear them sing," agreed Helen.

"Providing a cat or a hawk doesn't get them. That's the sort of thing nature doesn't trouble herself with. Well, it's soon over— with all of us, and that's a comfort. If men would only get rid of their notions that all their suffering comes from the will of a ma-levolent power! That is the kind of thing that makes the misery of the world!"

"I don't quite see—" began Helen.

"We were talking about the birds in winter," interrupted George, careful not to swell too suddenly any of the air bags on which he would float Helen's belief. He knew wisely how to leave a hint to work in her subconscious while it was yet not half un-derstood. By the time it was understood it would have grown a little familiar. The supposed kitten when it turned out to be a cub would not be so terrible as if it had presented itself at once as a baby lion.

And so they wandered across the park, talking easily.

"They've got on a good way since I was here last," said George, as they came within sight of the new house the earl was building. "But they don't seem much in a hurry with it."

"Aunt says it is twenty years since the uncle of the present earl laid the foundations," said Helen, "and then for some reason or other the thing was dropped."

"Was there no house on the place before?"

"Oh yes—not much of a house though."

"And they pulled it down, I suppose."

"No, it still stands there."

"Where?"

"Down in the hollow there—over those trees. Surely you have seen it! Poldie and I used to run all over it."

"No, I never saw it. Was it empty then?"

GEORGE MACDONALD

"Yes, or almost. I can remember some little attention being
paid to the garden, but none to the house. It is just slowly falling
to pieces. Would you like to see it?"

"That I should," Bascombe assured her.

In the hollow all the water of the park gathered into a lake
before finding its way to the river Lythe. This lake lay at the bottom of the old garden and the house at the top of it. The garden
was walled on the two sides, the walls running right down to the
lake. There were wonderful legends among the children of Glaston
concerning that lake, its depth, and the creatures in it. One terrible
story had inspired a ballad told about a lady drowned in a sack,
whose ghost might still be seen when the moon was old, haunting
the gardens and the house. Hence it was that no children generally
went near it, except those few whose appetites for adventure now
and then grew keen enough to prevent their imaginations from
rousing more fear than supplied the proper relish of danger. The
house itself even those bravest of children never dared to enter.

Not so had it been when Helen and Leopold were growing up.
When her brother had come visiting during the holidays, the place
was one of their favorite haunts, and they knew every cubic yard
in the house.

"Here," said Helen to her cousin as she opened a door in a
little closet. Inside was a dusky room which had only one small
window high up in the wall of a back staircase. "Here is one room
I could never get Poldie in without the greatest trouble. I finally
gave it up. He was always too scared to go in. I will show you such
a curious place at the other end of it."

She led the way to a closet similar to that by which they had
entered, and directed Bascombe to raise a trapdoor which filled
the whole floor of the closet, so that it did not show. Under the
floor was a sort of well, big enough to hold three in an emergency.

"If only you could breathe in there," said George. "It looks ugly.
If it but had a tongue, what tales that place could tell."

"Come," beckoned Helen. "I don't know why it is, but now I
don't like the look of it myself. Let's get back out into the open
air again."

Ascending from the hollow and passing through a deep belt of
trees that surrounded it, they came again to the open park. By and
by they reached the road that led from the lodge to the new build-

34

ing. As they walked along this road, they presently encountered a strange couple.

The moment they had passed, George turned to his cousin with a look of moral indignation mingled with disgust. The healthy instincts of the elect of his race were offended by the sight of such physical failures, such mockeries of humanity as those.

The woman was about four feet in height. She was deformed with one high shoulder, and walked with a severe limp, one leg being shorter than the other. Her companion walked quite straight, with a certain appearance of dignity which he neither assumed nor could have avoided, giving his gait the air of a march. He was not an inch taller than the woman, had broad, square shoulders, pigeon breast, and an invisible neck. He was twice her age, and they seemed father and daughter. George and Helen heard his breathing, loud with asthma, as they went by.

"Poor things!" Helen remarked with cold kindness.

"It is shameful!" George exploded in a tone of righteous anger. "Such creatures have no right to existence."

"But, George, the poor wretch can't help his deformity."

"No; but what right had he to marry and perpetuate such odious misery?"

"You are too hasty. The young woman is his niece."

"She ought to have been strangled the moment she was born—for the sake of *humanity*."

"Unfortunately they have all got mothers," said Helen, and something in her face made him fear he had gone too far.

"Don't mistake me, dear Helen," he assured her. "I would neither starve nor drown them after they had reached the age of being able to resent such treatment." He added, smiling, "I am afraid it would be hard to convince them of the justice of such action then. But such people actually marry. I have *known* cases. And that ought to be provided against by suitable laws and penalties."

"And so," rejoined Helen, "because they are unhappy already, you would heap further unhappiness upon them?"

"Now, Helen, you must not be unfair to me any more than to your dwarf hunchbacks. It is the good of the many I seek, and surely that is better than the good of the few."

"What I object to is that it should be at the expense of the few who are least able to bear it."

"The expense is trifling," said Bascombe. "Besides, we both agree it would be better for society that no such persons—or rather put it this way: that it would be well for each individual who makes up society that he were neither deformed, sickly, nor idiotic. A given space of territory under given conditions will maintain a certain number of human beings. Therefore, such a law as I propose would not mean, to take the instance before us as an illustration, that the number drawing the breath of heaven would be two less. It would merely mean that a certain two of them in that space of territory would not be as those who passed us now, creatures whose existence is a burden to themselves, but rather such as you and I, Helen, who are no disgrace to Nature's handicraft."

Helen was not particularly sensitive. His tenets, thus expounded, had nothing very repulsive in them so far as she saw, and she made no further objection.

As they walked into the garden again, through the many lingering signs of a more stately if less luxurious existence than their own generation, she calmly listened to his lecture. They seated themselves in the summerhouse—a little wooden room under the boughs of a huge cedar—and continued their conversation, or rather Bascombe pursued his monologue. A lively girl would in all probability have been bored to death by him, but Helen was not a lively girl, and was not bored at all. Before they finally went into the house she had heard, among a hundred other things of wisdom, his views of crime and punishment with which I shall not trouble my reader.

It was altogether a distinguished sort of discussion between two such perfect specimens of the race, and as at length they entered the house, they professed to each other to have much enjoyed their walk.

Holding the opinions he did, Bascombe was in one thing inconsistent: he went to church on Sunday with his aunt and cousin. He attended not to humor Helen's prejudices but those of Mrs. Ramshorn, for she had strong opinions as to the wickedness of not going to church. It was of no use, he admitted to himself, trying to upset her ideas. Even if he succeeded he would only make her miserable, and his design was to make the race happy. Therefore, in the grand old abbey, they together heard the morning prayers, the Litany, and the Communion according to weariful custom, followed by a dull, sensible sermon, short and tolerably well read, on the duty of forgiveness.

I dare say it did most of the people present a little good. I trust that on the whole their church-going tended to make them better rather than to harden them. But as to the main point of church, the stirring up of the children of the Highest to lay hold of the skirts of their Father's robe, the waking of the individual conscience to say *I will arise*, and the strengthening of the captive will to break its bonds and stand free in the name of the eternal creating Freedom—for that there was no special provision.

On the way home Bascombe made some objections to the discourse, partly to show his aunt that he had been paying attention. He admitted that one might forgive and forget individual grievances. But when it came within the scope of the law, a man was bound, he affirmed, to punish the wrong which may affect the community.

"George, I differ from you there," objected his aunt. "Nobody ought to go to law to punish an injury. I would forgive ever so many before I would run the risk of the law. But as to *forgetting* an injury—some injuries at least—no, that I never would!—And I don't believe, let the young curate say what he will, that *that* is required of anyone."

Helen said nothing. She had no enemies to forgive, no wrongs worth remembering, and was not particularly interested in the question. She thought it a very good sermon indeed.

When Bascombe left for London in the morning, he carried with him the lingering rustle of silk, the odor of lavender, and a certain blueness, not of the sky, which seemed to suggest something behind it, for the sky was empty to him. He had never met a woman so worthy of being his mate, either as regarded the perfection of her form or the hidden development of her brain—evident in her capacity for reception of truth as he saw it—as his own cousin, Helen Lingard.

Helen thought nothing correspondingly in the opposite direction. She considered George a fine, manly fellow with bold and original ideas about everything. She liked her cousin, was attached to her aunt, but loved only her brother Leopold and nobody else.

They wrote to each other often, but lately his letters had grown infrequent, and a rumor had reached her that he was not doing quite satisfactorily at Cambridge. She explained it away to the full contentment of her own heart, and went on building such castles as her poor imaginative skill could command.

4 The Curate

If we could understand the feelings of a fish of the northern ocean suddenly transplanted to tropical waters swarming with terrifying and threatening forms of life, we would have a fair idea of the mental condition in which Thomas Wingfold now found himself. The spiritual sea in which his being floated had become all at once uncomfortable. A certain intermittent stinging, as if from the flashes of some moral electricity, had begun to pass in various directions through that previously undisturbed mass he called himself, and he felt strangely restless. It never occurred to him—how should it?—that he might have begun undergoing the most marvelous of all possible changes. For a man to see its result ahead of time or understand what he was passing through would be more strange than if a caterpillar should recognize in the rainbow-winged butterfly hovering over the flower at whose leaf he was gnawing, the perfected idea of his own potential self. For it was the change of being born again.

A restless night had followed his reflections in the churchyard, and he had not awakened at all comfortable. Not that he had ever been in the habit of feeling comfortable. To him life had not been a land flowing with milk and honey. He had experienced few smiles and not many of those grasps of the hand which let a man know another man is near him in the battle—for had it not been something of a battle? He would not have piously said, "All these commandments I have kept from my youth up," but I can say that for several of them he had shown fight, although only One knew anything of it.

This morning, then, it was not merely that he did not feel comfortable: he was consciously uncomfortable. Things were getting too hot for him. That infidel fellow had poked several awkward questions at him—yes, into him—and a good many more had arisen from within himself to meet them. Usually he lay in bed a little while before he came fully to himself. But this morning he came face-to-face with himself all at once, and not liking the interview, jumped out of bed as if he had hoped to leave himself there behind him.

He had always scorned lying. However, one day, when still a boy at school, he suddenly found that he had told a lie, after which he hated it, and continued to hate it all the more. Yet now, if he were to believe Bascombe, and even his own conscience by now, was not his very life a lie? the very bread he ate grown on the fields of falsehood?

No, no—it could not be! What had he done to find himself damned to such a depth?

The thing must be looked to.

He bathed himself without even shivering, though the water in his tub was bitterly cold, then dressed with more haste than precision. He hurried over his breakfast, neglected his newspaper, and took down a volume of early church history. But he could not read it. The thing was utterly hopeless! The wolves of doubt and the jackals of shame howled at his heels. He must find some evidence with which to turn and face them. Yet whatever was to be found historically, one man received while another refused. What was popularly accepted could just as well prove Mohammedanism as Christianity.

And then Sunday loomed on the horizon as an awful specter. He did not so much mind reading the prayers: he was not accountable for what was in them. Happy thing he was not a dissenter; then he would have had to pretend to pray from his own soul which at this moment was too horrible to even contemplate. But there was the sermon to contend with! That at least was supposed to contain his own ideas and convictions. But now what were his convictions? For the life of him he could not tell. Did he even have any? Did he have any opinions, any beliefs, any unbeliefs? He had plenty of sermons to be sure—old, yellow, respectable sermons, neither composed by his mind nor copied by his hand, but in the neat writing of his old D.D. uncle. These were so legible that he never felt it necessary even to read them over beforehand. He only had to make sure he had the right one. A hundred and fifty-seven such sermons (the odd one for the year that began on a Sunday) of unquestionable orthodoxy, his kind old uncle had left him in his will. The man probably felt he was not only setting Thomas up with sermons for life, but giving him a fair start as well in the race for a stall in some high cathedral. For his own part, Wingfold had never written a sermon, at least never one he had judged worth preaching to a congregation, and these sermons of his uncle he considered really excellent. Some of them, however, were altogether doctrinal, a few quite controversial: of these he must now beware.

For this approaching Sunday he would see what kind was the next in order; he would read it ahead of time and make sure it contained nothing he was not, in some degree at least, prepared to hold his face to and defend—even if he could not absolutely swear that he believed it as purely true.

He did as resolved. The first he took up was in defense of the Athanasian creed. That would not do. He tried another. That was upon the inspiration of the Scriptures. He glanced through it—found Moses on a level with St. Paul, and Jonah with St. John. True, there might be a sense in which—but—! No, he could not meddle with it. He tried a third; that was on the authority of the church. It would not do. He had read each of all these sermons at least once to a congregation with perfect composure. But now he could hardly find one with which he was even in sympathy—not to say one of which he was certain was more true than false. At last he took up the odd one—that which could come into use but once in a week of years. This was the sermon Bascombe heard and commented on. Having read it over, and finding nothing to compromise him with his conscience, which was like an irritable man trying to find his way in a windy wood by means of a broken lantern, he laid all the rest aside and felt a little relieved.

Wingfold never neglected the private duty of a clergyman with regard to morning and evening devotions, but he was in the habit of dressing and undressing his soul with the help of certain chosen contents of the prayer book—a somewhat circuitous mode of communicating with Him who was so near. But that Saturday he knelt by his bedside at noon and began to pray or try to pray as he had never prayed or tried to pray before. The perplexed man cried out for some acknowledgment from God.

But almost the same moment he began to pray in this truer fashion, the doubts rushed in upon him like a spring torrent. Was there—could there be—a God at all? a real being who might actually hear his prayer? In this crowd of houses and shops and churches, amid buying and selling and ploughing and praising and backbiting, this endless pursuit of ends and of means to ends— was there, *could* there be a silent, invisible God working his own will in it all? Was there, could there be a living heart to the universe that heard him—poor, misplaced, dishonest, ignorant Thomas Wingfold, who had presumed to undertake a work he neither could perform nor had the courage to forsake—when out of the misery of the grimy little cellar of his consciousness he cried aloud for light and something to make a man of him? Now that Thomas had begun to doubt like an honest being, every ugly thing within him began to show itself to his awakened integrity.

But honest and of good parentage as the doubts were, no sooner had they shown themselves than the wings of the ascending prayers fluttered feebly and failed. They sank slowly, fell, and lay as dead, while all the wretchedness of his position rushed back upon him with redoubled force. Here he was, a man who could not pray, and yet he had to go and read prayers and preach the very next day, pretending that he knew something of the secrets of the Almighty. Wouldn't it be better for him to send round the bellman to announce that there would be no service? And yet what right did he have to lay his troubles on the shoulders of those who did faithfully believe and who looked to him to break for them their daily bread?

Thus into the dark pool of his dull submissive life, the bold words of the unbeliever had fallen—a dead stone perhaps, but causing a thousand motions in the living water. Question crowded upon question and doubt upon doubt until he could bear it no longer. Jumping up from the floor he rushed from the house, scarcely knowing where he was heading or even where he was until he came to himself some little distance from the town, wandering hurriedly along a path through the fields.

It was a fair day. The trees were nearly bare, but the grass was green and there was a memory of spring in the low, sad sunshine—even the sunshine, the gladdest thing in creation, is sad sometimes. There was no wind, nothing to fight with, nothing to turn his mind from its own miserable perplexities. He came to a stile where his path joined another that ran both ways, and there he seated himself. Just then the strange couple I have already described when met by Miss Lingard and Mr. Bascombe approached and walked by. After they had gone a good way, he caught sight of something lying on the path. He went to pick it up and found it was a small manuscript volume, apparently a journal.

With the instinct of service, he hastened after them. They heard him, and turning, waited for his approach. He took off his hat, and presenting the book to the young woman, asked if she had dropped it. Her face flushed terribly at the sight of the book. In order to spare her any further uneasiness, Wingfold could not help saying with a smile, "Don't be alarmed. I have not read one word of it."

She returned his smile sweetly, and replied, "I see I need not have been afraid."

Her companion joined in thanks and apologies for having caused him so much trouble. Wingfold assured them it had been but a pleasure. He did not scrutinize them carefully, but the interview left him with the feeling that their faces were refined and intelligent, and their speech was good. Again he lifted his rather shabby hat, and in return the man responded with equal politeness in removing from a great gray head one slightly better. They turned from each other and went their ways. The sight of their malformation did not arouse in the curate any such questions as those which had agitated the tongue of George Bascombe.

How he got through the Sunday he never could have told. How a man may endure certain events, he knows not! As soon as it was over, it was all a mist—from which gloomed large the face of George Bascombe with its keen unbelieving eyes and scornful lips. All the time he was reading the prayers and lessons, all the time he was reading his uncle's sermon, Wingfold had not only been aware of those eyes, but aware also of what lay behind them— seeing and reading the reflex of himself in Bascombe's brain.

Time passed, and Sunday after Sunday in like fashion Thomas struggled through the services. I will not request my reader to accompany me through the confused fog of Wingfold's dimly lit moorland journey. One who has ever gone through any such experience in which was blowing a wind whose breath was causing a world to pass from chaos to cosmos will be able to imagine it. To one who has not, my descriptions would be of small service.

The weeks passed and seemed to bring him no light, but only increased the earnestness of his search after it. He would have to find an answer before long, he thought, or he would have no choice but to resign his curacy and look for a position as a tutor.

Of course all this he ought to have gone through long ago. But how can a man go through anything till his hour is come? Wingfold had all this time been skirting the wall of the kingdom of heaven without even knowing there was a wall there, not to say seeing a gate in it. The fault lay with those who had introduced him to the church as a profession, just as they might introduce someone to the practice of medicine, or the bar, or the drapery business—as if the ministry were on the same level of choice with other human callings. Never had he been warned to take off his shoes for the holiness of the ground. And yet how were they to have warned him when they themselves had never discovered the treasure in that ground more holy than libraries, incomes, and the visits of royalty? As to visions of truth that make a man sigh with joy and enlarge his heart with more than human tenderness—how many of those men had ever found such treasures in the fields of the church? How many of them knew, except by hearsay, whether there be any Holy Ghost? How then could they warn other men from the dangers of following in their footsteps and becoming such as they? Where in a community of general ignorance shall we begin to blame? Wingfold had no time to accuse anyone. He simply had to awaken from the dead and cry for light, and was soon in the bitter agony of the paralyzing struggle between life and death.

He thought afterward, when the time had passed, that surely in this period of darkness he had been upheld by a power whose presence he was completely unaware of. He did not know how else he could have gotten through it. Strange helps came to him from time to time. The details of nature wonderfully softened toward him, and for the first time he began to notice her ways and shows and to see in them all the working of an infinite humanity. He later remembered how a hawthorn bud once set him weeping; and how once, as he was walking miserably to church, a child looked up in his face and smiled. In the strength of that smile, he had been able to confidently approach the lectern.

He never knew how long he had been in the agony of his most peculiar birth—in which the soul is at the same time both the mother that bears and the child that is born.

5   A Most Disturbing Letter

In the meantime, George Bascombe came and went. Every visit he showed clearer and clearer notions as to what he was for and what he was against. And every visit he found Helen more worthy and desirable than before and flattered himself that he was making progress in the transmitting of his opinions into her mind. His various talents went far to assist him in this design. There was hardly anything Helen could do that George could not do as well, if not better, and there were many things George was at home with which she knew nothing about. He found great satisfaction in teaching such a pupil. When at length he began to press his affections more openly, Helen found it agreeable. The pleasure of his attentions opened her mind favorably toward the theories and doctrines he would have her receive. Much that a more experienced mind would have rejected as impractical she accepted. Her regard for his propositions was limited to the intellectual arena, and this prevented her from looking at their practical impact on daily life. Therefore, when her cousin finally ventured to attack even those doctrines which most women would be expected to revere the most, she listened unshocked.

There are those, like George, who believe men will be happy to learn there is no God. To them I would say, preach it then, and prosper in proportion to its truth. No; that from my pen would be a curse. Do not preach it until you have searched all the expanse of the universe, lest what you should consider a truth should turn out to be false and there should be after all somewhere, somehow, a living God, a Truth indeed who has created and governs the universe. You may be convinced there is no God such as this or that in whom men *imagine* they believe. But you cannot be convinced there is no God.

In the meantime, George continued to be particular about his cigars and his wine, and ate his dinners with what some would call a good conscience. (I would call it a dull one were I not sure it was a good digestion they really meant.) Matters between the two made no rapid advance. Geroge went on loving Helen more than any other woman, and Helen went on liking George next best to anyone but her brother Leopold.

One Tuesday morning in the spring, the curate received by the local post the following letter dated from the park gate:

Respected Sir:

An obligation on my part which you have no doubt forgotten gives me courage to address you on a matter which seems to me of some consequence.

I sat in the abbey church last Sunday morning. I had not listened long to the sermon before I began to fancy I knew what was coming before you said it, and in a few minutes more I seemed to recognize it as one of Jeremy Taylor's. When I came home I found that the best portions of one of his sermons had, in the one you read, been worked in with other material.

If, sir, I imagined you to be one of such as would willingly have something taken as his own which another had produced, I should feel I was only doing you a wrong if I aided you in avoiding detection. For the sooner the truth concerning such a one was known, and the judgment of society brought to bear upon it, the better for him. But I have read in your face and demeanor that which convinces me that, however custom and the presence of worldly elements in the community to which you belong may have influenced your judgment, you require only to be set thinking of a matter to follow your conscience with regard to it. I have the honor to be, respected sir, your obedient servant and well-wisher,

Joseph Polwarth

Wingfold sat, slightly stunned, staring at the letter. The feeling which first flew through his mental chaos was vexation at having committed such a blunder. Next, he experienced annoyance with his dead old uncle for having led him into such a scrape. There in the good doctor's own handwriting lay the sermon, looking in no way different from the rest. Had the man forgotten his quotation marks? Or to this particular sermon, did he always add a few words of extempore introduction? This could not be his uncle's usual manner of making his sermons. Was it possible they could *all* be pieces of counterfeit literary mosaic? It was very annoying.

If the fact came to be known, parishioners would certainly say he had tried to pass off Jeremy Taylor's ideas for his own. What was he to do, try to lay the blame on his departed uncle? Was it any worse of his uncle to use Jeremy Taylor than for him to use his uncle? What would the church-going inhabitants of Glaston think when they discovered that he had never once preached a sermon of his own? Yet what could it matter to anyone where it came from, so long as a good sermon was preached? He did not occupy the pulpit by virtue of his personality but by his office, and it was not a place to display originality but to dispense the bread of life. From the stores of other people? Yes—if their bread was better and no one was the worse for taking it.

Then why should he object so to being found out? Why had the letter made him so uncomfortable? What did he have to be ashamed of? What did he want to conceal? Didn't everybody know that very few clergymen really wrote their own sermons? Was it not ridiculous, this silent agreement everyone knew not to be true that it had to appear a man's sermons were absolutely his own? It was nothing but the old Spartan game of steal as you will and enjoy it as you can, but woe to you if you are caught in the act! There was something contemptible about the whole thing. He was a greater humbug than he had thought.

He had, however, one considerate parishioner whom he must at least thank for his openness. He stopped pacing the room, sat down at his writing table, and acknowledged Mr. Polwarth's letter. He expressed his obligation for its contents, and said he would like to call upon him that afternoon, in the hope of being allowed to say for himself what little could be said, and of receiving counsel with regard to the difficulty he found himself in. He sent the note by his landlady's boy, and as soon as he had finished his lunch, he set out to find park gate, which he took for some row of dwellings in the suburbs.

Going in the direction pointed out, and finding he had left all the houses behind him, he stopped at the gate of Osterfield Park to make further inquiry. The door of the lodge was opened by one whom he took, for the first second, to be a child. The next moment he recognized her as the same young woman whose book he had picked up in the fields a few months before. He had never seen her since, but her deformity and her face together had made it easy to remember her.

"We have met before," he stated, in answer to her courtesy and smile, "and you must now do me a small favor if you can."

"I shall be most happy to, sir," she answered.

"Can you tell me where Mr. Polwarth of the park gate lives?"

The girl's smile of sweetness changed to one of amusement as she answered in a gentle voice through which ran a thread of suffering, "Come in, sir, please. My uncle's name is Joseph Polwarth, and this is the gate to Osterfield Park. People know it as the park gate."

The house was not one of those trim modern park lodges, all angles and peaks, but a low cottage, with a very thick thatch into which rose two astonished eyebrows over the stare of two half-awake dormer windows. On the front of it were young leaves and old hips enough to show that in summer it must be covered with roses.

Wingfold at once followed her inside. His first step through the door planted him in the kitchen, a bright place, with stone floor and shining things on the walls. She led him to a neat little parlor, cozy and rather dark, with a small window looking out on the garden behind, and a smell of last year's roses.

"My uncle will be here in a few minutes," she said, placing a chair for the curate. "I would have had a fire here, but my uncle always talks better among his books. He expected you, but my lord's steward sent for him up to the new house."

He took the chair she offered him and sat down to wait. He had not much of the gift of making talk—a questionable accomplishment anyway—and he never could approach his so-called inferiors as anything but as his equals. In their presence he never felt any difference.

"So you are the warders of the gate here, Miss Polwarth?" he concluded, assuming that to be her name.

"Yes," she answered. "We have kept it now for about eight years, sir. It is not hard, but I imagine there will be more to do when the house is finished."

"It is a long way for you to go to church."

"It would be, sir; but I do not go."

"Your uncle does."

"Not very often, sir."

She left the door open and kept coming and going between the kitchen and the parlor, busy about house affairs. As Wingfold sat he watched her with growing interest.

She had the full-sized head that is so often set on a dwarf's body, and it seemed even larger because of the quantity of rich brown hair upon it—hair which some ladies would have given fortunes to possess. Clearly too it gave pleasure to its owner, for it was carefully and modestly arranged. Her face seemed more interesting to Wingfold every fresh glance he had of it, until at last he concluded to himself that it was one of the sweetest he had ever seen. Its chief expression was placidity, and something that was not merely contentment: I would term it satisfaction. Her hands and feet were both about the size of a child's.

He was still studying her like a book which a boy reads by stealth, when at last her uncle entered the room with a slow step.

Wingfold rose and held out his hand.

"Welcome, sir," said Polwarth modestly, with the strong grasp of his small firm hand. "Will you walk upstairs with me where we shall be undisturbed? My niece has, I hope, already apologized for my not being at home when you came.—Rachel, my child, will you get us a cup of tea, and by the time it is ready I dare say we will have got through our business."

The face of Wingfold's host resembled that of his niece a good deal, but bore traces of yet greater suffering—bodily to be sure, but possibly mentally as well. It did not look quite old enough to account for the whiteness of the plentiful hair that crowned it, and yet there was that in its expression which might account for the whiteness.

His voice was a little dry and husky, streaked with the asthma whose sounds made that big disproportioned chest seem like the cave of the east wind. But it had a tone of dignity and decision in it quite in harmony with both the manner and style of his letter. Before Wingfold had followed him to the top of the steep, narrow, straight staircase, all sense of incongruity or of being out of place had vanished from his mind.

6   Polwarth's Plan

The little man led the way into a large room with sloping ceiling on both sides. Light came from a small window in the gable near the fireplace and a dormer window as well. The low walls up to the slope were filled with books; books lay on the table, on the bed, on the chairs, and in corners everywhere.

"Aha!" said Wingfold as he entered and looked about, "it is no surprise that you should have found me out so easily, Mr. Polwarth! Here you have a legion of detectives for such rascals as I."

The little man turned and for a moment looked at him with a doubtful expression, as if he had not been quite prepared for such a beginning to such a solemn question. But a moment's reading of the curate's honest face, which by this time had a good deal more print upon it than would have been found there six months earlier, sufficed. The cloud melted into a smile, and he said cordially, "It is very kind of you, sir, to take my presumption so well. Please sit down. You will find that chair comfortable."

"Presumption!" exclaimed Wingfold. "The presumption was all on my part, and the kindness on yours. But you must first hear my explanation, such as it is. It doesn't make the matter look a bit better; only a man would not willingly look worse than he is. And besides, we must understand each other if we would be friends.

However unlikely it may seem to you, Mr. Polwarth, I really do share the common weakness of wanting to be taken for exactly what I am, neither more nor less."

"It is a noble weakness, and far enough from common, I am sorry to say," returned Polwarth.

The curate then told the gatekeeper of his uncle's legacy and his own ignorance of Jeremy Taylor.

"But," he concluded, "since you set me thinking about it, my judgment has turned over on itself and it now seems worse to me to use my uncle's sermons than to have used the bishop's."

"I see no harm in either," said Polwarth, "provided it be above board. I believe some clergymen think the only evil lies in detection. I doubt if they ever escape it in the end. Many a congregation can tell, by a kind of instinct I think, whether a man is preaching his own sermons or not. The worst of it appears to me to lie in the unspoken understanding that a sermon must *seem* to be a man's own, although everyone in the congregation knows, and the would-be preacher knows, that it is not."

"Then you mean, Mr. Polwarth, that I should solemnly tell my congregation next Sunday that the sermon I am about to read is one of many left me by my worthy uncle Jonah Driftwood, who on his deathbed expressed the hope that I should support their teaching by my example? Having gone over them some ten or fifteen times in the course of his ministry, and bettered each every time he gave it, he did not think I could improve further upon the truths they contained: shall I tell them all that?"

Polwarth laughed with merriment, which, however, took nothing from his genuineness.

"It would hardly be necessary to enter so fully into the particulars," he replied. "It would be enough to let them know that you wished it understood that you did not profess to teach them anything of your own, but merely were bringing to them teaching of others. It would raise complaints and objections undoubtedly, but you must be prepared for that whenever you would do anything right."

Wingfold was silent, thoughtfully saying to himself, *How straight an honest bow can shoot!*—But this would involve some-

thing awful. To stand up in that pulpit and speak about himself—
he gave a forlorn little laugh.

"But," resumed the small man, "have you never preached a
sermon of your own thinking? I don't mean of your own making—
one that came out of the commentaries. I am told that commentaries are the mines where some of our most noted preachers go
to dig for their first inspirations. But have you never offered one
that came out of your own heart, from your delight in something
you had discovered, or from something about which you felt very
strongly?"

"No," answered Wingfold. "I have nothing. I never have had
anything worth giving to another."

"You must know about some things which might do your people good to be reminded of—even if they know them already,"
prodded Polwarth. "I cannot imagine that a man who looks things
straight in the face as you do has never met with anything which
has taught him something other people need to be taught. Of
course a man to whom no message has been personally given has
no right to take the place of a prophet. But there is room for
teachers as well as prophets. And a man might honestly be a clergyman who teaches the people, though he makes no claim to be
gifted in prophecy."

"I do not see where you are leading me," responded Wingfold,
considerably astonished at both the frankness and fluency with
which a man in his host's position was able to express himself.

"I will come to the point practically: a man who does not feel
that he has something in his own soul to tell his people should turn
his energy to the providing of such food for them as he finds feeds
himself. In other words, if he has nothing new in his own treasure,
let him bring something old out of another man's."

"Then you do think a man should make up his sermons from
the books he reads?"

"Yes, if he can do no better. But then I would have him read
much—not with his sermon in his thoughts, but with his *people* in
his *heart*. Most people have so little time for reading or thinking.
The office of preaching is meant first of all to wake them up, next
to make them hungry, and finally to give them food for that hunger. And the pastor has to take thought for all these things. For

if he doesn't feed God's flock, then he is no shepherd."

At this moment Rachel entered with a small tea tray. She cast a loving glance at the young man who now sat before her uncle with his head bowed in humble thought. She looked at her uncle with an expression almost of earnest pleading, as if interceding for a culprit and begging the master not to be too hard on him. But the little man smiled—such a sweet smile of reassurance that her face returned at once to its contented expression. She cleared a place on the table, set down her tray, and went to bring cups and saucers.

"I think I understand you now," acknowledged Wingfold, after the little pause. "You would have a man who cannot be original deal honestly in secondhand goods. Or perhaps, rather, he should say to his congregation, 'This is not homemade bread I offer you, but something better. I got it from this or that baker's shop. I have eaten of it myself, and it has agreed with me and done me good.'— Is that something like what you would have, Mr. Polwarth?"

"Precisely," assured the gatekeeper with enthusiasm. "But," he added after a moment's delay, "I would be sorry if you stopped there."

"Stopped there!" echoed Wingfold. "The question is whether I can *begin* there. You have no idea how ignorant I am—how little I have read."

"I have some idea of both, I think. I'm sure I knew considerably less than you at your age, for I never attended a university."

"But perhaps even then you had more of the knowledge which, they say, only life can give."

"I have it now in any case. But of that everyone has enough who lives his life. Those who gain no experience are those who shirk the king's highway for fear of encountering the Duty seated by the roadside."

"You ought to be a minister yourself, sir," proposed Wingfold humbly.

"I hope I ought to be just what I am, neither more nor less," replied Polwarth. "But if you will let me help you, I shall be most happy to. For lately I have been oppressed with the thought that I serve no one but myself and my niece. I am in mortal fear of growing selfish under the weight of all my blessings."

A fit of asthmatic coughing seized him, and grew so severe he seemed struggling for his life. His niece entered, but she showed no alarm, only concern. She did nothing but go up to him and lay her hand on his back between his shoulders till the spasm was over. The instant the convulsion ceased, its pain dissolved in a smile.

Wingfold uttered some lame expression of regret that he should suffer so much.

"It is really nothing to distress you, or me either, Mr. Wingfold," said the little man. "Shall we have a cup of tea, and then resume our talk?"

"The fact is, Mr. Polwarth," conceded the curate, "I must not give you half-confidences. I will tell you all that troubles me, for it is plain that you know something of which I am ignorant—something which, I have great hope, will turn out to be the very thing I need to know. Will you permit me to talk about myself?"

"Certainly. I am entirely at your service, Mr. Wingfold," returned Polwarth. Seeing that the curate did not touch his tea, he placed his own cup again on the table.

The young woman slipped down like a child from the chair upon which she had perched herself at the table, and with a kind look at Wingfold was about to leave the room.

"No, no, Miss Polwarth," insisted the curate, rising. "I wouldn't be able to go on if I felt I had sent you away—and your tea untouched too. What an ungrateful fellow I am. I didn't even notice that you have given me tea. If you don't mind staying, we can talk and drink our tea at the same time. But I am afraid I may have to say some things that will shock you."

"I will stay then," replied Rachel with a smile, and climbed back onto her chair. "I am not afraid of what you may say. My uncle says things sometimes fit to make a Pharisee's hair stand on end, but somehow they make my heart burn inside me.—May I stay, uncle? I would very much like to."

"Certainly, my child, if Mr. Wingfold will not feel your presence a restraint."

"Not in the least," declared the curate.

Miss Polwarth helped them to bread and butter, and a brief silence followed.

"I was brought up for the church," began Wingfold at length, playing with his teaspoon, and looking down at the table. "It's an awful shame such a thing should have been, but I don't think anybody particular was to blame for it. I passed all my examinations with decency, distinguishing myself in nothing. I went before the bishop and became a deacon, after a year was ordained, and after another year or two of false preaching and parish work, suddenly found myself curate in charge of this grand old abbey church. But as to what the whole thing means in practical terms, I am ignorant. Do not mistake me. I think I could stand up to an examination on the doctrines of the church as contained in the creeds and the prayer book. But for all they have done for me I might as well never have heard of them."

"Don't be quite sure of that, Mr. Wingfold. At least they have brought you to ask if there is anything in them."

"Mr. Polwarth," returned Wingfold abruptly, "I cannot even prove there is a God."

"But the Church of England exists to teach Christianity, not to prove there is a God."

"What is Christianity then?"

"God in Christ, and Christ in man."

"What is the use of that if there be no God?"

"None whatever!"

"Can *you* prove there is a God?"

"No."

"Then, if you don't believe there is a God . . . I don't know what is to become of it all," said the curate in a tone of deep disappointment, and rose to go.

"Mr. Wingfold," assured the little man, with a smile and a deep breath of delight at the thought that was moving him, "I know him in my heart, and he is everything to me. You did not ask whether I *believe* in him, but whether I could *prove* there was a God."

"Pardon me. You must have patience with me," replied Wingfold, resuming his seat. "I am a fool. But understanding this has suddenly become very important to me."

"I wish we were all such fools! But please ask me no more questions, or ask me as many as you wish but expect no answers just yet. I want to know more of your mind first."

"Well, I will ask questions, but press for no answers. If you cannot prove there is a God, do you know for certain that such a man as Jesus Christ ever lived? Can it be proved with positive certainty? I am not talking about what they call the doctrines of Christianity, or the authority of the church, or anything of that sort. Right at the moment, all that is of no interest to me. And yet the very fact that they do not interest me is enough to prove me as false a man who ever occupied the pulpit. I would rather be despised than excused, Mr. Polwarth."

"I shall do neither, Mr. Wingfold. Go on, if you please. I am more deeply interested than I can tell you."

"A few months ago I met a young man who takes for granted the opposite of all that up to that time I had taken for granted, and which I now want to be able to prove. He spoke with contempt of my profession. I could not defend my position and thus began to despise myself. I began to think. I began to pray. My whole past life began to grow dim. A cloud gathered about me and hangs there still. I call, but no voice answers me out of the darkness. At times I am in despair. For the love of honesty I would give up the ministry, but I don't want to leave what I may yet possibly find to be true. Nevertheless, I would have abandoned everything months ago if I had not felt bound by my agreement to serve my rectory for a year. You are the only one of the congregation who has shown me any humanity. Will you be my friend, and help me?"

"Of course," answered the dwarf humbly.

"Then again comes the question, what shall I do? How am I to know that there is a God?"

"It would be a more pertinent question," returned Polwarth, "to ask—if there *is* in fact a God, how am I to find him? And, as I have hinted at before, there is still another question—one you have already asked: Was there ever such a man as Jesus Christ?— Those, I think, were your own words. What do you mean by *such* a man?"

"Such as he is represented in the New Testament."

"From that representation, what description would you give of him? What sort of person, supposing the story true, would you take this Jesus to have been?"

Wingfold thought for a while.

"I am a worse humbug than I thought," he confessed. "I do not know what he was. My thoughts of him are so vague and indistinct that it would take me a long time to find an answer to your question."

"Perhaps even longer than you think. It took me a very long time." There was a slight pause, then the gatekeeper went on, "Shall I tell you something of my life, in return for the confidence you have honored me with?"

"Nothing could please me more," answered Wingfold.

"Indeed, it is not that I know so much," responded the little man. "On the contrary, I am the most ignorant person I know. You would be astonished to discover all that I don't know. But I do know what is really worth knowing. Yet I get not a crumb more than my daily bread by it—I mean the bread by which the inner man lives. The man who gives himself to making money will seldom fail to become a rich man. I tried to make a little money by bookselling once. I failed—not to pay my debts, but to make money. I could not enter into the business heartily, so it was only right I should not succeed.

"My ancestors, as my name indicates, were from Cornwall, where they held large property. Forgive the seeming boast—it is just a fact and reflects little enough on one like me. Scorn and pain mingled with great hopes are a grand prescription for weaning the heart from the ambitions of this world. Later ancestors, not many generations ago, were the proprietors of this very property of Osterfield, which the uncle of the present Lord de Barre bought, and to which I, their descendant, am gatekeeper. What with gambling, drinking, and worse, they deserved to lose it. The harvest of their lawlessness is ours: we are what and where you see us. But with the inherited poison, the Father gave the antidote.—Rachel, my child, am I not right when I say that you thank God with me for having thus visited the iniquities of the fathers upon the children?"

"I do, Uncle. You know I do," replied Rachel in a low, tender voice.

A great solemnity came upon the spirit of Wingfold, and for a moment he felt as if he sat wrapped in a cloud of sacred marvel. But presently Polwarth resumed: "My father was a remarkably fine-appearing man, tall and stately. I have little to say about him. If he did not do well, my grandfather must be censured first. He had a sister very much like Rachel here. Poor Aunt Lottie! She was not as happy as my little one. My brothers were all fine men like himself, yet they all died young except my brother Robert. He too is dead now, thank God, and I trust he is in peace. He left me my Rachel with her twenty pounds a year. I have thirty of my own and this cottage we have rent free for attending to the gate. There are none of the family left now but myself and Rachel. God in his mercy is about to let it cease.

"I was sent to one of our smaller public schools—mainly, I believe, because I was an eyesore to my handsome father. There for the first time I felt myself an outcast. I was the butt of all the coarser-minded of my schoolfellows, and the kindness of some could but partially make up for it. On the other hand, I had no fierce impulse to retaliate on those who injured me or on the society that scorned me. The isolation that belonged to my condition worked instead to intensify my individuality. My longing was mainly for a refuge, for some corner into which I might creep, where I could be concealed and at rest. The only triumph I coveted over my persecutors was to know that they could not find me. It is hardly any wonder that I cannot remember when I began to pray and hope that God heard me. I used to imagine that I lay in his hand and looked through his fingers at my foes. That was at night, for my deformity brought me one blessed comfort—that I did not have to share a bed. This I felt at first as both a sad deprivation and a painful rejection, but I learned to pray all the sooner for the loneliness of it.

"What field I would have been prepared for had I been like other people, I do not know. But it soon became clear, as time passed and I grew no taller but more and more misshapen, that there could be no profession suitable for it. Therefore, the first few years after I left school I spent at home, keeping out of my father's way as much as possible. When my mother died, she left her little property between me and my brother. He had been brought up to be an engineer like my father. My father could not touch the principal of this money, but neither could we, while he lived, benefit from the interest. I hardly know how I lived for the next three or four years—it must have been almost entirely on charity, I think. My father was never at home, and but for an old woman who had been our only attendant all my life, I think I would very likely have starved. I spent most of my time reading—whatever I could get my hands on.

"Somewhere in this time I began to feel dissatisfied with myself. At first the feeling was vague, altogether undefined. As it went on and began to gather roots, it grew toward something more definite. I began to be aware that, heavy affliction as it was to be made so different from others, my outward deformity was but a picture of my inward condition. There—inside me—nothing was right. I discovered with horror that I was envious and revengeful and conceited. I discovered that I looked down on people whom I thought less clever than myself. All at once one day, with a sickening conviction it came upon me, *What a contemptible little wretch I am!*

"I now concluded that I had been nothing but a Pharisee and a hypocrite, praying with a bad heart, and that God saw me just as detestable as I saw myself, and despised me and was angry with me. I read my Bible more diligently than ever for a while, found in it nothing but judgment and wrath, and soon dropped it in despair. I had already stopped praying.

"One day a little boy made fun of me. I flew into a rage and ran after him and caught him. When the boy found himself in my clutches, he turned on me with a look of such terror that it disarmed me at once. I would have let him go instantly, but I did not want him to run away without at first comforting him. But every word of kindness I tried to utter sounded to him like a threat. Nothing would do but to let him go. The moment he found himself free, he fled headlong into a nearby pond, got out again, and ran home. He told, with perfect truthfulness I believe, though absolute inaccuracy, that I threw him in. After this I tried to control my temper, but I found that the more I tried the less I could subdue the wrath in my soul. Always I was aware of the lack of harmony in my heart. I was not at peace. I was sick.

"One twilight, I lay alone, not thinking really, but with my mind passive and open to whatever might come into it. It was very hot—indeed sultry. My little skylight was open, but not a breath of air came in. All at once the face of the terrified little boy rose before me and I found myself eagerly, painfully, at length almost in an agony, trying to persuade him that I would not hurt him, but meant well toward him. Again, in my daydream, I had just let him go in despair, when the sweetest, gentlest, most refreshing little waft of air came in at the window. Its greeting was more delicate even than my mother's kiss, and it cooled my whole body. Now, whatever the link between that breath of air and what came next I do not know, but I immediately thought, *What if I misunderstood God in the same way the boy had misunderstood me!* So I took my New Testament from the shelf where I had laid it some time before.

"Later that same summer I said to myself that I would begin at the beginning and read it through. I had no definite idea in the resolve. It simply seemed a good thing to do, and I would do it. It would perhaps serve toward keeping up my connection with *things above*. I began, but did not that night get even through the first chapter of Matthew. Conscientiously I read every word of the genealogy. But when I came to the twenty-first verse and read, 'Thou shalt call his name JESUS; *for he shall save his people from their sins*,' I fell on my knees. No system of theology had come between me and a common-sense reading of the book. I did not for a moment imagine that to be saved from my sins meant to be saved from the punishment of them. My sinfulness remained clear to my eyes, and my sins too. I hated them, yet could not free myself from them. They were in me and of me, and how was I to get rid of them? But here was news of one who came to deliver me from that in me which was bad.

"Ah! Mr. Wingfold, what if, after all the discoveries are made, and all the theories are set up and pulled down—what if, after all this, the strongest weapon a man can wield is prayer to the one who made him!

"To tell you all that followed, if I could recall it in order, would take hours. Suffice it to say that from that moment on I became a student, a disciple. Before long there came to me also the two same questions you asked: *How do I know there is a God at all?* and *How am I to know that such a man as Jesus ever lived?* I could answer neither. But in the meantime I was reading the story—was drawn to the Man, and was trying to understand his being, and character, and the principles of his life and action. To sum it all up, not many months had passed before I had forgotten to seek an answer to either question: they were in fact no longer questions. I had seen the man Jesus Christ, and in him had known the Father of him and of me.

"My dear sir, no conviction can be got—or if it could be got, would be of any lasting value—through that dealer in secondhand goods, the intellect. If by it we could prove there is a God, it would be of small avail indeed. *We must see him and know him.* And I know of no other way of knowing that there is a God but that which reveals *what* he is—and that way is Jesus Christ as he revealed himself on earth, and as he is revealed afresh to every heart that seeks to know the truth about him."

A pause followed—a solemn one—and then again Polwarth spoke.

"Either the whole frame of existence," he declared, "is a wretched, miserable chaos of a world, or it is an embodied idea growing toward perfection in him who is the one perfect creative Idea, the Father of Lights, who himself suffers that he may bring his many sons and daughters into his own glory."

"But," interjected Wingfold, "—only do not think I am opposing you; I am now in the mental straits you have left so far behind—how am I to know that I have not merely talked myself into the believing of what I would like to be true?"

"Leave that question until you know what that really is which you want to believe. I do not imagine you have yet more than the faintest glimmer of the nature of that which you find yourself doubting. Is a man to refuse to open his curtains lest some flash in his own eyes should deceive him with a vision of morning while it is still night? The truth to the soul is as light to the eyes: you may be deceived, and mistake something else for light, but you can never fail to know the light when it really comes."

"What, then, would you have of me? What am I to *do*?" inquired Wingfold.

"Your business," emphasized Polwarth, "is to acquaint yourself with the man Jesus: he will be to you the one to reveal the Father. Take your New Testament as if you had never seen it before, and read to find out. The point is, there was a man who said he knew

God and that if you would give heed to him, you should know him too. The record left of him is indeed scanty, yet enough to disclose what kind of man he was—his principles, his ways of looking at things, his thoughts of his Father and his brothers and the relations between them, of man's business in life, his destiny, and his hopes."

"I see plainly," answered the curate, "what you say I must do. But how can I carry out such a mission of inquiry while on duty as a clergyman? How am I, with the sense of the unreality of my position growing ever more strongly upon me, and with my utter inability to supply the needs of my congregation except from my uncle's store of dry provender—with all this pressing upon me, making me restless and irritable, how am I to set myself to such solemn work? Surely to carry it out a man must be clear-eyed and single-hearted if he would succeed in his quest. What am I to do but resign my curacy?"

Mr. Polwarth thought a little.

"I think it would be well to retain it for a while longer while you search," he advised. "If you do not within a month see any prospect of finding him, then resign. In any case, your continuance must depend on your knowledge of the Lord and his will concerning you."

"I will try," replied Wingfold, rising. "But I am afraid I am hardly the man to make discoveries in such high spiritual regions."

"You are the man to find what fits your own need if the answer exists," insisted Polwarth. "But to ease your mind, I know pretty well some of our best English writers in theology, and if you would like to come again tomorrow, I think I shall be able to provide you means to feed your flock for a month at least."

"I will not attempt to thank you," said Wingfold, "but I will try to do as you tell me. You are one of the first real friends I have had—except my brother, who is dead."

"Perhaps you have had more friends than you are aware of. You owe something to the man, for instance, who with his outspoken antagonism first roused you to a sense of what you were lacking."

"I hope I shall be grateful to God for it someday," returned Wingfold. "I cannot say that I now feel much obligation to Mr.

Bascombe. And yet, when I think of it—perhaps—I don't know—what ought a man to be more grateful for than honesty?"

The curate took his leave, with a stronger feeling of simple, genuine respect than he had ever yet felt for anyone. Rachel bade him good-night with her fine eyes filled with tears, which suited their expression, for they always seemed to be looking through sorrow to something beyond it.

I will not count the milestones along the road on which Wingfold now began to journey. Some of the stages, however, will appear in the course of my story. Every day during the rest of that week he saw his new friends.

7   A Strange Sermon

On Sunday the curate walked across the churchyard to the morning service as if the bells, instead of ringing the people to church, had been tolling for his execution. But if he was going to be hanged, he would at least die like a gentleman, confessing his sin. When he stood up to read, he trembled so that he could not tell whether or not he was speaking in a voice audible to the congregation. But as his hour drew near, the courage to meet it drew near also. When at length he ascended the pulpit stairs for the sermon, he cast a glance across the sea of heads to discover whether the little man was present. But he looked for the large head in vain.

When he read his text it was to a listless and indifferent congregation. He had not gone far into the sermon, however, before a marked change gradually became visible on the faces before him. If the congregation had been a troop of horses, they would have shown their new attentiveness by a general forward swivelling of the ears. They were actually listening! But in truth it was no wonder, for seldom in any, and certainly never in that church, had there been heard such a sermon.

His text was, "Confessing your faults one to another." Having read it, trembling once again, he paused. For a moment his brain suddenly seemed to reel under a wave of oblivion, annihilating both his thoughts and his speech altogether. But with a mighty effort of the will, he recovered himself and went on. To fully understand this effort, you must remember that Wingfold was a shy man. It had been difficult enough to persevere in his intentions when alone in his study. But to carry out his resolve in the face of so many people, and in spite of a cowardly brain, was an effort and a victory indeed.

From the manuscript before him he read: " 'Confess your faults one to another.'—This command of the apostle ought to justify me in doing what I fear some of you may consider almost a breach of morals—talking of myself in the pulpit. But in this pulpit a wrong has been done, and in this pulpit it shall be confessed." His faltering voice grew stronger.

"From Sunday to Sunday since I came to you, standing on this very spot, I have read to you without a word of explanation the thoughts and words of another. Undoubtedly these sermons were better than any I could have given you from my own mind or experience. And if I had told you the truth concerning them, my actions would have been perfectly acceptable. But in fact I did not tell you. This week, through words of honest reproach from a friend whose wounds are faithful, I have been aroused to an awareness of the wrong I have been doing. I now confess it to you. I am sorry. I will do so no more."

His eyes swept the congregation for an understanding face. He continued, "But, brethren, my own garden is but small, and is in the middle of a bare hillside. It has borne no fruit fit to offer any of you. And also my heart is troubled about many things, and God has humbled me. I ask you, therefore, to bear with me for a time while I break through the bonds of custom in order to try to provide you with food. Should I fail in this, I shall make room for a better man. But for your bread today, I go gleaning openly in other men's fields. I will lay before you what I have discovered with the help of the same friend I mentioned earlier—with the name of the field where I gathered it. Together they will show what some of the wisest and best shepherds of the English flock have believed concerning the duty of confessing our faults."

He then proceeded to read the extracts which Mr. Polwarth had helped him to find. His voice steadied and strengthened as he read. Renewed contact with the minds of those vanished teachers infused a delight into the words as he read them, and if the curate preached to no one else in the congregation, certainly he preached to himself. Before it was done, he had entered into a thorough enjoyment of the sermon.

A few of the congregation were disappointed. A few others were scandalized at such innovation on the part of a young man who was only a curate. Many, however, said it was the most interesting sermon they had ever heard in their lives—which perhaps was not saying much.

Mrs. Ramshorn was in a class by herself. She had not yet learned to like Wingfold and had herself a knowledge of not a few of the secrets of the clerical ways. She was indignant with the presumptuous young man who degraded the pulpit to such a level. "What is it to a congregation of respectable people, many of them belonging to the first families of the county, that he, a mere curate, should have committed what he fancied a crime against them? He should have waited until it had been found out and laid to his charge against him. Couldn't he repent of his sins, whatever they were, without making a boast of them in the pulpit and exposing them to the eyes of a whole congregation? I have known people to make a stock-in-trade of their sins! What was it to the congregation whether the washy stuff he gave them by way of sermons was his own foolishness or someone else's? Nobody would have bothered to ask about his honesty if he had but held his foolish tongue. Better men than he have preached other people's sermons and never thought it worth mentioning. And what worse were the people? The only harm lies in letting them know it; that has brought the profession into disgrace and prevented the good the sermon would otherwise have done, besides giving the enemies of the truth a handle against the church!" Thus she fumed half the way home without giving either of her companions an opportunity to say a word.

"I am sorry to differ with you, Aunt," countered Helen mildly. "I thought the sermon a very interesting one."

"For my part," submitted Bascombe, who was now a regular visitor from Saturdays to Mondays, "I used to think the fellow a dolt, but, by Jove! if ever there was a plucky thing to do, that was one," he exulted enthusiastically. "There aren't many men, let me tell you, Aunt, who would have the pluck for it.—It's my belief, Helen," he went on, turning to her and speaking in a lower tone, "that I've done that fellow some good. I gave him my mind about honesty pretty plainly the first time I saw him. And who can tell what may come next when a fellow once starts thinking in the right direction? We shall have him with *us* before long. I must keep an eye out for something for him to do, for of course he'll be in a devil of a fix without his profession."

"There was always something I was inclined to like about Mr. Wingfold," confessed Helen. "Indeed, I should have liked him even if he had *not* been so painfully honest."

"Except for his sheepishness, though," returned Bascombe, "there was a sort of quiet self-satisfaction about him. The way he always said, *'Don't you think?'* made me set him down as conceited, but I am beginning to change my mind. By Jove! he must have worked pretty hard too in the dust bins to get together all those bits he read."

"You heard him say he had help," Helen pointed out.

"No, I don't remember that."

"It came just after that pretty simile about gleaning in old fields."

"I remember the simile, for I thought it a very absurd one— as if fields would lie gleanable for generations!"

"To be sure—now that you point it out," acquiesced Helen slowly.

"The grain would have sprouted and borne harvests by now. If a man wants to use analogies, he should be careful to use them correctly.—I wonder who he got to help him? Not the rector, I suppose?"

"The rector!" echoed Mrs. Ramshorn, who had been listening to the young people's remarks with a smile of quiet scorn on her lips, thinking what an advantage was her experience, even if it could not make up for the loss of youth and beauty. "He would be the last man in the world to lend himself to such a miserable and makeshift pretense! Without brains enough even to fancy himself able to write a sermon of his own, the man steals from the dead!"

"I like a man to hold his face to what he does or thinks," declared Bascombe.

"Ah! George," returned his aunt in tones of wisdom, "by the time you have had my experience, you will have learned a little prudence."

In the meantime, as far as his aunt was concerned, George did use prudence, for in her presence he did not hold his face to what he thought, and said nothing further. He justified this to himself, *It would do her no good. She is so prejudiced!* And it might interfere with his visits. She, for her part, never had the slightest doubt of George's orthodoxy. Was he not the son of a clergyman—a grandson of the church itself?

8   Leopold

Sometimes a thunderbolt will shoot from a clear sky; and sometimes into the life of a peaceful individual, without warning of gathered storm, something terrible will fall. And from that moment everything is changed. That life is no more what it was. Better it ought to be, worse it may be. The result depends on the life itself and its response to the invading storm of trouble. Forever after, its spiritual weather is altered. But for the one who believes in God, such rending and frightful catastrophes never come but where they are turned around for good in his own life and in other lives he touches.

I cannot report much progress in Helen during the months of winter and spring. But if one wakes at last, who shall say that one ought to have waked sooner? What man who is awake will dare say that he roused himself the first moment it became possible? The only condemnation is that when people do wake they do not get up. At the same time, however, I can hardly doubt that Helen was keeping the law of progress as slow as the growth of an iron tree. She seemed in no particular hurry to be roused from her mental and spiritual slumber.

Nothing had ever troubled her. She had never been in love, and it could hardly be said that she was in love now. She went to church regularly, and I believe said her prayers at night—yet she felt no indignation at the opposing doctrines and theories propounded by George Bascombe. She regarded them as "George's ideas," and never cared enough to wonder whether they were true or not. Truth to her had not yet become a factor of existence. At the same time, George's ideas were becoming to her by degrees as like truth as falsehood can ever be. For to the untruthful mind the false *can* seem to be true.

One night Helen was up late as she sat making her aunt a cap. The one sign of originality in her was the character and quality of her millinery. She wanted to complete it before the next morning, her aunt's birthday. They had entertained friends at dinner who had stayed rather late and it was now very late. But Helen was not yet tired, so she sat working away and thinking, not of George Bascombe but of one she loved better—her brother Leopold. However, she was not thinking of him quite so comfortably as usual. Her anxieties had grown stronger, for she had not heard from him for a very long time.

All at once she stopped her work and her posture grew rigid; was that a noise she had heard outside her window?

Helen was not frightened very easily. She stopped her needle, not from fear but only to listen better. She heard nothing. Her hands went on again with their work. But there it came again, very much like a tap at the window! And now her heart began to beat a little faster, if not with fear exactly, then with something very much like it, perhaps mingled with some foreboding. She quietly rose, and, saying to herself it must be one of the pigeons which were constantly about the balcony, she laid her work on the table and went to the window. As she drew one of the curtains a little aside to look, the tap was plainly and hurriedly repeated. At once she swept the rest of the curtain back.

There was the dim shadow of a man's head upon the blind, made by the light of an old withered moon low in the west. She pulled up the blind hurriedly—there was something in the shape of the shadow. Yes, there was a face!—frightful as a corpse.

Helen did not scream. Her throat closed tightly and her heart stopped. But her eyes continued their fixed gaze on the face even after she recognized it as her brother's. And the eyes of the face kept staring back into hers through the glass with a look of concentrated eagerness. The two gazed at each other for a moment of rigid silence. Helen came to herself and slowly, noiselessly, though with a trembling hand, undid the sash and opened the window. Leopold stood, still staring into her face. Presently his lips began to move, but no words came from them.

Some unknown horror had already roused the instinct of secrecy in Helen. She put out her two hands, took his face between them, and said in a hurried whisper, calling him by the pet name she had given him when a child, "Come in, Poldie, and tell me all about it."

Her voice seemed to wake him. Slowly, with the movements of one half paralyzed, he dragged himself over the windowsill, dropped on the floor inside, and lay there looking up in her face like a hunted animal that hoped he had found a refuge, but doubted. Seeing him so exhausted, she turned to get some brandy, but a low cry of agony drew her back. His head was raised from the floor and his hands were stretched out, while his face seemed to beg her to stay as plainly as if he had spoken. She knelt and would have kissed him, but he turned his face from her with an expression of seeming disgust.

"Poldie," she assured him, "I *must* go and get you something. Don't be afraid. Everyone is sound asleep."

The grasp with which he had clutched her dress relaxed, and his hand fell by his side. She rose at once and went, creeping through the house as lightly and noiselessly as a shadow, but with a heart that seemed not her own. As she went, she had to struggle to compose herself, for she could not think clearly. An age seemed to have passed since she heard the clock strike midnight.

One thing was clear: her brother had done something wrong and had fled to her. The moment this conviction made itself plain to her, she drew herself up with the great, deep breath of a vow, as strong as it was silent and undefined, that he had not come to her in vain. Silent-footed as a beast of prey, silent-handed as a thief, lithe in her movements, her eye flashed with the new-kindled instinct of motherhood to the orphan of her father.

As she reentered the room, her brother was still where she had left him. He raised himself on his elbow, seized the glass she offered him with a trembling hand, swallowed the brandy in one gulp, and sank again on the floor. The next instant he sprang to his feet, cast a terrified look toward the window, bounded to the door and locked it, then ran to his sister, threw his arms about her, and clung to her like a trembling child.

Though now twenty years of age, and at his full height, he was barely as tall as Helen. Swarthy of complexion, his hair was dark as the night. Helen tried to quiet him, unconsciously using the same words and tones with which she had soothed him when he was a child. All at once he raised his head and drew himself back from her arms with a look of horror. Then he put his hand over his eyes as if her face had been a mirror and he had seen himself in it.

"What is that on your wristband, Leopold?" she asked. "Have you hurt yourself?"

The youth cast an indescribable look at his hand, but it was not that which turned Helen so deadly sick. Rather, with her question had come to her the ghastly suspicion that the blood she saw was not his. But she would never, never believe it! Yet her arms dropped and let him go. She stepped back a pace, and of their own will, as it were, her eyes went wandering and questioning all over him. His clothes were torn and dirty—stained, who could tell with what?

He stood still for a moment, submissive to her searching eyes, his face downcast. Then suddenly flashing his eyes on her, he said in a voice that seemed to force its way through earth that choked it back, "Helen, I am a murderer, and they are after me. They will be here before daylight."

He dropped on his knees.

"Oh, Sister! Sister! Save me, save me!" he cried in agony.

Helen stood silently, for to remain standing took all her strength. How long she fought that horrible sickness she could never even guess. All was dark before her and her brain swayed senseless. At length the darkness thinned and the face of her boy-brother glimmered up through it. The mist thinned, and she caught a glimmer of his pleading, despairing, horrified eyes. All the mother in her nature rushed to the aid of her struggling will. Her heart gave a great heave; the blood rose to her white brain; her hands went out, took his head between them, and pressed it against her.

"Poldie, dear," she comforted, "be calm and reasonable, and I will do all I can for you. Here, take this. Now, answer me one question."

"You won't give me up, Helen?"

"No. I will not."

"Swear it, Helen."

"Ah, my dear Poldie, has it come to this between you and me?"

"Swear it, Helen."

"So help me God, I will not," vowed Helen, looking upward.

Leopold rose, and again stood quiet before her, but again with his head bent down like a prisoner about to be sentenced.

"Do you mean what you said a moment ago—that the police are searching for you?" asked Helen with forced calmness.

"They must be. They must have been after me for days—I don't know how many. They will be here soon! I can't imagine how I have escaped them for so long. I did not try to hide her; they must have found her long ago."

"My God!" cried Helen, but checked the scream that tried to follow the cry.

"There was an old mine shaft nearby," he went on hurriedly. "If I had thrown her down that, they would never have found her. But I could not bear the thought of sending the lovely thing down there—even to save my life."

He was growing wild again. With renewed horror clutching at her, she stood speechless, staring at him.

"Hide me, hide me, Helen!" he pleaded. "Perhaps you think I am mad. Oh, if only I were! Sometimes I think I must be. But, I tell you, this is no madman's fancy. If you take it for that, you will send me to the gallows. So if you will see me hanged—"

He sat down and folded his arms.

"Hush, Poldie, hush!" cried Helen in an agonized whisper. "I am only thinking what would be best for me to do. I cannot hide you here. If my aunt knew, she would be so terrified she would betray you without saying a word."

Again she was silent for a few moments, then, seeming suddenly to have made up her mind, she went softly to the door.

"Don't leave me!" cried Leopold.

"Hush! I must. I know what to do now. Be quiet here until I come back."

Cautiously she unlocked the door and left the room. In three or four minutes she returned, carrying a loaf of bread and a bottle of wine. To her dismay Leopold had vanished. Presently he came creeping out from under the bed, looking so miserable that Helen could not help feeling a pang of shame about him. But the next moment the love of the sister, the tender compassion of the woman, returned. The more abject he was, the more he was to be pitied and ministered to.

"Here, Poldie," she said, "you carry the bread and I will take the wine. You must eat something, or you will become ill."

As she spoke, she locked the door again. Then she put a dark shawl over her head and fastened it under her chin. Her white face shone out from it like the moon from a dark cloud.

"Follow me, Poldie," she instructed, and putting out the candles, went to the window. He obeyed without a question, carrying the loaf she had put into his hands. The window sash rested on a little door. She opened it and stepped onto the balcony. As soon as her brother had followed her, she closed it again, drew down the sash, and led the way to the garden. And so, by the door in the sunk fence, they came out upon the meadow.

9 The Refuge

The night was very dusky, but Helen knew perfectly the way she was going. A strange excitement possessed her and lifted her above fear. The instant she found herself in the open air, her faculties seemed to awaken. There had been no rain, so the ground would not betray their steps. There was enough light in the sky to see the trees, and she guided herself to the door in the park fence and then straight to the deserted house. Remembering well her brother's old dislike of the place, she said nothing of their destination; but when he suddenly stopped, she knew it had dawned upon him. For one moment he hung back, but a stronger and more definite fear lay behind, and he continued on.

Emerging from the trees on the edge of the hollow, it was too dark to see the mass of the house or the slight gleam from the surface of the lake. All was silent as a deserted churchyard when they went down the slope. Through the straggling bushes they forced their way with their arms and felt their way with their feet to the front door of the house. The steps, from the effects of various floods, were all out of level in different directions. The door was unlocked as usual, needing only a strong push to open it, and they entered. How awfully still it seemed!

They groped their way through the hall and up the wide staircase. Helen had taken Leopold by the hand, and she now led him straight to the closet where the hidden room opened. He made no resistance, for the covering wings of darkness had protection in them. When at last she knew that no ray could reach the outside, Helen struck a match. As the spot where he had so often shuddered was laid bare before his eyes, he gave a cry and would have rushed away. Helen grabbed him. He yielded, and allowed her to lead him into the room. There she lit a candle, and as it came gradually alive, it shed a pale yellow light around, revealing a bare room with a bedstead and the remains of a moth-eaten mattress in a corner. Leopold threw himself upon it, uttering a sound that more resembled a choked scream than a groan.

Helen tried to soothe him. She took from her pocket a piece of bread and tried to make him eat, but in vain. Then she poured out a cup of wine. He drank it eagerly, and asked for more, but she refused. The wine, instead of comforting him, seemed only to rouse him to fresh horror. She consoled him as best she could, and assured him that for the present he was perfectly safe. Thinking it would encourage him, she reminded him of the trapdoor in the floor of the closet and the little chamber underneath. But at the mention of it he jumped up, his eyes glaring.

"Helen! I remember now!" he cried. "I knew it at the time. Don't you know I never could endure the place? I always dreamed, as plainly as I see you now, that one day I would be crouching here with a hideous crime on my conscience. I told you so, Helen, at the time. Oh, how could you bring me here?"

He threw himself down again and hid his face on her lap.

With new dismay Helen thought he must be going mad, for surely this was but some trick of his imagination. Certainly he had always dreaded the place, but he had never said a word of any special premonition to her. Yet there was a shadow of possible comfort in the thought—for what if the present crime should prove to be but a hallucination?—But whether real or not, she must know his story.

"Come, dearest Poldie, darling brother!" she entreated. "You have not yet told me what it is. What is the terrible thing you have done? I dare say it's nothing so very bad after all."

"There's the light coming!" he muttered in a dull, hollow voice. "The morning! Always the morning is coming again!"

"No, no, dear Poldie!" she returned. "There is no window here—at least it opens only onto the back stairway, and the morning is still a long way off."

"How far?" he asked, staring into her eyes. "Twenty years? That was just when I was born! Why are we sent into this cursed world? I wish God had never made it. What was the good?"

He was silent. She realized the futility of a rational report from him and decided she must get him to sleep.

With an effort of her will, she controlled the anguish of her own spirit and softly stroked the head of the poor lad. She began singing him a lullaby he had been very fond of in his childhood, and in a few minutes the fingers which clutched her hand relaxed, and she knew by his breathing that he was asleep. She sat still as a stone, not daring to move, hardly daring to breathe, lest she should rouse him from a few blessed minutes of self-nothingness. She sat motionless until it seemed as if she would drop from sheer weariness on the floor. How long she sat that way she could not tell—she had no means of knowing, but it seemed hours. At length some involuntary movement woke him. He started to his feet with a look of wild gladness. But there was scarcely time to recognize it before it vanished.

"My God, it is true, then!" he shrieked. "Oh, Helen! I dreamed that I was innocent—that I had but dreamed I had done it. Tell me that I'm dreaming now. Tell me! tell me! Tell me that I am not a murderer!"

As he spoke he seized her shoulders with a fierce grasp and shook her as if trying to wake her from the silence of lethargy.

"I hope you are innocent, my darling. But in any case I will do all I can to protect you," promised Helen. "Only I shall never be able to unless you control yourself enough to let me go home."

"No, Helen!" he cried. "You must not leave me. If you do, I will go crazy. *She* will come instead."

Helen shuddered.

"If I stay with you, just think what will happen," she reasoned. "I will be missed, and everyone in the countryside will come out to look for me. They will think I have been—" She checked herself.

"And so you might be—so might anyone be," he cried, "as long as I am on the loose. O God!" He hid his face in his hands.

"And then, my Poldie," Helen went on as calmly as she could, "they would come here and find us, and I don't know what might happen next."

"Yes, yes, Helen! Go," he agreed hurriedly, turning her by the shoulders as if he would push her from the room. "But you will come back to me as soon as you can? How will I know when to begin looking for you? What time is it? My watch has never been—since— The light will be here soon." As he spoke he had been feeling in one of his pockets. "I will not be taken alive.—Can you whistle, Helen?"

"Yes, Poldie," answered Helen, trembling. "Don't you remember teaching me?"

"Yes, yes. Then, when you come near the house, whistle, and keep whistling, for if I hear a step without a whistle, I will kill myself."

"What have you got there?" she asked, in a voice of renewed terror, noticing that he kept his hand in the breast pocket of his coat.

"Only the knife," he answered calmly.

"Give it to me," she said, calmly too.

He laughed, and the laugh was more terrible than any cry.

"No, I'm not so foolish as that," he responded. "My knife is my only friend! Who is to take care of me when you are away?"

She saw that the comfort of the knife must not be denied him. Nor did she fear any visit that might drive him to use it—*except indeed were the police to come upon him—and then what better could he do anyway?* she thought mournfully.

"Well, I will not plague you about it," she conceded. "Lie down and I will cover you with my shawl, and you can imagine my arms around you. I will come to you as soon as I can."

He obeyed. She spread her shawl over him and kissed him.

"Thank you, Helen," he whispered.

"Pray to God to deliver you, dear Poldie," she said.

"He can do that only by killing me," he returned. "I will pray for that."

He followed her from the room with eyes out of which peered the very demon of silent despair.

I will not further attempt to set forth the poor boy's feelings. He who knows the relief of waking from a dream of crime into the sunlight and jubilation of recovered innocence may conceive the misery of a delicate nature suddenly filled with the assurance of horrible guilt. Such a misery no waking could ever console unless it annihilated the past.

The moment Helen was out of sight, Leopold drew a small silver box from an inner pocket and eyed it with the eager look of a hungry animal. He took from it a certain potion, put it in his mouth, closed his eyes, and lay still.

When Helen came out into the hallway, she saw the day was breaking. A dim, dreary light filled the dismal house, but the candle had prevented her from perceiving the little of it that could enter the other room. A pang of renewed fear shot through her and she fled across the park. It was all like a horrible dream. Her darling brother lay in that frightful house, and if anyone should see her it might be death for him. But it was still very early; two hours would pass before any of the workmen would be on their way to the new house. When she was safe in her own room, before she could get into bed, she turned deathly sick, and next knew by the agonies of coming to herself that she had fainted.

A troubled, weary, excited sleep followed. She woke with many starts and then dozed off again. How kind is weariness sometimes! It is like the Father's hand laid a little heavy on the heart to make it still. But her dreams were full of torture, and even when she had no definite dream, she was haunted by the vague presence of blood. It was considerably past her usual time for rising when at length she heard her maid in the room. She got up wearily, but except for a heavy heart and a general sense of misery, nothing ailed her. She did not even have a headache.

Her chief business now was to keep herself from thinking until breakfast was over. She hurried to her bath for strength; the friendly water would rouse her to the present, make the past recede like a dream, and give her courage to face the future. But she must not think!

All the time she was dressing, her thoughts kept hovering round the awful thing—like moths around a flame. Ever and again she kept saying to herself that she must not think on it. Nevertheless, she found herself peeping through the chinks of the thought chamber at the terrible thing inside—the form of which she could not see. She could see only the color red—red mingled with ghastly whiteness. In all the world her best loved, her brother, the child of her father, was the only one who knew how that thing came there.

But while Helen's being was in such tumult that she could never again be the indifferent, self-contented person she had always been, her old habits were now a help in retaining her composure and covering her secret. A dim gleam of gladness woke in her at the sight of the unfinished cap, and when she showed it to her aunt with the wish of many happy returns, no second glance from Mrs. Ramshorn added to her uneasiness.

But, oh! How terribly time crept. She had no friend to help her. *George Bascombe?* She shuddered at the thought of his involvement. With his grand ideas of duty, he would be all for Leopold's giving up that very moment! Naturally the clergyman was the one to go to—and Mr. Wingfold had himself done wrong. But he had confessed it. No—he was a poor creature, and would not hold his tongue! She shook at every knock on the door, every ring of the bell, afraid it might be the police.

All the time her consciousness was like a single intense point of light in the middle of a darkness it could do nothing to illuminate. She knew nothing but that her brother lay in that horrible empty house and that, if his words were not the ravings of a maniac, the law, whether it yet suspected him or not, was certainly after him. And if it had not yet struck upon his trail, it was every moment on the point of finding it and must sooner or later come up with him. She *must* save him—all that was left of him to save! But poor Helen knew very little about saving.

She could not rest. When would the weary day be over? She wandered into the garden and looked out over the meadow. Not a creature was in sight, except a red and white cow, a child gathering buttercups, and a few rooks crossing from one field to another. It was a glorious day. The sun seemed the very center of conscious peace. And now for the first time, strange to say, Helen began to know the bliss of bare existence under a divine sky, in the midst of a divine air—but as something apart from her now, something she had possessed without knowing it but had lost, and which could never again be hers. How could she ever be happy again? For away there beyond those trees lay her unhappy brother in the lonely house, now a haunted house indeed. Perhaps he lay there dead! The horrors of the morning or his own hand might have slain him. She must go to him! She would defy the very sun and go. Was he not her brother?

What did people do when their brothers did awful deeds? She

heard of praying to God—had indeed herself told her brother to pray, but it seemed all folly. Yet even with the thought of denial in her mind, she looked up and gazed earnestly into the wide, innocent, mighty-looking space, as if by searching she might find someone. Perhaps she *ought* to pray. She could see no likelihood of a God, and yet something pushed her toward prayer. What if all this had come upon her and Poldie because she never prayed! If there were such horrible things in the world, although she had never dreamed of them, might there not be a God also, though she knew nothing of his whereabouts or how to reach him?

In the form of wordless feelings, hardly even of thoughts, fragments like these passed through her mind as she stood on the top of the sunk fence and gazed across the flat of sunny green lying before her. She *must* go to him. "God, hide me!" she cried within herself. "But how can he hide me," she answered herself, "when I am hiding a murderer?" "O God!" she cried again, and this time in an audible murmur. Then she turned, walked back to the house, and went looking for her aunt.

"I have a little headache," she said coolly, "and I need a long walk. Don't wait lunch for me. It is such a glorious day! I think I will go by the Millpool road, and across the park. Goodbye till tea, or perhaps even dinnertime."

"Hadn't you better have a ride and be back for lunch?" her aunt inquired, mournfully. Although she had almost given up birthdays, she thought her niece need not quite desert her on the disagreeable occasion.

"I'm not in the mood for riding. Nothing will do me but a good, long walk."

She went quietly out by the front door, walking slowly, softly along the street and out of the town, and eventually entering the park by the lodge gate. She saw Rachel at her work in the cottage kitchen as she passed, and heard her singing in a low and weak but very sweet voice, which went to her heart like a sting, making the tall, attractive rich lady envy the poor, distorted dwarf. But indeed, if all her misery had been swept away like a dream, Helen might yet have envied her ten times more than she did now had she but known how they actually compared with each other. For the being of Helen to that of Rachel was as a single primary cell to a finished brain; as the peeping of a chicken to the song of a lark.

"Good day, Rachel," she said, calling as she passed. It seemed to poor Helen a squalid abode, but it was a homelike palace to Rachel and her uncle. There was no sound all along the way as she walked except the noise of the birds and an occasional clank from the new building far away.

She entered the dismal house trembling, and the air felt as if death had been there before her. With slow step she reached the hidden room. Leopold lay as she had left him. She crept near and laid her hand on his forehead. He started to his feet in an agony of fright.

"You didn't whistle," he accused her.

"No, I forgot," answered Helen, shocked at her own carelessness. "But if I had, you wouldn't have heard me. You were sound asleep."

"A good thing I was! And yet I wish I had heard you, for then by this time I would have been beyond their reach."

Impulsively he showed her the weapon he carried. Helen stretched out her hand to take it, but he hurriedly replaced it in his pocket.

"I will find some water for you to wash with," she said. "There used to be a well in the garden, I remember. Here, I have brought you a shirt."

With some difficulty she found the well, all but lost in matted weeds under a clump of ivy. She carried him some water and put the garment with the horrible spot in her bag, to take it away and destroy it. Then she made him eat and drink. He did whatever she told him with a dull obedience. His condition was greatly changed. He wore a stupefied look and seemed only half awake to his terrible plight. He answered what questions she put to him with an indifference more dreadful than any passionate outburst. But at the root of the apparent apathy lay despair and remorse. Only the dull creature of misery was awake, lying motionless on the bottom of the deepest pool of his spirit.

The mood was favorable to the drawing of his story from him, but there are more particulars in the narrative I am now going to give than Helen learned at that time.

10   Leopold's Story

While yet a mere boy, scarcely more than sixteen, Leopold had become acquainted with the family of a certain manufacturer. The businessman had retired some years before and had purchased an estate a few miles from Goldswyre, his uncle's place. Leopold's association with them began just after he had left Eton, between which time and his going to Cambridge he spent a year reading with his cousin's tutor. It was at a ball he first saw Emmeline, the eldest of the family. He fell in love with her, if not in the noblest way, yet in a very genuine though at the same time passionate way. Had she been truehearted, being at least a year and a half older than he, she would have been too much of a woman to encourage his approaches. And yet to be just, to English eyes he did look older than he was. And then he was very handsome, distinguished-looking, of a good family, and at the same time was a natural contrast to herself and personally attractive to her. The first moment she saw his great black eyes blaze, she accepted the homage, laid it on the altar of self-worship, and ever after sought to see them alight in fresh worship of her. To be aware of her power over him, to play with him and make his cheek pale or glow or his eyes flash as she pleased was a game for the young woman too delightful to be ignored.

One of the most potent means for producing the human game of passion in which her soul thus rejoiced was jealousy, and for that she had all possible facilities. Emmeline consoled and irritated and reconsoled Leopold until he was her very slave. From that moment on he did badly at school, and finally went to Cambridge with the conviction that the woman to whom he had given his soul would be doing things in his absence the sight of which would drive him mad. Yet somehow he continued to live, reassured now and then by the loving letters she wrote to him, and relieving his own heart while he fostered her falsehood by the passionate replies he made to them.

From a tragic accident of his childhood, he had become acquainted with the influences of a certain baneful drug, to which one of his Indian attendants was addicted. Now at college, partly from curiosity but chiefly to escape from gnawing and passionate thought about Emmeline, he began to experiment with it. Experiment called for repetition, and repetition led first to a longing after its effects, and next to a mad appetite for the thing itself. By the time of my narrative he was on the verge of absolute slavery to its use.

He knew from Emmeline's letters that her family was going to give a ball, at which as many as pleased should be welcome in fancy dress, masked if they chose. The night before it, under the influence of his familiar drug, he had a dream. The dream made him so miserable and jealous that he longed to see her as a wounded man longs for water, and the thought suddenly came to him of going to the ball. The same moment the thought became a resolve.

For concealment he contented himself with a large traveling cloak, a tall felt hat, and a black silk mask. He entered the grounds with a group of guests, and, knowing the place perfectly, contrived to see something of her movements and behavior while he watched for an opportunity to speak to her alone—a quest of unlikely success. Hour after hour he watched, alternating between the house and the garden, and all the time he never spoke to anyone else or was spoken to.

Now Leopold had taken a dose of the drug on his journey, and it was later than usual before it began to take effect, possibly because of the motion of the carriage. He had indeed stopped looking for any result from it, when all at once, as he stood among the lilacs of a rather late spring, something fairly burst in his brain.

Made bold by his new condition, he again drew near the house. The guests were then passing from the supper to the ballroom. He had in his pocket a note ready, if needed, to slip into her hand, containing only the words, "Meet me for one long minute at the circle," a spot well known to both. He threw his cloak Spanish fashion over his left shoulder, slouched his hat, entered, and stood in a shadowy spot she would have to pass. There he waited, the note hidden in his hand, for a long time, yet not a weary one. At

GEORGE MACDONALD

length she passed, leaning on the arm of someone, but Leopold
never even looked at him. He slid the note into her hand, which
hung ungloved as inviting confidences. With an instinct quickened
and sharpened by much practice, her fingers instantly closed upon
it, but not a muscle belonging to any other part of her betrayed
the intrusion of a foreign object. I do not believe her heart gave
one beat more the next minute. She passed gracefully on, her
swan's neck shining, and Leopold hastened out to one of the windows of the ballroom, there to feast his eyes upon her loveliness.
But when he caught sight of her whirling in the waltz with the
officer whose name he had heard coupled with hers, and saw her
flash on him the light and power of her eyes, eyes which were to
him the windows of all the heaven, suddenly the whole frame of
his dream trembled, shook, and fell. With the suddenness of the
dark that follows the lightning, the music changed. He found himself lying on the floor of a huge vault. His soul fainted within him,
and the vision changed.

When he came to himself, he lay on the little plot of grass
among the lilacs where he had asked Emmeline to meet him. Fevered with jealousy and the horrible drug, his mouth was parched
like a chapped leather purse, and he found himself chewing at the
grass to ease its burning draught. But presently the evil thing resumed its sway, and fancies usurped facts. He was lying in an Indian jungle, close to the cave of a beautiful tigress which crouched
inside it waiting for the first sting of reviving hunger to devour
him. He could hear her breathing as she slept, but he was paralyzed and could not escape, knowing that, even if with some mighty
effort he succeeded in moving a finger, that motion would suffice
to wake her, and she would spring upon him and tear him to pieces.
Aeons of time seemingly passed thus, and still he lay on the grass
in the jungle and still the beautiful tigress slept. Suddenly an angel
in white stood over him. His fears vanished. The waving of her
wings cooled him, and she was the angel whom he had loved, and
loved to all eternity. She lifted him to his feet, gave him her hand,
and they walked away, and the tigress was asleep forever. For
miles and miles, as it seemed to his great joy, they wandered away
into the woods.

"Have you nothing to say now that I have come?" asked the angel.

"I have said all. I am at rest," answered the mortal.

"I am going to be married to Captain Hodges," announced the angel.

And with that word, the forest of heaven vanished. A worse hell suddenly appeared—the cold reality of an earth abjured, and a worthless maiden strolling by his side. He turned to her. The shock had mastered the drug. They were in the little wooded hollow only a hundred yards from the house. The blood began to throb in his head as from the piston of an engine. A horrid sound of dance music was ringing in his ears. Emmeline, his own, stood in her white dress gazing up in his face, with the words just parted from her lips, "I am going to be married to Captain Hodges." The next moment the foolish girl threw her arms round his neck, pulled his face to hers, kissed him and clung to him.

"Poor Leopold!" she uttered, looking in his face with her electricity at full power, "does it make him miserable, then?—But you know it could not have gone on like this between you and me forever. It was very dear while it lasted, but it had to come to an end."

Was there a glimmer of real pity and sadness in those wondrous eyes? She laughed, and hid her face on his chest. And what was it that awoke in Leopold? Had the drug resumed its power over him? Was it rage at her mockery, or infinite compassion for her despair? Would he slay a demon, or ransom a spirit from hateful bonds? Would he save a woman from disgrace and misery to come? or punish her for the vilest of falsehood? Who can tell? Leopold himself never knew. Whatever the feeling was, its own violence erased it from his memory and left him with a knife in his hand and Emmeline lying motionless at his feet. It was a knife the Scottish highlanders call a *skean-dhu*, sharp-pointed as a needle, sharp-edged as a razor. With one blow of it he had cleft her heart, and she never cried or laughed anymore in that body whose charms she had degraded to serve her own vanity. The next thing he remembered was standing on the edge of the shaft of a deserted coalpit, ready to throw himself down. From whence came the change of resolve he could not tell, but he threw in his cloak and mask, and fled. The one thought in his miserable brain was his sister. Having murdered one woman, he was fleeing to another for refuge. Helen would save him.

How he had found his way to his haven he had no idea. By searching the newspapers, Helen learned that a week had elapsed between the "mysterious murder of a young lady in Yorkshire" and the night on which Leopold had come to her window.

11   Sisterhood

Listening to the halting fragments of his story, her brother's sin broke wide the feebly flowing springs of Helen's conscience. Many things passed through her mind. She saw that in idleness and ease and drowsiness of soul, she had been forgetting and neglecting even the one she loved best in all the universe. Watching him again in exhausted slumber, she saw it would be impossible for her to look after him sufficiently where he was. The difficulty of feeding him would be great and that very likely he was on the edge of an illness which would require constant attention. If she only had some friend to talk to! But she had no one on whose counsel or discretion she could depend.

When at last he opened his eyes, she told him she must leave him now, but when it was dark she would come again and stay with him till dawn. Feebly he assented, seeming but half aware of what she said, and again closed his eyes. While he lay thus she managed to take his knife. She slipped it out of its sheath and put it naked in her pocket. As she went from the room, feeling like a mother abandoning her child, his eyes opened and followed her to the door with a longing, wild, hungry look. She felt the look following her still as she passed through the wood and across the park and into her room, while the knife in her pocket felt like a spell-bound demon waiting his chance to work them both some further mischief. She locked her door and took it out to hide it away somewhere, and then saw her brother's name engraved on the silver mounting of the handle. *What if he had left it behind him!* she thought with a shudder.

But a reassuring strength had risen in her mind with Leopold's disclosure. More than once on her way home she caught herself reasoning that the poor boy was not actually to blame at all, that he could not help it. But her conscience told her that love her brother she must, excuse him she might, but to uphold the deed would be to take the side of hell against heaven. Still, the murder did not seem so frightful now that she had heard the tale, as sketchy as Leopold's recounting of it had been, and she found it now required far less effort to face her aunt.

She lay down and slept until dinnertime, woke refreshed, and calmly sustained her part of the conversation during the slow meal. She talked to her aunt and a lady who was dining with them as if there were nothing on her mind at all. The time passed, the conversation waned, the hour arrived, and adieus were exchanged. All the world of Glaston lay asleep, the moon was draped in darkness, and the wind was blowing upon Helen's hot forehead as she moved like a thief across the park.

Her mind was in a tumult of mixed feelings, all gathered about the form of her precious brother. The sum of it all was a passionate devotion of her entire being to his service. I suspect that the loves of the noble wife, the great-souled mother, and the true sister flow from a single root. Anyhow, they are all but glints on the ruffled waters of humanity of the one, changeless, enduring Light.

She reached the little iron gate, which hung on one hinge only, and was lifting it from the ground to push it open when suddenly through the stillness came a frightful cry. When she hurried into the hall, however, the place was as silent as a crypt. Could it have been her imagination? Again, curdling her blood with horror, came the tearing cry, a shout of agony. In the dark she flew up the stair, calling him by name, fell twice, and finally reached the room. With trembling hands she found her matchbox and struck a light, uttering all the time every soothing word she could think of. Another shriek came just as the match flamed up in her fingers. Her brother was sitting on the edge of the bed staring ahead with unseeing eyes and terror-stricken face. She lit the candle quickly, talking to him all the while, but the ghastly face continued unchanged, and the wide-open eyes remained fixed. She seated herself at his side and threw her arms around him. It was like embracing a marble statue. But presently he gave a kind of shudder and the tension in his frame abated.

"Is it you, Helen?" he asked, shuddering. Then he closed his eyes and laid his head on her shoulder. His breath felt like a furnace and his skin seemed on fire. She felt his pulse. It was galloping wildly under her fingers. He was in a fever—brain fever probably—and what could she do? A thought came to her. Yes, it was the only possible thing. She would take him home.

"Poldie, dear," she persuaded, "you must come with me. I am going to take you to my own room where I can nurse you properly and won't have to leave you. Do you think you could walk that far?"

"Walk. Yes, quite well. Why not?"

"I am afraid you are going to be ill, Poldie. But however ill you may feel, you must promise me to try to make as little noise as you can, and never cry out if you can help it. When I do like this," she went on, laying her finger on his lips, "you must be altogether silent."

"I will do whatever you tell me, Helen, if you will only promise not to leave me, and when they come for me to give me poison."

She promised, breathing a prayer that the latter would never be required, and then hastily obliterated every sign that the room had been occupied. She took his arm and led him out into the night. He was very quiet—too quiet and submissive, she thought. They were soon in Helen's room, where she left him to get into bed himself while she gathered her thoughts and went to tell her aunt of his presence in the house. When the lady heard Helen's story, how her brother had come to her window, that he was, she thought, ill with brain fever and talked wildly, Mrs. Ramshorn quite approved of Helen's having put him to bed in her own room and would immediately have risen to help nurse him. But Helen persuaded her to have a good night's rest, and begged her to warn the servants not to mention his presence in the house so that it would not get out that he was out of his mind. They were all old and tolerably faithful, and Leopold had been from childhood such a favorite that she hoped thus to secure their silence.

"But, child, he must have the doctor," insisted her aunt.

"Yes, but I will manage him. What a good thing old Mr. Bird is gone!" Helen rattled on. "He was such a gossip. We will have to call in the new doctor, Mr. Faber. I will see that he understands. He has to build up his practice and will mind what I say."

"Why, child, you *are* cunning!" exclaimed her aunt. "What helpless creatures men are," she continued. "Out of one scrape into another. Would you believe it, my dear?—your uncle, one of the best men and most exemplary of clergymen—why, I had to put on his stockings for him every day. Not that my services stopped there, either," she went on, warming to her subject. "I wrote more than half his sermons for him. He never would preach the same sermon twice, you see. He made it a point of honor, and the result was that he ran out of ideas and had to come to me.—Poor dear boy, we must do what we can for him."

"I will call you if I find it necessary, Aunt. I must go to him now, for he cannot stand to have me out of his sight. Don't send for the doctor till I see you again."

When she was back in her room, to her great relief she found Leopold asleep. But when he woke, he had a high fever and Mr. Faber was summoned. He found the state of his patient so severe that no amount of wild raving could have surprised him. His brain was burning and he tossed from side to side, talking vehemently, but it was unintelligible even to Helen.

Mr. Faber had attended medical classes and walked the hospitals but not without undergoing the influences of the unbelief prevailing in those places. So when he came to practice in Glaston, he brought his quota of the yeast of unbelief into that ancient and slumberous town. Since he had to gain for himself a practice, he was prudent enough to make no display of his godless views. He did not fancy himself the holder of some commission for the general annihilation of belief like George Bascombe. He had a cold, businesslike manner, which however admirable on some grounds, destroyed any hope Helen might have had in finding in him someone to whom she might reveal the awkward facts of the situation.

He proved himself both wise and skillful, yet it was weeks before Leopold began to mend. By the time the fever left him, he was in such a weakened condition that it was very doubtful whether he would live. Helen's exhausting ministration continued. Yet now she thought of her life as she had never thought of it before—namely, as a thing of worth. It had grown precious to her since it had become the mainstay of Leopold's. Despite the terrible state of suspense in which she now lived, seeming to herself at times an actual sharer in her brother's guilt, she would yet occasionally find herself exulting in the thought of being the guardian angel he called her.

During all this time she scarcely saw her cousin George. Neither did she attend church, for Leopold's sake. Her physical being certainly suffered during this time. But one morning the curate saw in the midst of the congregation her face, and along with its pallor and look of suppressed trouble, gathered the expression of a higher existence. Not that she had drawn a single consoling drink from any one of the wells of religion, or now sought out the church for the sake of anything precious it might have to offer. The great quiet place drew her merely with the offer of its two hours of restful stillness. The thing which had elevated her instead was simply that, without any thought of him, she had yet been doing the will of the Heart of the world. True, she had been but following her instinct, yet it was the beginning of the way of God, and therefore the face of the maiden had begun to shine with a light which no physical health or beauty could have kindled there.

12 The Curate Makes a Discovery

Wingfold's visits to the little people at the gate became not only more frequent but more and more interesting to him. As Polwarth's position as gatekeeper made few demands on his attention, he had plenty of time to give the curate. He had never yet had any pupil but his niece, and to find another, and one whose soul was so eager, was pure delight. The curate was an answer to that for which he had so often prayed—an outlet for the living waters of his spirit into dry and thirsty lands. In Wingfold he had found a man docile and obedient, both thirsting after and recognizing the truth.

For two or three Sundays the curate, largely assisted by his new friend, fed his flock with his gleanings from other men's harvests. Though it had not yet come to his knowledge, the complaints of some already had led to a semi-public meeting at which they discussed the possibility of communicating with the rector on the subject. Others felt that since the rector paid so little attention to his flock, it would be better to appeal directly to the bishop. But before the group could take any action, things took a new turn, at first surprising to all, soon alarming to some and, finally, appalling to many.

Obedient to Polwarth's instructions, Wingfold had taken to his New Testament. At first as he read and tried to understand, small difficulties would shoot out at him. Initially it was a discrepancy in the genealogies—I mention this merely to show the sort of difficulty I mean. Some of these he pursued until he had solved the apparent inconsistency, but then found he had gained nothing by the victory. Polwarth soon persuaded him to ignore such things for the present, since they involved little concerning the man whom he was trying to understand. With other difficulties, Polwarth told him that understanding them depended on a more advanced knowledge of Jesus himself. Polwarth did not want to say or explain too much, for he did not want to weaken by *presentation* the force of a truth which, in *discovery*, would have its full effect.

On one occasion when Wingfold had asked him whether he saw the meaning of a certain saying of our Lord, Polwarth answered wisely: "I think I do; but whether I could at present make you see it I cannot tell. I suspect it is one of those concerning which I have already said that you have to understand Jesus better before you can understand what the text means. Let me just ask you one question, to make the nature of what I say clear to you: Tell me, if you can, what primarily did Jesus, from his own account of himself, come into the world to do?"

"To save it," answered Wingfold readily.

"I think you are wrong," returned Polwarth. "Mind, I said *primarily*. I think you will come to the same conclusion yourself by and by. An honest man will never ultimately fail to get at what Jesus means if he studies Jesus' life and teachings long enough. I have seen him described somewhere as a man dominated by the passion of humanity—or something like that. But, another passion was the light of his life, and dominated even that which would yet have been enough to make him lay down his life."

Wingfold went away pondering.

Though Polwarth read little concerning religion except the New Testament, he could have directed Wingfold to several books which might have lent him good aid in his quest after the real likeness of the man he sought. But he desired instead that when the light should first dawn for Wingfold, it should flow from the words of the Son of Man himself. And little did Wingfold suspect that, now and again when his lamp was burning far into the night while he was struggling with some hard saying, the little man was going round and round his house praying for his young friend.

Before long Jesus' miracles grew troublesome to Wingfold's modern mind. Could Mr. Polwarth honestly say that he found no difficulty in believing things so altogether out of the common order of events, and so buried in antiquity that investigation was impossible?

Mr. Polwarth could not say that he found no such difficulty.

"Then why should the weight of the story," pressed Wingfold, "rest upon such improbable things as miracles, which even a man like yourself has found difficulty believing? I presume you will admit that they *are* at best improbable."

"Having said that I believe every one recorded," stated Polwarth, "I heartily admit their improbability. But the weight of proof is not, and never was, laid upon the miracles themselves. Our Lord did not make much of them. He did them more out of concern for the individual than for the sake of the onlookers.—But it is not through the miracles that you will find the Lord; though, having found him, you will find him there also. The question for you is not: Are the miracles true? but, Was *Jesus* true? Again I say, you must find him—the man himself. When you have found him, I may perhaps be able to discuss with you in more depth the question about how one can believe in such improbable things as the miracles."

At length one day, as the curate was comparing certain passages in the gospels, he fell into a half-thinking, half-dreaming mood in which his eyes rested for some time on the verse, "Ye will not come unto me that ye might have life." It mingled itself with his brooding, and by and by the form of Jesus gathered in the stillness of his mind with such reality that he found himself thinking of him as a truehearted man, earnestly desiring to help his fellowmen and women, but who could not get them to obey what he told them.

"Ah!" said the curate to himself, "if I had but seen him, I would have minded him, would have followed him with question after question until I got at the truth!"

Again his thoughts drifted into a reverie for some time, until suddenly the words rose from deep in his memory, *"Why do you call me, Lord, Lord, and do not the things which I say?"*

"Good God!" he exclaimed. "Here I am bothering over words, and questioning about this and that, as if I were examining his fitness for a job, while he has all the while been claiming my obedience! I have not once in my life done a single thing because he told me.—But then, how am I to obey him until I am sure of his right to command? I just want to know whether I am to call him Lord or not. Here I have all these years been calling myself a Christian, even ministering in the temple of Christ as if he were some heathen divinity who cared for songs and prayers and sacrifices, and yet I cannot honestly say I ever once in my life did a thing because he said so. I have *not* been an honest man! Is it any wonder that the things he said are too high and noble to be recognized as truth by such a man as me?"

With this another saying dawned upon him, *"If any man will do his will, he shall find out whether my teaching comes from God, or whether I speak on my own."*

After thinking for a few more minutes, Thomas went into his room and shut the door. He came out again not long afterward and went straight to visit a certain grieving old woman.

The next visible result showed on the following Sunday. The man who went up to the pulpit believed for the first time in his life that he now had something to say to his fellow sinners. It was not the sacred spoil of others that he brought with him, but the message given him by a light in his own heart.

He opened no notebook, nor read words from any book except, with shaky voice, those of his text: "*Why do you call me, Lord, Lord, and do not the things which I say?*"

He looked around upon his congregation as he had never dared to until now and saw face after face. He saw among the rest that of Helen Lingard, now so sadly altered; and trembling a little with a new excitement, he began, "My hearers, I come before you this morning to say the first word of truth ever given to *me* to utter."

"Is he going to deny the Bible?" muttered some to themselves. "If the rector hears how you have been disgracing his pulpit, it will surely be your last week in it."

"In my room, three days ago," the curate went on, "I was reading the strange story of the man who appeared in Palestine saying that he was the Son of God. And I came upon those words of his which I have just read to you. All at once my conscience awoke and asked me, 'Do you do the things he says to you?' And I thought to myself, 'Have I today done a single thing he has said to me? When was the last time I did something I heard from him? Did I *ever* in all my life do one thing because he said to me, "Do this?"' And the answer was, 'No, never.' Yet there I was, not only calling myself a Christian, but presuming to live among you and be your helper on the road toward the heavenly kingdom. What a living lie I have been!"

"What a wretch!" mumbled one man to himself. "A hypocrite, by his own confession!" concluded others. *Exceedingly improper!* thought Mrs. Ramshorn; *unheard-of and most unclerical behavior!* Helen woke up a little, began to listen, and wondered what Wingfold had been saying to cause such a wind to come rustling among the heads of the congregation.

"Having made this confession," Wingfold proceeded, "you will understand that whatever I now say, I say to myself as much as to any among you to whom it may apply."

He then proceeded to show that faith and obedience are one and the same spirit: what in the heart we call faith, in the will we call obedience. He showed that the Lord refused the so-called faith which found its vent at the lips in worshipping words and not at the limbs in obedient action. Some of his listeners immediately pronounced his notions bad theology, while others said to themselves that at least it was common sense.

"A Socinian!" grumbled Mrs. Ramshorn; though rather proud of her learned description; "trying to deny and rationalize the sacred doctrines!"

"There's stuff in the fellow!" admitted the rector's churchwarden, who had been brought up a Wesleyan.

"He'd make a fellow think he *did* believe all his grandmother told him!" concluded Bascombe.

As he went on, the awakened curate grew almost eloquent. His face shone with earnestness. Even Helen, in the middle of her own trouble, found her gaze fixed upon him, though she did not have a single idea what he was talking about. At length he closed with these words: "I request anyone who agrees with my confession to make it to himself and his God. It follows from my confession that I dare not call myself a Christian. How could such a one as myself know anything about that which, if it is indeed true, must be the one all-absorbing truth in the universe?

"No, my hearers, I do not call myself a Christian. But I call everyone here who obeys the word of Jesus—who restrains anger, who avoids judgment, who practices generosity, who does good to his enemies, who prays for his slanderers—to witness my vow, that I will from this day on try to obey him. I commit myself to this in the hope that he whom Jesus called God and his Father will reveal to me him whom you call your Lord Jesus Christ, that into my darkness I may receive the light of the world."

"A professed infidel!" was Mrs. Ramshorn's shocked assessment; she barely managed to keep her profound indignation to herself. "A clever one too! Laying a trap for us to prove us all atheists as well as himself. As if any mere mortal *could* obey the instructions of the Savior!"

But there was one shining face in that congregation. Its eyes were full of tears and the heart behind it was giving that God and

Father thanks, for this was far more than he had even hoped for except in the distant future. The light was now shining into the heart of his friend, to whom now, praised be God! the way lay open into all truth. And when the words of the benediction came, in a voice that once more shook with emotion, he bent down his face and the poor, stunted, distorted frame and great gray head were shaken with the sobs of a mighty gladness. It mattered not how the congregation would receive this. Those whom the Father had drawn would hear.

Polwarth did not seek the curate in the vestry or wait for him at the church door, nor did he follow him to his home after the service. He was not one of those who compliment a man on his fine sermon. How grandly careless are some men of the ruinous risk their praises are to their friends. "Let God praise him!" said Polwarth. "I will only dare to love him." He would not toy with his friend's awakening spirit.

13   The Ride

This had been the first Sunday Helen had gone to church since her brother had come. On the previous Sunday Leopold had begun to improve and by the end of the week was so quiet that, longing for a change of atmosphere, she had gone to church. On her return she heard he was no worse, although he had been anxiously asking for her. She hurried upstairs to him.

"Why do you go to church?" he asked when she entered. "What's the use of it?"

"Not much," replied Helen. "I like the quiet and the music, that's all."

He seemed disappointed and lay still for a few moments.

"In old times," he said finally, "the churches used to be a refuge. I suppose that is why one can't help feeling as if some safety were to be gotten from them. Was your cousin George there this morning?"

"Yes, he went with us," answered Helen.

"I would like to see him. I want somebody to talk to."

Helen was silent. She was more occupied wondering why she shrank from bringing Bascombe into the sickroom than in thinking what to answer Leopold. Why should she object to Leopold's being told as well as herself that he need fear no punishment in the next world, whatever he might have to encounter in this? That there was no frightful God to be terrified of? Ought it not to encourage the poor fellow? But encourage him to what? To live on and endure his misery, or to put an end to it and himself at once?

I will not say that exactly such a train of thoughts passed through her mind, but whatever her thoughts, they brought her no nearer desiring George Bascombe's presence by the bedside of her guilty brother. At the same time, her partiality for her cousin made her justify his exclusion, thinking, "George would not in the least understand my poor Poldie, and would be too hard on him."

Since her brother's appearance, she had seen very little of her cousin. She had felt, almost without knowing it, that his character was unsympathetic, and that his loud, cold, casual nature could never recognize or justify such love as she felt for her brother. Nor was this all; she remembered how he had once expressed himself about criminals. She feared to look in his face lest his keen, questioning, unsparing eye might read in her soul that she was the sister of a murderer.

Before this time, however, a hint of light had appeared in her mind, and she had begun to doubt whether he had really committed the crime after all. There had been no inquiry about him, except from his uncle, concerning his absence from Cambridge. And his sudden attack of brain fever served as more than sufficient excuse for that. That there had been such a murder, the newspapers left no room for doubt. But might not the horror of his beloved's death, the insidious approaches of the fever, and the influences of that hateful drug all have combined to create a hallucination of guilt? And what finally all but satisfied her of the truth of her hoped conjecture was that when he began to recover, Leopold seemed himself in doubt at times whether his sense of guilt did not have its origin in one of the many dreams which had haunted him throughout his illness. He knew only too well that because of the drug, dreams had long since become often more real than what was going on around him. To this blurring confusion it probably added that in the first stages of the fever, he was still under the influence of the same drug which had been working on his brain up to the very moment when he committed the crime.

During the week, Helen's hope had almost settled into conviction. One consequence was that, although she was not a whit more inclined to bring George Bascombe to the sickroom, she found herself no longer adverse to meeting him. So on the following Saturday when he presented himself as usual, she consented to go out for a ride with him in the evening.

A soft west wind met them the instant they turned out of the street, walking their horses toward the park gate. Something had prevailed to momentarily silence George Bascombe; it may have been but the influence of the cigar which Helen had begged him to finish quickly. Helen too was silent.

It was a perfect English summer evening—warm, but not sultry. As they walked their horses up the carriageway the sun went down, and Helen became aware that the whole evening was thinking around her. As the dusk grew deeper and the night drew closer, the world seemed to have grown dark with its contemplations. Lately Helen herself had been driven to think—if not deeply, yet intensely—and so she knew what it was like and felt at home with the twilight.

They turned from the drive onto the turf. Their horses tossed up their heads and set off at a good pelting gallop across the park. On Helen's cheek the wind blew cool, strong and kind. As if flowing from some fountain above, it seemed to bring to her a vague promise, almost a precognition, of peace—which only set her longing after something—she knew not what—which would fill the longing the wind had brought her. The longing grew as they galloped, and soon tears were running down her face. For fear Bascombe would see them, she gave her horse the rein and fled into the friendly dusk.

Suddenly she found herself close to a clump of trees which overhung the deserted house where she had first hidden Leopold.

She had made a great circle without knowing it. A pang shot to her heart and her tears stopped. The night, silent with thought, held Leopold's secret also in its bosom! She drew rein, turned, and waited for Bascombe.

"What a chase you've given me, Helen!" he cried while yet pounding away some yards off.

"A wild goose chase, you mean?"

"It would have been if I had tried to catch you on this ancient beast."

"Don't abuse the old horse, George; he has seen better days.— Shall I tell you what I was thinking about?"

"If you like."

"I was thinking how pleasant it would be to ride on and on into eternity," sighed Helen.

"That feeling of continuity," returned George, "is a proof of the painlessness of departure. No one can ever know when he ceases to be, because then he is not; that is how some men come to believe they are going to live forever. But the worst of it is that they no sooner fancy it than it seems to them a probable as well as a delightful thing to go on and on and never cease. The fools very conveniently take their longing for immortality, which they call an idea innate in the human heart, for a proof that immortality is their rightful inheritance."

"How then do you account for the existence and universality of the idea?" asked Helen, who had happened lately to come upon some arguments on the other side.

"I account for its existence as I have just said. And, for its universality, by denying it myself. It is *not* universal, because I for one don't share it."

Helen said nothing in reply. She thought her cousin very clever, but could not enjoy what he said—not in the face of that sky and in the lingering reflection of the feelings it had awakened in her. He might be right, but now at least she wanted no more of it.

"And what were you thinking of, George?" inquired Helen, anxious to change the subject.

"I was thinking," he answered, "—let me see!—oh, yes! I was thinking of that very singular case of murder. You must have seen it in the newspapers. I have long wondered whether I was better fit for a lawyer or a detective. I can't keep my mind off a puzzling case. You must have heard of this one—the girl they found lying in her ball-dress in the middle of a wood, stabbed to the heart?"

"I do remember something of it," answered Helen, gathering a little courage from the fact that her cousin could not see her face. "Then the murderer has not been discovered?"

"That is the interesting point. There is not a trace of him. There is not even a soul suspected!"

Helen drew in a deep breath.

"Had it been in Rome, now—" George went on. "But in a quiet country place in England! The thing seems incredible. So artistically done! No struggle—just one blow right to the heart, and the assassin gone as if by magic. No weapon. Nothing to give a clue. I *should* like to try to unravel it."

"Has nothing been done, then?" asked Helen with a gasp, moving in her saddle to hide it.

"Oh, everything that can be done has been done. There was an instant chase, but they seem to have got on the track of the wrong man—or indeed, for anything certain, of no man at all. A coast guardsman says that on the night, or rather morning, in question, he was approaching a little cove on the shore not more than a mile from the scene. As he watched what seemed to be two fishermen preparing to launch their boat, he saw a third man come running down the steep slope from the pastures above and jump into the stern of it. Before he could reach the spot, they were off and had hoisted two lug-sails. The moon was in her last quarter and gave light enough for what he reported. But when inquiries were made, nothing whatever could be discovered concerning boat or men. The next morning no fishing boat was missing, and no fishermen would confess to having gone from that cove. The marks of the boat's keel and of the men's feet on the sand, if there ever were any, had been washed out by the tide. It was concluded that the thing had been prearranged and that the murderer had escaped, probably to Holland. Telegrams were sent to the mainland in all directions, but no news could be gathered of any suspicious landing on the opposite coast. There the matter rests. Neither parents, relatives, nor friends appear to have a suspicion of anyone."

"Are there no conjectures as to motives?" asked Helen, masking the rising joy she felt at his words.

"No end of them. She was beautiful, they say, sweet-tempered as a dove, and of course, fond of admiration. Thus most of the conjectures turn on jealousy. The most likely thing seems that she had some squire of low degree, of whom neither parents nor friends knew anything. I must say, I am strongly inclined to take the matter in hand myself."

We must get him out of the country as soon as possible, thought Helen. "I should hardly have thought it worthy of your gifts, George," she reproached him, "to turn policeman. For my part, I should not relish hunting down some poor wretch."

"The sacrifice of individual choice is a claim society has upon each of its members," returned Bascombe. "Every murderer imprisoned for life or hanged is a benefit to the community."

Helen said no more, and presently turned homewards, thinking that she must not be away any longer from her invalid.

14   A Dream

It was nearly dark when Helen and Bascombe arrived again at the lodge, and Rachel opened the gate for them. Without even a *thank you,* they rode out. She stood for a moment gazing after them through the dusk, then turned with a sigh and went into the kitchen where her uncle sat by the fire with a book in his hand.

"How I would like to be as well made as Miss Lingard!" she remarked, seating herself by the lamp that stood on the pine table. "It must be a fine thing to be strong and tall and able to look this way and that without turning all your body along with your head. And what it must be to sit on a horse as she does! I'm dreadfully envious, Uncle."

"No, my child. I know you better than you do yourself. There is a great difference between *I wish I were* and *I would like to be.* To be content is not to be satisfied. No one ought to be satisfied with the imperfect. It is God's will that we should contentedly bear what he gives us. But at the same time we can look forward with hope to the redemption of the body."

"Yes, Uncle. I understand. You know I enjoy life. How could I help it with you to share it with? But how am I to tell whether I may not be crooked in the next life as well. And that's what troubles me at times. There might be some necessity for it, you know."

"Then there will also be patience to bear it, that you may be sure of. But do not fear. It is more likely that those who have not thanked God but have prided themselves that they were beautiful in this world will be crooked in the next. But God does what is best for them as well as for us. We may find one day that beauty and riches were the best things for those to whom they were given, as deformity and poverty were the best for us."

"I wonder what sort of person I would have been if I'd had a straight spine!" said Rachel, laughing.

"Hardly one so dear to your deformed uncle."

"Then I am glad I am as I am."

"I don't mind being God's dwarf," she went on after a thoughtful silence. "But I would rather be made after his own image. And this can't be it. I should like to be made over again."

"And if the hope we are saved by is no mockery, if St. Paul was not the fool of his own radiant imaginings, you *will* be made over again, my child.—But now let us forget our miserable bodies. Come up to my room, and I will read you a few lines that came to me this morning in the park."

But before they had climbed to the top of the stairs, Rachel heard Mr. Wingfold's step outside, then his knock on the door, and went down again to receive him.

Invited to ascend, Wingfold followed Rachel to her uncle's room. From the drawer of his table, Polwarth took a scratched and scored half sheet, and—not in the most melodious of voices—read the lines he had written.

When he was finished, Rachel understood her uncle's verses with sufficient ease to enjoy them at once. But Wingfold confessed,

"Mr. Polwarth, where poetry or any kind of verse is concerned, I am simply stupid. I did not understand half of what you read. Will you let me take those verses home with me?"

"I can hardly do that, for they are not legible. But I will copy them out for you."

"Will you give me them tomorrow? Will you be at church?"

"That will depend on you: would you rather have me there or not?"

"A thousand times rather," answered the curate. "To have one man there who knows what I mean is to have a double dose of courage. But I came tonight mainly to tell you something else. I have been greatly puzzled this last week about how I ought to regard the Bible—I mean as to its inspiration. What am I to say about it?"

"Those are two very distinct things. Why do you want to say something about it before you have anything to say? For yourself, however, let me just ask if you have not already found in that book the highest means of spiritual education and development you have yet met with? It is the man Christ Jesus we have to know, and the Bible we must use to that end—not for theory or dogma. In that light, it is the most practical and useful book in the world.— But let me tell you a strange dream I had not long ago."

Rachel's face brightened. She rose, got a little stool, and setting it down close by the chair on which her uncle was perched, seated herself at his feet to listen.

"About two years ago," related Polwarth, "a friend sent me Tauchnitz's edition of the English New Testament, which has the different readings of the three oldest known manuscripts translated at the foot of the page. I received it with such exultation that it brought on an attack of asthma, and I could scarcely open it for a week but lay with it under my pillow. Any person who loves books would understand the ecstasy I felt. Why, Mr. Wingfold, just to hold that book in my hands—I can scarcely describe the pleasure it brought me, such a prize did I consider that gift. I suppose a cherished possession of any kind would have that same effect on anyone. But for me there has never been anything quite like an old book or a revered edition of the Scriptures. In any case, such was my reaction to the New Testament I received. And when I eventually was able to study it more closely, my main surprise was to find the differences from the common version so *few* and so *small*.

"You can hardly imagine my delight in the discoveries this edition gave me. The contents within its handsome leather covers outran the anticipation I had felt as I first held it between my hands. I mention all this because it goes to account for the dream that followed and to enforce its truth. Do not, however, imagine me a believer in dreams more than any other source of mental impressions. If a dream reveals a principle, that principle is a revelation, and the dream is neither more nor less valuable than a waking thought that does the same. The truth conveyed is the revelation, not the dream.

"The dream I am now going to tell you was clearly led up to by my waking thoughts. I dreamed that I was in a desert. It was neither day nor night. I saw neither sun, moon, nor stars. A heavy yet half-luminous cloud hung over the earth. My heart was beating fast and high, for I was journeying toward an isolated Armenian convent, where I had good ground for hoping I would find the original manuscript of the fourth gospel, the very handwriting of the apostle John. That the old man did not actually write it himself, I never considered in my dream. The excitement mounting inside me was the same dreaming sensation as the gift from my friend had caused in my waking emotions.

"After I had walked on for a long time, I saw the level horizon before me broken by a rock, as it seemed, rising from the plain of the desert. I knew it was the monastery. It was many miles away, and as I journeyed on, it grew and grew, until it became huge as a hill against the sky. At length I came to the door, iron-clamped, deep-set in a low, thick wall. It stood wide open. I entered, crossed a court, reached the door of the monastery itself, and again entered. Every door to which I came stood open, but no guide came to meet me. I used my best judgment to get deeper and deeper into the building, for I scarce doubted that in its innermost chamber I should find the treasure I sought. At last I stood before a huge door hung with a curtain of rich workmanship, torn in the middle from top to bottom. Through the rent I passed into a stone cell. In the cell stood a table. On the table was a closed book.

"Oh! how my heart beat! Never but in that moment had I

known the feeling of utter preciousness in a thing possessed. What doubts and fears would not this one lovely, oh! unutterably beloved volume, lay at rest forever! How my eyes would dwell upon every stroke of every letter formed by the hand of the dearest disciple! Nearly eighteen hundred years—and there it lay! Here was a man who actually *heard* the Master say the words and then wrote them down!

"I stood motionless and my soul seemed to wind itself among the pages, while my body stood like a pillar of salt, lost in amazement. At last, with sudden daring, I made a step toward the table. Bending with awe, I stretched out my hand to lay it on the book. But before my hand reached it, another hand, from the opposite side of the table, appeared upon it—an old, blue-veined, but powerful hand. I looked up.

"There stood the beloved disciple! His countenance was as a mirror which shone back the face of the Master. Slowly he lifted the book and turned away. Then I saw behind him as it were an altar where a fire of wood was burning, and a pang of dismay shot to my heart, for I knew what he was about to do. He laid the book on the burning wood, and regarded it with a smile as it shrank and shriveled and smouldered to ashes. Then he turned to me and said, while a perfect heaven of peace shone in his eyes: 'Son of man, the Word of God lives and abides forever, not in the volume of the book, but in the heart of the man that in love obeys him.' And then I awoke weeping, but with the lesson of my dream."

A deep silence settled on the little company. Finally Wingfold said, "I trust I have the lesson too."

He rose, shook hands with them, and, without another word, went home.

15   Another Sermon

There are those who in their very first seeking of it are nearer to the kingdom of heaven than many who have for years believed themselves in it. In the former there is more of the mind of Jesus, and when he calls them, they recognize him at once and go after him. The others examine him from head to foot, and finding him not sufficiently like the Jesus of their conception, turn their backs, and go to church to kneel before a vague form mingled of tradition and imagination.

Wingfold soon found that his nature was being stirred to depths unsuspected before. His first sermon showed that he had begun to have thoughts of his own. The news of that strange outpouring of honesty had of course spread through the town, and the people came to church the next Sunday in crowds—twice as many as the usual number—some who went seldom, some who went nowhere, some who belonged to other congregations. Mostly they were bent on witnessing whatever eccentricity the very peculiar young man might be guilty of next.

His second sermon was like the first. Proposing no text, he spoke the following:

"This church stands here in the name of Christianity. But what is Christianity? I know but one definition. Christianity does not mean what you think or what I think concerning Christ, but who *Christ is*. Last Sunday I showed you our Lord's very words—that anyone is his disciple who does what he commands. I said, therefore, that I dared not call myself a disciple, a Christian. Yet it is in the name of Christianity that I stand here. I have signed my name as a believer to the articles of the Church of England, with no better reason than that I had no particular dissent with any of the points of it at the time. Thus, knowing no better, I was ordained as one of her ministers. So it remains my business, as an honest man in the employment of the church, to do my best to set forth the claims of Jesus Christ, upon whom the church is founded and in whose name she exists. As one standing on the outskirts of a listening Galilean crowd, a word comes now and then to my hungry ears and hungrier heart. I turn and tell it again to you—not that you have not heard it also. If anything, I certainly am behind you rather than ahead of you in the hearing of these things. I tell you what I have learned only that I may stir you up to ask yourselves, as I ask myself, 'Do I then obey this word? Have I ever, have I once, sought to obey it? Am I a pupil of Jesus? Am I a Christian?' Hear then his words. For me, they fill my heart with doubt and dismay.

"The Lord says, '*Love your enemies.*' Do you say, '*It is impossible*'? Do you say, '*Alas, I cannot*'? But have you tried to see whether he who made you will not increase your strength when you step out to obey him?

"The Lord says, '*Be perfect.*' Do you then aim for perfection, or do you excuse your shortcomings and say, '*To err is human*'? If so, then you must ask yourself what part you have in him.

"The Lord says, '*Lay not up for yourselves treasures on earth.*' My part is not now to preach against the love of money, but to ask you, '*Are* you laying up for yourselves treasures on earth?' As to what the command means, the honest heart and the dishonest must each settle it in his own way. No doubt you can point to other men who are no better than you, and of whom yet no one would dare question the validity of their Christianity. But all that matters not a hair. All that does is confirm that you may all be pagans together. Do not mistake me. I am not judging you. For my finger points at myself along with you. But I ask you simply to judge yourselves by the words of Jesus.

"The Lord says, '*Take no thought for your life. Take no thought for tomorrow.*' Explain it as you may, but ask yourselves, '*Do I take no thought for my life? Do I take no thought for tomorrow*?'

"The Lord says, '*Judge not.*' Did you judge your neighbor yesterday? Will you judge him again tomorrow? Are you judging him now in the very heart that sits hearing the words, '*Judge not*'? Or do you side-step the command by asking, 'Who is my neighbor?' Does not your own profession of Christianity counsel you to fall upon your face, and cry to him, 'I am a sinful man, O Lord'?

"The Lord said, '*All things you would that men should do to*

you, do also to them.' You that buy and sell, do you obey this law?
Examine yourselves and see. You would want men to deal fairly to
you: do you deal just as fairly to them as you would count fairness
in them toward you? If conscience makes you hang your head inwardly, however you sit with it erect in the pew, can you dare to
add to your crime against the law and the prophets the insult to
Christ of calling yourselves his disciples?

"'Not every one that says unto me, "Lord, Lord," shall enter
into the kingdom of heaven, but he that does the will of my Father
who is in heaven.'"

I have of course given but the spine and ribs of the sermon.
There is no room for more. But this is enough to show that he
was certainly making the best of the accident that had led him into
that pulpit in the first place. And whatever the various opinions
of his hearers, many of them did actually feel that he had been
preaching to them. Even Mrs. Ramshorn was more silent than
usual as they went home. Although she was profoundly convinced
that such preaching was altogether contrary to the tradition of the
English Church, of which her departed dean remained to her the
unimpeachable embodiment, the only remark she made was that
Mr. Wingfold took quite too many pains to prove himself a pagan.

Mr. Bascombe was of the same opinion as before. "I like the
fellow," he said. "He says what he means. It's all great rubbish, of
course. Why don't you ask him home to dinner, Aunt?"

"Why should I, George?" returned his aunt. "Has he not been
abusing us all at a most ignorant and furious rate?"

"Oh, I didn't know," returned her nephew, and held his peace.
Nor did the aunt perceive the sarcasm. But George was paid in
full by the flicker of a faint smile across Helen's face.

As for Helen, the sermon had laid a sort of feeble electrical
hold upon her by its influx of honesty and earnestness. But she
could not accuse herself of having ever made a prominent profession of Christianity, confirmation and communion aside. And besides, had she not now all but rejected the whole thing in her
heart? If every word of what he said was true, not a word of it
could be applied to her. Anyway, what time did she have to think
about things that had happened eighteen centuries ago when her
brother was pining away with a black weight on his heart?

For although Leopold was gradually recovering, a supreme dejection which seemed to linger upon him gradually prompted Mr. Faber to ask Helen if she knew of any source of mental suffering that could explain it. She told him of the drug habit he had formed and asked if his being deprived of the narcotic might not be the cause. He accepted the suggestion and set himself to repair the injury the abuse had caused. Still, although Leopold's physical condition plainly improved, the dejection continued.

The earnestness of the doctor's quest for a cause added greatly to Helen's uneasiness. Also, as his health returned, his sleep became more troubled. He dreamed more, and his condition was always worse between two and three o'clock in the morning. Having perceived this, Helen would never allow anyone except herself to sit up with him during the first part of the night.

Increased anxiety and continued nighttime watching soon affected her health and she lost her appetite and color. Still she slept well during the latter part of the morning, and was always down before her aunt finished breakfast. During the day, also, she spent every available moment by Leopold's bedside, reading and talking to him, but yet not a single allusion had been made to their frightful secret.

16   The Linendraper

Outside, the sun rose and set, never a crimson thread less in the garment of his glory, though the spirit of one of the children of the earth was stained with the guilt of blood. The moon came up and knew nothing of the matter. The stars minded their own business. And the people of Glaston were all talking about their curate's sermons. Alas! it was about his sermons and not the subject of them that men talked. Their interest was roused by their peculiarity, and what some called the oddity of the preacher.

What had come upon him? He had not been at all like that for months after his appointment, and the change had come about so suddenly! Yes, it began with those extravagant notions about honesty in writing his own sermons. It might have been a sunstroke, but it took him too early in the year for that. Poor man!

Others said he was a clever fellow, and farsighted enough to know that that sort of thing attracted attention and might open the way to an engagement in London, where eloquence was more important than in a country place like Glaston from which the tide of grace had ebbed, leaving that great ship of the church, the abbey, high and dry on the shore.

Still others judged him a fanatic—a dangerous man. They did not all venture to assert that he had erred from the way, but what was more dangerous than one who went too far? Possibly they forgot that the narrow way can hardly be one to sit down in comfortably, or indeed to be entered at all except by him who tries the gate with the intent of going all the way—even should it lead to the perfection of the Father in heaven. "But," they would have argued, "is not a fanatic dangerous? Is not an enthusiast always in peril of becoming a fanatic? Whatever the direction his enthusiasm may take toward Jesus Christ, even toward God himself—such a man is dangerous, most dangerous!"

In such a fashion so did the wind of words in Glaston rudely seize and flack hither and thither the spiritual reputation of Thomas Wingfold, curate. And all the time the young man was wrestling, his life in his hands, with his own unbelief. At one moment he was ready to believe everything, even that strangest miracle of the fish and the piece of money, and the next to doubt whether any man had ever dared utter the words, "I and the Father are one." Tossed he was in spirit, calling even aloud sometimes to know if there was a God anywhere hearing his prayer. He was sure only of this, that whatever else any being might be, if he heard not prayer, he could not be God. Sometimes there came to him what he would gladly have taken for an answer, but it was nothing more than a sudden descent of a calmness on his spirit, which, for anything he could tell, might but be the calm of exhaustion. His knees were sore with kneeling, his face white with thinking, for when a man has set out to find God, he must find him or die.

This was the inner reality whose outcome had set the public of Glaston babbling. It was from this that George Bascombe magisterially pronounced the curate a hypochondriac, worrying his brain about things that had no existence—as George himself could confidently testify, not once having seen the sight of them, heard the sound of them, or imagined in his heart that they ought to be, or even might possibly be true. The thought had never rippled the gray mass of his self-satisfied brain that perhaps there was more to himself than he yet knew. Poor, poverty-stricken, misguided, weak-brained, hypochondriacal Wingfold could be contented with nothing less than the fulfillment of the promise of a certain man who perhaps never existed: "The Father and I will come to him and make our abode with him."

But there was yet another class among those who on that second day heard the curate. So far as he learned, however, that class consisted of one individual.

On the following Tuesday morning Thomas went into the shop of the chief linendraper of Glaston. A young woman waited on him, but Mr. Drew, seeing him from the other end of the shop, came and took her place. When he had paid for his purchase, two new tea towels, and was turning to leave, the draper suddenly leaned over the counter and said, "Would you mind walking upstairs for a few minutes, sir? I ask it as a great favor. I would very much like to speak with you."

"I shall be happy to," answered Wingfold, anticipating some argument. The curate followed Mr. Drew up a stair and into a comfortable dining room which smelled strongly of tobacco. There Mr. Drew placed a chair for him and seated himself also.

The linendraper was a middle-aged, average-sized, stoutish man, with plump rosy cheeks and keen black eyes. His dark hair was a little streaked with gray. His manner, which in the shop had been of the shop, settled into one more resembling that of a country gentleman. It was courteous and friendly, but clouded with a little anxiety.

After an uncomfortable pause, Wingfold stumbled with the question, "I hope Mrs. Drew is well," without reflecting whether he had really ever heard of a Mrs. Drew.

The draper's face flushed.

"It's twenty years since I lost her, sir," he returned. There was something peculiar in his tone and manner as he spoke.

"I beg your pardon," said Wingfold with sincerity.

"I will be open with you, sir," continued his host. "She left me for another—nearly twenty years ago."

"I am ashamed of my inadvertence," apologized Wingfold.

"Do not mention it. How could you possibly have known? Besides, the thing did not take place here, but a hundred miles away. But if I could, I would like to speak to you about something else."

"I am at your service," offered Wingfold.

"I was in your church last Sunday, but I am not one of your regular congregation. Your sermon that day set me thinking. And instead of thinking less when Monday came, I have been thinking more and more ever since, and when I saw you in the shop I could not resist the sudden desire to speak to you—if you have the time, sir?"

Wingfold assured him that his time could not be better occupied. Mr. Drew thanked him and went on.

"Your sermon, I must confess, made me uncomfortable— through no fault of yours. It is all to do with me, though how much the fault is I hardly know: use and custom are hard on a man. But I have been troubled since hearing your words, Mr. Wingfold, for I am not altogether at ease in my own mind as to the way I have made my money—what little money I have. It is no great sum, but enough to retire on when I please. I would not have you think me worse than I am, but I sincerely would like to know what you would have me do."

"My dear sir," advised Wingfold, "I am the very last to look to for help. I am as ignorant of business as a child. I can say only one thing. If you have been in the habit of doing anything you are no longer satisfied with, don't do it anymore."

"But just there is my need of help. One must *do* something with one's business, and *don't do it* doesn't tell me what to do. I don't say I have done anything the trade would count wrong or which is not done in the larger establishments. What I now question, in fact, I learned in one of the most respectable of the London houses. I would never have dared confess it to you but for the confession you made in the pulpit some time ago. I was not there, but I heard of it. It made me want to go hear you preach, for it was a plucky thing to do, and we all like pluck in a man, sir."

"Then you know the sum and substance of what I can do for you, Mr. Drew: I can sympathize with you, but not a whit more or less am I capable of. I am the merest beginner and dabbler in doing things right myself, and have more need to ask you to teach me than to try to teach you."

"That's the beauty of it!—excuse me, sir," cried the draper triumphantly. "You don't pretend to teach us anything, but you make us so uncomfortable that we go about afterward asking ourselves what we ought to do. Till last Sunday I had always considered myself a perfectly honest man.—Let me see, it would be more correct to say I looked on myself as *quite honest enough.* I feel differently now, and that is your doing. You said in your sermon last Sunday, and especially to businessmen, 'Do you do to your neighbor as you would have your neighbor do to you? If not, how can you suppose that the Lord will acknowledge you as a disciple of his, that is, as a Christian?' Now, I was even surer of being a Christian than of being an honest man. I had satisfied myself, more or less, that I had gone through all the necessary stages of being born again, and it has now been many years since I was received into a Christian church. At first, I was indignant at being called to question from a church pulpit whether or not I was a Christian. But I was driven from the theologians' tests who reduce the question to one of formulas and so-called belief. You sent me to try myself by the words of the Master instead—for he must be the best theologian of all, mustn't he? And so there and then I tried the test of doing to your neighbor as you would be done by. But I could not get it to work. I could not quite see how to apply it, and in thinking about it, I lost all the rest of the sermon.

"Now, whether it was anything you said coming back to me I cannot tell, but the next day—that was yesterday—all at once in the shop here, as I was serving Mrs. Ramshorn, the thought came to me, *What would Jesus Christ have done if he had been a draper instead of a carpenter?* When she was gone, I went up to my room to think about it. First I determined I must know how he behaved as a carpenter. But we are told nothing about that. And so my thoughts turned again to the original question, What would he have done had he been a draper? And strange to say, I seemed to know far more about that than the other. In fact, I had a sharp and decisive answer concerning several things soon after I asked myself that question. And the more I thought, the more dissatisfied I became. That same afternoon, after hearing one of my clerks trying to persuade an old farmer's wife to buy some fabric pieces she didn't need, I called all my people together and told them that if I ever heard one of them doing such a thing in the future, I would turn him or her away at once. But unfortunately, I had some time before introduced the system of a small percentage to my clerks in order to induce them to do that very thing. I shall be able to rectify that at once, however. But I do wish I had something more definite to follow than merely doing as I would have others do to me."

"Would not more light inside do as well as clearer law outside?" suggested Wingfold.

"How can I tell till I have a chance of trying?" returned the draper with a smile, which quickly vanished as he went on. "Then again, there's the profits! How much should I take? Am I to do as others do and be ruled by the market? How much should I mark up my goods? What is fair and reasonable? Am I bound to give my customers any special bargain I may have made on a good purchase from the wholesaler in London? And then again—for I myself do a large wholesale business with the little country shops—if I learn that one of my accounts is going downhill, have I or have I not a right to pounce on him and make him pay me, to the detriment of his other creditors? There's no end to the questions, you see, about how to apply these principles in a business such as mine?"

"I am the worst possible man to ask," returned Wingfold again. "I might, though it be from ignorance, judge something wrong which is actually right, or right which is really wrong. But one thing I am beginning to see, that before a man can do right by his neighbor, he must love him as himself. Only I am such a poor scholar in these high things that, as you have just said, I cannot pretend to teach anybody. That sermon was but an appeal to men's own consciences. Except for you, Mr. Drew, I am not aware that anyone in the congregation has taken it to heart."

"I am not sure of that," returned the draper. "Some talk among my own people has made me think that, perhaps, though talk be but froth, the froth may rise from some hot work down below. I think more people may be listening to you than you imagine."

Wingfold looked him in the face. The earnestness of the man was plain in his eyes. The curate thought of Zacchaeus and thought of Matthew at his tax office. Now it was clear that a tradesman might just as soon have Jesus behind the counter with him, teaching him to buy and sell as he would have done it, as an earl riding over his lands might have Jesus with him, teaching him how to treat his farmers and cottagers—all depending on how the one did his trading and the other his earling.

A mere truism, is it? Yes, but what is a truism? What is it but a truth that ought to have been buried long ago in the lives of men—to send up forever the corn of true deeds and the wine of lovingkindness. But, instead of being buried in friendly soil, it is allowed to lie about, kicked hither and thither in the dry and empty attic of men's brains till they are sick of the sight and the sound of it. Then, to be rid of the thought of it, they declare it to be no living truth but only a lifeless truism. Yet in their brain that truism will rattle until they shift it to its rightful quarters in their heart, where it will rattle no longer but take root. To the critic the truism is a sea-worn pebble; to the obedient scholar, a radiant topaz, which, as he polishes it with the dust of its use, may turn into a sparkling gem.

"Jesus buying and selling!" exclaimed Wingfold to himself. "And why not? Did Jesus make chairs and tables, or boats perhaps, which the people of Nazareth wanted, without any mixture of business in the matter? Was there no transaction? No passing of money between hands? Did they not pay his father for them? No, there must be a way of handling money that is as noble as the handling of the sword in the hands of the patriot."

Wingfold had taken a kindly leave of the draper, promising to call again soon, and had reached the room-door on his way out, when he turned suddenly and said, "Did you think to try praying, Mr. Drew? Men whose minds seem to me, from their writings, of the very highest order, have positively believed that the loftiest activity of a man's being lies in prayer to the unknown Father; that in very truth not only does the prayer of the man find the ear of God, but the man finds God himself. I have no right to an opinion, but I have a slendid hope that I shall one day find it true. The Lord said a man must go on praying and not lose heart."

With those words he walked out, and the deacon thought of his many prayers at prayer meetings and family worships. The words of a young man who seemed to have only just discovered that there was such a thing as prayer, who could not pretend to be sure about it, made him ashamed of them all.

17   Rachel and Mr. Drew

Wingfold went straight to his friend Polwarth and asked if he might bring Mr. Drew to tea some evening.

"You mean the linen merchant?" asked Polwarth. "Certainly, if you wish."

"Some troubles are catching," said the curate. "Drew has caught my disease."

"I am delighted to hear it. It would be hard to catch a better one. I always liked his round, good-humored, honest face. If I remember rightly, he had a sore trial with his wife. It is generally understood that she ran away with some fellow or other. But that was before he came to live in Glaston.—Would you mind looking in on Rachel for a few minutes, sir? She is not feeling so well today, and has not even been out of her room."

"Certainly," answered Wingfold. "I am sorry to hear she is suffering."

"She is always suffering more or less," replied the little man. "But she enjoys life in spite of it, as you can clearly see. Come this way."

He led the curate to the room next to his own.

It also was a humble little garret, but dainty with whiteness. One who did not thoroughly know her might have said it was like her life, colorless, but bright with innocence and peace. The walls were white; the boards of the uncarpeted floor were as white as scrubbing could make old pine; the window curtains and bed were whiteness itself.

"I cannot give you my hand," she apologized, smiling, as the curate went softly toward her, feeling like Moses when he took off his shoes, "for I have such a pain in my arm, I cannot raise it so well."

The curate bowed reverently, seated himself in a chair by her bedside, and, like a true comforter, said nothing.

"Don't be sorry for me, Mr. Wingfold," said her sweet voice after a few moments. "The 'poor dwarfie,' as the children call me, is not a creature to be pitied. You don't know how happy I am as I lie here, knowing my uncle is in the next room and will come the moment I call him—and that there is One nearer still," she added in a lower voice, almost in a whisper, "whom I haven't even to call. I am his and he shall do with me just as he likes. I imagine some- times, when I have to lie still, that I am a little sheep, tied hands and feet—I should have said all four feet if I am a sheep"—and here she gave a little merry laugh—"lying on an altar—the bed here—burning away in the flame of life that consumes the death- ful body, burning heart and soul and sense, up to the great Fa- ther.—But forgive me, Mr. Wingfold, for talking about myself!"

"On the contrary, I am greatly obliged to you for honoring me by talking so freely," responded Wingfold. "It gives me great sat- isfaction to find that suffering is not necessarily unhappiness. I could be well content to suffer also, Miss Polwarth, if with the suffering I might have the same peace."

"Sometimes I am troubled," she answered, "but generally I am in peace, and sometimes too happy to dare speak about it. There are of course sad thoughts sometimes, which in their season I would not lose, for I would have their influences with me always. In their season they are better than a host of happy ones, and there is joy at the root of all. But if they did come from physical causes, would it necessarily follow that they did not come from God? Is he not the God of the dying as well as the living?"

"If there be a God, Miss Polwarth," returned Wingfold eagerly, "then he is God everywhere, and not a maggot can die any more than a Shakespeare be born without him. He is either all in all, or he is not at all."

"That is what I think, because it is best. I can give no better reason."

"If there be a God, there can be no better reason," agreed Wingfold.

This "if" of Wingfold's was an if of bare honesty and did not come from any desire to shake Rachel's confidence. Their talk continued on for some time, after which Wingfold could not help almost envying the dwarf girl whose face shone with such a radiant peace.

As he walked home that afternoon, he thought much of what he had heard and seen. "If there be a God," he said to himself, "then all is well, for certainly he would not give being to such a woman, and then throw her aside and forget her. It is strange to see, though, how he permits his work to be thwarted. To be the perfect God, notwithstanding, he must be able to turn the very thwarting to higher good. Is it presumptuous to imagine God saying to Rachel, 'Trust me and bear it, and I will do better for you than you can think'? Certainly the one who most needs the comfort of such a faith, in this case *has* it. I wish I could be as sure of him as Rachel Polwarth! But then," he added, smiling to himself, "she has her crooked spine to help her!"

As he walked and thought, a fresh wave of doubts washed over him. "The ideas of religion are so grand," he said to himself, "and the things all around it in life so ordinary. They contradict each other from morning to night—in my mind, I mean. Which is the true: a loving, caring Father, or the grinding of cruel poverty? What does nature have in common with the Bible and its metaphysics? Yet there I am wrong: she has a thousand things. The very wind on my face seems to rouse me to fresh effort after a pure, healthy life! Then there is the sunrise! The snowdrop in the snow! There is the butterfly! And the rain of summer and the clearing of the sky after a storm! There is the hen gathering her chicks under her wing! I begin to doubt whether anything is in fact *ordinary* except in our own mistrusting nature. I have been thinking like the disciples when they were for the time rendered incapable of understanding the words of the Lord about forgetting

116

to take bread in the boat: they were so afraid of being hungry that they could think of nothing but bread."

Such were some of the curate's thoughts as he walked home, and they drove him to prayer, in which came still more thoughts. When he was through, having arrived at no conclusions, he caught up his hat and stick and hurried out again, thinking he would combat the demon of doubts better in the open air.

It was evening, and the air was still and warm. Pine Street was almost empty except for the red sun. All but a few of the shops were closed, but among the open ones he was surprised to find the linendraper's, though he had always been a strong advocate of early closing. He peered into the shop. It looked very dark, but he thought he saw Mr. Drew talking to someone, and so he entered. He was right—it was the draper himself and a poor woman with a child on one arm and a dress print she had just bought on the other. The curate leaned against the counter and, waiting until their business was over to greet his friend, fell to thinking. His reverie was interrupted by a merchant's voice nearby.

"I cannot tell you how it goes against my grain to take that woman's money," said Mr. Drew.

The curate looked around and saw that the woman and the child had left the shop.

"I did let her have it at cost," Mr. Drew went on, laughing merrily. "That was all I could venture."

"What was the danger?"

"Ah, you don't know as well as I do the good of having some difficulty in getting what you need! To remove the struggles of the poor can sometimes prove to be a cruel sort of kindness. Although I try to do what I can."

"Then you don't always sell to that woman at cost?"

"No. Only to the soldier's wives. They have a very hard life of it, poor things."

"That is your custom then?"

"For the last ten years. But I don't let them know it."

"Is it for the soldier's wives that you keep your shop open so late?" asked the curate.

"Let me explain how it happened tonight," answered the draper. "As the sun was going down and I was getting ready to close, it came upon me that the shop felt like a chapel—had the very air of one, somehow, and so I fell to thinking, and forgot to shut the door. My past life began coming into my mind, and I remembered how, when a young man, I used to despise my father's business to which he was preparing me as I grew. Then I saw that must have been partly how I fell into the mistake of marrying Mrs. Drew. She was the daughter of a doctor in our town, a widower. He was in poor health and unable to make much of his practice. So when he died she was left destitute, and for that reason alone, I do believe, she accepted me. Later she went away with a man who traveled for a large Manchester manufacturing house. I have never heard of her since.

"After she left me, something which I call the disease of self-preservation laid hold upon me. When she was gone I was aware of a not-unwelcome calm in the house, and in the emptiness of that calm the demon of selfishness came sevenfold to torment me, and I let him into my heart. From that time I busied myself with only two things: the safety of my soul and securing provisions for my body. I joined the church I had mentioned to you before, grew a little harder in my business dealings, and began to accumulate money. And so I have been living ever since till I heard your sermon the other day, which I hope has awakened me to something better. All this long story is but to let you understand how I was feeling when that woman came into the shop. I told you how, in the dusk and the silence, it was as if I were in the chapel. And with that thought a great awe fell upon me. Could it be—might it not be that God was actually in my place of business? I leaned over the counter, with my face in my hands, and went on half thinking, half praying. All at once the desire rose burning in my heart: if only my house could in truth be a holy place, haunted by his presence! 'And why not?' rejoiced something within me. God knows I want to follow him.

"Just then I heard a step in the shop. Lifting my head, I saw a poor woman with a child in her arms. My first reaction was annoyance that I had been found leaning over the counter with my face in my hands. But suddenly I realized a great principle: God was waiting to see what truth was in my words. I could see that the poor woman looked uncomfortable, probably misjudging my looks. I quickly received her and listened to her errand as if she had been a duchess—rather, an angel of God, for such I felt her in my heart to be. She wanted a bit of dark print with a particular kind of pattern. She had seen it in the shop some months before, but had not had money to buy it. I looked through everything we had, and at last found the very piece she wanted. But all the time I sought it, I felt as if I were doing God service—or at least something he wanted me to do. It sounds like such a trifle now!"

"But who with any heart would call it a trifle to please the fancy of a poor woman," commented Wingfold. "She had been thinking about the dress she wanted to make. You took the trouble to content her. Who knows what it may do for the growth of the woman? I know what you've done for me by telling me about it."

"She did seem pleased when she walked out," admitted the draper, "and left me even more pleased—and grateful to her for coming."

"I am beginning to suspect," declared the curate after a pause, "that the common transactions of life are the most sacred channels for the spread of the heavenly leaven. There was ten times more of the divine in selling her that material in the name of God as you did than there would have been in taking her into your pew and singing out of the same hymnbook with her."

"I would be glad to do that next, though, if I had the chance," replied Mr. Drew.

The curate had entered the fabric shop in the full blaze of sunset. When he left some time later, the sun was far below the horizon. And as he went he talked thus with himself: "Either there is a God, and that God is perfect truth and loveliness, or else all poetry and art is but an unsown, unplanted, rootless flower crowning a somewhat symmetrical heap of stones. The man who sees no beauty in its petals, finds no perfume in its breath may well accord it the parentage of the stones; the man whose heart swells in looking at it will be ready to think it has roots that reach below them."

The curate's search had already greatly widened the sphere of his doubts. But if there be such a thing as truth, every fresh doubt is yet another fingerpost pointing toward its dwelling. So reasoned the curate with himself as he rounded the corner of a street and met George Bascombe.

The young lawyer held out his large hospitable hand and they went through the ceremony of shaking hands.

"I have not yet had an opportunity of thanking you for the great service you have done me," said Wingfold sincerely.

"I am glad to know I have such an honor, but—"

"I mean in opening my eyes to my true position."

"Ah, my dear fellow! I was sure you only required to have your attention turned in the right direction. Are you thinking of resigning, then?"

"Not yet," replied Wingfold. "The more I look into the matter, the more reason I find for thinking the whole thing may be true after all and I may be able to keep my appointment to the church."

"But what if you find it is not true?" pressed Bascombe.

"What if I should find it *is* true, even though you might never be able to see it?" returned the curate.

After a somewhat uncomfortable pause, each of the two men continued on his own way. Bascombe had said nothing more, for his mind was only directed at finding holes in another's consistency rather than seeing whether truth had anything to teach his own self. Meanwhile, Wingfold's honest heart continued its quest for truth, wherever and however he could unearth it.

"If I can't prove there is a God," said Wingfold to himself, "then surely just as little can Bascombe prove there isn't."

But then came the thought, "But the fellow would say that, there being no sign of a God, the burden of proof lies with me."

And with that he saw how useless it would be to discuss the question with anyone who, not seeing God, had no desire to see him. The only good to be gleaned out of any discussion would have to come by sharing doubts and conjectures with another who shared the common desire of knowing and finding the truth. Otherwise, discussion would be but the vain exchange of differing viewpoints, leading nowhere.

"No!" he concluded at length, "my business is not now to *prove* to any other man that there is a God, but *to find him for myself.* If I should find him, then there will be time enough to think of showing him to others."

18 The Sheath

One evening Polwarth took what he usually left to his young friend—the initiative.

"Mr. Wingfold," he said in a low voice, the usual salutations over, "I want to tell you something I don't wish even Rachel to hear."

He led the way to his room and the curate followed. Seated there, in the shadowy old attic, through the very walls of which the ivy grew and into which, by the open window in the gable, blew the lovely scent of honeysuckle to mingle with that of old books, Polwarth recounted a strange adventure.

"I am going to make a confidante of you, Mr. Wingfold," announced the dwarf, his face troubled. "You will know how much I have learned to trust you when I say that I am about to confide to you what plainly involves the secret of another."

His large face grew paler as he spoke. His eyes looked straight into those of the curate and his voice did not tremble.

"One night, some weeks ago, I was unable to sleep. That is not an uncommon thing with me. Sometimes, when such is the case, I lie as still and happy as any bird under the wing of its mother. At other times I must get up. That night, nothing would serve my spirits but the outside air. So I rose, dressed, and went out.

"It was a still, warm night, no moon, but plenty of stars, the wind blowing gentle and sweet and cool. I got into the open park, avoiding the trees, and wandered on and on without thinking where I was going. The turf was soft under my feet, the dusk soft to my eyes, and the wind gentle to my soul. I had been out perhaps an hour, when through the soft air came a cry, apparently from far off. There was something in the tone that seemed unusually frightful. The bare sound made me shudder before I had time to say to myself it was a cry. I turned in the direction of it, as far as I could tell, and headed for it.

"I had not gone very far before I found myself approaching the hollow where the old house of Glaston stands, uninhabited for twenty years. I stood and listened for a moment, but all seemed still as the grave. But I knew I had to go in to see if there was someone there in need of help, for it seemed as though the sound may have come from the house. It may strike you as humorous, the thought of my helping anyone, for what could I do if it came to a struggle?"

"On the contrary," interrupted Wingfold. "I was smiling with admiration at your pluck."

"At least," resumed Polwarth, "I have this advantage over some, that I cannot be fooled into thinking my body worth much. So down the slope I went and fought through the tangled bushes to the house. I knew the place perfectly, for I had often wandered all over it, sometimes spending hours there.

"Before I reached the door I heard someone behind me in the garden, and instantly I stepped into a thicket of gooseberry and currant bushes. That same moment the night seemed torn in two by a second most hideous cry from the house. Before I could catch my breath again, the tall figure of a woman rushed past me, tearing its way through the bushes toward the door. I followed instantly, saw her run up the steps, and heard her open and shut the door. I opened it as quietly as I could, but just as I stepped into the dark hall came a third fearful cry. I cannot describe the horror of it. It was the cry of a soul in torture—unlike any sound of any human voice I had ever heard before. I shudder now at the recollection of it. I had by now lost all sense of the interior of the house when I caught a glimpse of a light shining from under a door. I approached it softly and knew again where I was. Laying my ear against the door, I heard what was plainly enough a lady's voice. She soothed and condoled and coaxed. Mingled with hers was the voice of a youth, as it seemed. It was wild, yet so low as sometimes to be all but inaudible, and not a word from either could I distinguish. It was plain, however, that the youth spoke either in delirium or with something terrible on his mind, for his tones were those of one in despair. I stood for a time bewildered and terrified. At length I became convinced that I had no right to be there. Undoubtedly the man was in hiding, and where a man hides there must be a reason; but was it any business of mine? I crept out of the house and up to the higher ground. There I drew a deep breath of the sweet night air, and then went straight home and to bed again, resolving to discover what I could the next day. For I thought there must be some simple explanation of the matter. I might in the morning be of service to these people, whoever they might be.

"As soon as I awoke I had a cup of tea and then set out for the old house. As I walked, I heard the sounds of the workmen's hammers on the new house. All else was silence. The day looked so honest it was difficult to believe the night had shrouded such an awful meeting. Yet in the broad light of the morning, a cold shudder seized me when I first looked down on the broken roofs of the old house. When I got into the garden I began to sing and knock the bushes about, then opened the door noisily, and clattered about in the hall and the lower rooms before going up the stairs, in order to give good warning before I approached the room where I had heard the voices. Finally I stood at the door and knocked. There was no answer. I knocked again. Still no answer. I opened it and peeped in. There was no one there! An old bedstead was all I saw. I searched every corner, but not one trace could I discover of any human being having been there, except this behind the bed—and it may have lain there as long as the mattress, which I remember since the first time I ever went into the house."

As he spoke, Polwarth handed the curate a small leather sheath, which, from its shape, could not have belonged to a pair of scissors, although neither of the men knew any sort of knife it would have fitted.

"Would you mind taking care of it, Mr. Wingfold?" the gatekeeper continued as the curate examined it. "I don't like having it. I can't even bear to think of it in the house, and yet I don't quite think I should destroy it."

"I don't mind in the least taking charge of it," answered Wingfold.

Why did the face of Helen Lingard suddenly rise before his mind's eye as he had seen it now twice in the congregation at the abbey—pale with inward trouble? Why should he think of her now? He had never till then thought of her with the slightest interest, and what should have reminded him of her? Could it be that—

good heaven! There was her brother ill. And had not Faber said there was something unusual about the character of his illness? What could it mean?

"Do you think," he asked, "that we are in any way bound to inquire further into the affair?"

"If I had thought so, I should have mentioned it before now," answered Polwarth. "But to tell you the truth, I am uneasy, and that may be a sign that what you say is right. But without being busybodies, we might be prepared in case the thing should unfold and we could be useful. In the meantime, I have the relief of the confessional."

As Wingfold walked back to his lodgings, he found a new element mingling in his thoughts. Human suffering laid hold upon him in a way that was new to him. He realized there were hearts in the world from whose agony broke terrible cries, hearts which produced sad faces like Miss Lingard's. Such hearts might be groaning and writhing in any of the houses he passed, and even if he knew the hearts, he could do nothing for their relief. What multitudes there must be in the world—how many even in Glaston— whose hearts were overwhelmed, who knew their own bitterness, and yet had no friend radiant enough to bring sunshine into their shady places! He fell into a mournful mood over the troubles of his race. Though always a kindhearted fellow, he had not been used to thinking about such things; he had experienced troubles enough of his own. But now that he had begun to hope, he saw a glimmer of light somewhere at the end of the dark cave in which he had all at once discovered that he was buried alive. He began also to feel how wretched those must be who were groping on without any hope in their dark eyes.

If he had never committed any crime, he had yet done enough wrong to understand the misery of shame and dishonor. How much more miserable must those be who had committed some terrible deed? What relief, what hope was there for them? What a breeding nest of cares and pains was the human heart! Oh, surely it needed some refuge! If no Savior had yet come, the tortured world of human hearts cried aloud for one. The world certainly needed a Savior to whom anyone might go, at any moment, without a journey, without letters or commendations or credentials. And yet, what was the good of the pardon such a one might give if still the consciousness of the deeds of sin or the misery of loneliness kept on stinging? And who would wish one he loved to grow callous to a sin he had committed?

But if there was a God—such a God as, according to the Christian story, had sent his own Son into the world, had given him to appear among us, clothed in the garb of humanity, to take all the consequences of being the Son of obedience among the children of disobedience, engulfing their wrongs in his infinite forgiveness, and winning them back, by slow and unpromising and tedious renewal, to the heart of his Father, surely such a God would not have created them knowing that some of them would commit such horrible sins from which he could not redeem them. And as he thought, the words rose in his mind, *"Come unto me, all you that labor and are heavy laden, and I will give you rest."*

His heart filled! He pondered the words. When he got home, he sought and found them in the book. *Did a man ever really say them?* he wondered to himself. Such words they were! If a man did utter them, either he was the most presumptuous of mortals, or *he could do what he said.* He had to have been either sent from God himself, or a fool. There could be no middle ground.

19   A Sermon to Helen

All the rest of the week his mind was full of thoughts like these. Again and again the suffering face of Helen Lingard arose, bringing with it the growing suspicion that behind it must lie some oppressive secret. When he raised his head on Sunday and cast his eyes around on his congregation, they rested for one brief moment on her troubled countenance whose reflection so often lately had looked out from the mirror of his memory. Next they flitted across the satisfied, healthy, clever face of her cousin, behind which plainly sat a seared conscience in an easy chair. The third moment they saw the peevish autumnal visage of Mrs. Ramshorn. The next they roved a little, then rested on the draper's good-humored face on which brooded a cloud of thoughtfulness. Last of all they found the faces of both the dwarfs. It was the first time he had seen Rachel there, and it struck him that her face expressed greater suffering than he had read in it before. *She ought to be in bed rather than church*, he thought. The same seemed to be the case with her uncle's countenance also.

With these fleeting observations came the conclusion that the pulpit was a wonderful watchtower from which to study human nature, for people lay bare more of their real nature and condition to the man in the pulpit than they know. Their faces had fallen into the shape of their minds, for the church has an isolating as well as a congregating power. This all flashed through the curate's mind in the briefest of moments before he began to speak. The tears rose in his eyes as he gazed, and his heart swelled toward his own flock, as if his spirit would break forth in a flood of tenderness. Then he quickly began to speak. As usual his voice trembled at first, but then gathered strength as it found its way. This is a good deal like what he said:

"The marvelous man who is reported to have appeared in Palestine, teaching and preaching, seems to have suffered far more from sympathy with the inward sorrows of his race than from pity for their bodily pains. These last could he not have swept from the earth with a word? And yet it seems to have been mostly, if not always, only in answer to prayer that he healed them. Even then he did so for the sake of some deeper spiritual healing that should go with the bodily cure. His tears could not have flowed for the dead man whom he was about to call from the tomb. What source could they have but compassion and pitiful sympathy for the dead man's sisters and friends in their sorrows?

"Yet are there not more terrible troubles than mourning a death? There is the weight of conscious wrong-being and wrong-doing: that is the gravestone that needs to be rolled away before a man can rise to life. The guilt of sin, that is the great weight which rests upon us. Call to mind how Jesus used to forgive men's sins, thus lifting from their hearts the crushing load that paralyzed them—the repentant woman who wept sore-hearted from very love, the publicans who knew they were despised because they were despicable. With him they sought and found shelter. He received them, and the life within them rose up, and the light shone—despite shame and self-reproach. If God be for us, who can be against us? In his name they rose from the hell of their own heart's condemnation, and went forth into truth and strength and hope. They heard and believed and obeyed his words. And of all words that ever were spoken, were there ever any gentler, tenderer, humbler, lovelier than these? *'Come unto me, all you that labor and are heavy laden, and I will give you rest. Take my yoke upon you, and learn of me; for I am meek and lowly in heart: and you shall find rest for your souls. For my yoke is easy, and my burden is light.'*

"Surely these words, could they but be believed, are such as every human heart might gladly hear! You who call yourselves Christians profess to believe such rest is available, yet how many of you take no single step toward him who says 'Come,' lift not an eye to see whether a face of mercy may not be gazing down upon you? Is it that you do not believe there ever was such a man they call Jesus? Or is it that you are doubtful concerning the whole significance of his life? If the man said the words, he must have at least believed he could fulfill them. Who that knows anything about him can for a moment say that this man did not believe what he spoke?

"Hear me, my friends: I dare not yet say I know there is a Father. I can only say with my whole heart I hope we indeed have a Father in heaven. But this man says *he knows*. If he tells me he knows, I must listen and observe that it is his own best he wants to give; no bribe to obedience to his will, but the assurance of bliss if we will but do as he does. He wants us to have peace—*his* peace—peace from the same source as his. For what does he mean by, 'Take my yoke upon you and learn of me'? He does not mean, *Wear the yoke I lay upon you.* I do not say he might not have said what amounts to the same thing at other times, but that is not the truth he would convey in these words. He means, *Take upon you the yoke that I wear; learn to do as I do, who submits everything and refers everything to the will of my Father. Yea, have my will only insofar as I carry out his will; be meek and lowly in*

127

heart, and you shall find rest for your souls. With all the grief of humanity in his heart, in the face of the death that awaited him, he yet says, 'For my yoke, the yoke I wear, is easy, the burden I bear is light.'

"What made that yoke easy—that burden light? That it was the will of the Father. If a man answer, 'Any good man who believed in a God might say the same thing, and I do not see how that can help me,' my reply is that this man says, 'Come unto me, and I will give you rest'—asserting the power to give perfect help to him that comes. No one else can do that. Does all this seem too far away, my friends, and very distant from the things about us? The things close by do not give you peace. Peace has to come from somewhere else. And do not our souls themselves cry out for a nobler, better, more beautiful life?

"Alas! for poor men and women and their aching hearts! Come, then, sore heart, and see whether his heart can heal yours. He knows what sighs and tears are, and if he knew no sin himself, the more pitiful must it have been to look on the sighs and tears that guilt wrung from the tortured hearts of his brothers and sisters. Beloved, we *must* get rid of this misery of ours. It is slaying us. It is turning the fair earth into a hell, and our hearts into its fuel. There stands the man who says he knows: take him at his word. Go to him who says in the power of his eternal tenderness and his pity, 'Come unto me, all you that labor and are heavy-laden, and I will give you rest. Take my yoke upon you, and learn of me; for I am meek and lowly in heart: and you shall find rest for your souls. For my yoke is easy, and my burden is light.' "

Long before he came to a close, Wingfold was blind to all before him. He felt only the general suffering of the human soul. He did not see that Helen was sobbing convulsively. The word had touched her and had unsealed the fountain of tears, if not of faith. Neither did he see the curl on the lip of Bascombe, or the glance of annoyance which, every now and then, he cast upon the bent head beside him. *What on earth are you crying about?* flashed in Bascombe's eyes, but Helen did not see them. One or two more in the congregation were weeping, and here and there shone a face in which the light seemed to prevent the tears. Polwarth shone and Rachel wept. For the rest, the congregation listened only with varying degrees of attention and indifference. The majority looked as if neither Wingfold nor anyone else ever meant anything—at least in the pulpit.

The moment Wingfold reached the vestry, he quickly took off the garments of his profession, sped from the abbey, and all but ran across the churchyard to his home. There he shut himself up in his room, afraid that he had said more than he had a right to say. He turned his thoughts away from the congregation, from the church, from the sermon, and from the past altogether. Toward the hills of help he turned his face—to the summits over whose tops he looked for the dayspring from on high to break forth. If only Christ would come to him!

At length he sat down at a side table, while his landlady prepared his dinner. She too had been at church that morning and she moved about and set the things on the table with unusual softness, trying not to interrupt him while he wrote down a line here and there of what afterward grew into the following verses—born in the effort to forget the things that were behind, and reach toward the things that lay before him:

Yes, master, when you come you shall find
    A little faith on earth, if I am here.
You know how often I turn to you my mind,
    How sad I wait until your face appear!

Have you not ploughed my thorny ground full sore,
    And from it gathered many stones and sherds?
Plough, plough and harrow till it needs no more—
    Then sow your mustard seed, and send your birds.

I love you, Lord; and if I yield to fears,
    And cannot trust with triumph that doubt defies,
Remember, Lord, 'tis nearly two thousand years,
    And I have never seen you with my eyes.

And when I lift them from the wondrous tale,
    See, all about me so strange, so beautiful a show!
Is that *your* river running down the vale?
    Is that *your* wind that through the pines does blow?

Couldn't you appear again,
　The same who walked the paths of Palestine;
And here in England teach your trusting men,
　In church and field and house, with word and sign?

Here are but lilies, sparrows, and the rest!
　My hands on some dear proof would light and stay!
But my heart sees John leaning on your breast,
　And sends them forth to do what you did say.

20　Reactions

"What an unusual young man!" exclaimed Mrs. Ramshorn as they left the church, with a sigh that expressed despair.

"If he would pay a little more attention to his composition," pointed out Bascombe indifferently, "he might in time make a good speaker of himself. I'm not sure there aren't elements of an orator in him. He might in time become a great man. But he could hardly make himself a great preacher—and that seems to be his intention."

"If that is his object, he ought to join the Methodists," replied Mrs. Ramshorn shortly.

"That is not his object, George. How can you say so?" remarked Helen quietly, but with some latent indignation.

George smiled a rather unpleasant smile, and held his peace.

Little more was said until they reached the house. Helen went to take off her hat, but did not reappear until she was called to their early Sunday dinner.

Now George had counted on a walk in the garden with her before dinner and was annoyed to be left alone. When she came into the drawing room, it was plain she had been weeping. Although they were alone and would probably have to wait a few minutes before their aunt joined them, he resolved to say nothing till after dinner, lest he should spoil her appetite. When they rose from the table she would again have escaped, but when George followed her, she consented, at his almost urgent request, to walk once round the garden with him.

As soon as they were out of sight of the windows, he began: "How *could* you, my dear Helen, take so little care of your health, already so much disturbed with nursing your brother, as to yield your mind to that silly ecclesiastic and allow his false eloquence to untune your nerves? If you *must* go to church, you ought to remember that the whole thing is but part of a system—part of a false system. That preacher has been brought up in the trade of religion. That is his business and he has to persuade people of the truth—himself first if he can, but his congregation anyhow—of everything contained in that medley of priestly absurdities called the Bible. Think for a moment, how soon, if it were not for their churches and prayers and music, and their tomfoolery of preaching, the whole precious edifice would topple about their ears? So what is left them but to play on the hopes and fears and diseased consciences of men as best they can.

"The idiot! To tell a man when he is depressed, 'Come unto me!' Bah! Does the fool really expect any grown man or woman to believe that the one who spoke those words, if ever there was a man who spoke them, can at this moment, *anni domini*"— George liked to be correct—"1870, hear whatever silly words the Rev. Mr. Wingfold or any other human may think proper to address to him? Not to mention, they would have you believe, or be damned to all eternity, that every thought vibrated in the depths of your brain is known to him as well as to yourself! The thing is really too absurd! Ha! ha! ha!" His laughter was loud and seemed forced.

"The man died, and his body was stolen from his grave by his followers that they might impose thousands of years of absurdity upon the generations to come after them. And now, when a fellow feels miserable, he is to cry to that dead man who said of himself that he was meek and lowly in heart, and immediately the poor beggar shall find rest for his soul! All I can say is that if he finds rest in that way, it will be the rest of an idiot! Believe me, Helen, a good cigar and a bottle of claret would be considerably more to the purpose; for ladies, perhaps a cup of tea and a little Beetho-ven!" Here he laughed more genuinely, for the rush of his elo-quence had swept away his bad humor. "But really," he went on, "the whole thing is *too* absurd to talk about. To go whining after an old Jewish fable in these days of progress!"

"You will allow this much in excuse for their being so misled," returned Helen with some bitterness. "The old fable at least pre-tends some help for sore hearts."

"Do be serious, Helen," protested George. "I don't object to joking, you know, but this has to do with the well-being of the race. We must think of others. However, your 'Jew gospel' would set everybody to the saving of his *own* wind-bubble of a soul. Believe me, to live for others is the true way to lose sight of our own imagined sorrows."

Helen gave a deep sigh. "Imagined sorrows!" Yes, gladly indeed would she live for one other at least! She would even die for him. But, alas! What would that do for the one whose very being was consumed with grief?

"There are real sorrows," she insisted. "They are not all imag-ined."

"There are few sorrows," returned George, "in which imagi-nation does not exercise a stronger influence than even a woman of sense will be prepared to admit. I can remember bursts of grief when I was a boy, in which it seemed impossible anything would ever console me. But in one minute all would be gone. Believe that all is well, and you will find all will be well—very tolerably well considering."

"Considering that there is no God to look after the business!" retorted Helen. According to the state of the tide in the sea of her trouble, she either resented or accepted her cousin's teaching at any given time.

"You perplex me, my dear cousin," said Bascombe. "It is plain your nursing has been too much for you. You see everything with a jaundiced eye."

"Thank you, Cousin George," returned Helen. "You are even more courteous than usual."

She turned from him and went into the house. Bascombe walked to the bottom of the garden and lit his cigar, confessing to himself that for once he could not understand Helen.

Helen ran upstairs, dropped on her knees by her brother's bedside, and fell into a fit of sobbing which no tears came to relieve.

"Helen! Helen!" cried a voice of misery from the pillow.

She jumped up, wiping her eyes.

"Oh, Poldie!" she wept. "It is all the fault of the sermon I heard this morning. It was the first sermon I ever really listened to in my whole life—certainly the first I ever thought about again after I was out of the church. Somehow or other, Mr. Wingfold has been preaching so strangely lately! But this was the first time I have cared to listen. He spoke so differently and looked so different. I never saw any clergyman look like that; and I never saw such a change on a man as there has been on him. He speaks as if he really believes the things he is saying. There must be something to account for it. His text was: 'Come unto me, all you that labor and are heavy laden'—a common enough text, you know, Poldie. But somehow it seemed fresh to him, and he made it look fresh to me. I felt as if it hadn't been intended for preaching about at all, but for going straight into people's hearts. He first made us feel the sort of person that said the words. Then he made us feel that he *did* say them, and so made us want to see what they could really mean. But of course what made them so different to me was"—here Helen did burst into tears, but she fought with her sobs and went on—"was—was—that my heart is breaking for you, Poldie."

She buried her face on his pillow.

"Just think, Poldie," she went on when she was able, "what if there should be some help in the universe somewhere—a heart that feels for us both, as my heart feels for you? Oh! wouldn't it be lovely to be at peace again? 'Come unto me,' he invited, 'all you that labor and are heavy laden, and I will give you rest.' That's what he said.—Oh, if only it could be true!"

"Surely it is—for you, best of sisters!" cried Leopold. "But what does that have to do with me? Nothing. She is *dead*. Even if God were to raise her to life again, he could not make it that I didn't drive the knife into her heart. O my God! my God!" cried the poor youth, and stared at his thin, wasted hand as at an evil thing that was still stained with blood.

"God couldn't be so very angry with you, Poldie," sobbed Helen, feeling about blindly in the dark forest of her thoughts for some herb of comfort, and offering any leaf upon which her hand fell first.

"Then he wouldn't be fit to be God!" retorted Leopold fiercely. "I wouldn't have a word to say to a God that didn't cut a man in pieces for such a deed! Oh, Helen, she was so *lovely*—and what is she now!"

"Surely if there were a God, he would do something to set it right somehow! You aren't half as bad as you make yourself out," pleaded Helen.

"You had better tell that to the jury, Helen, and see how they will take it," said Leopold bitterly.

"The jury!" Helen almost screamed.

"All God can do to set it right," he insisted, after a pause, "is to damn me forever as one of the blackest creatures in creation."

"*That* I don't believe!" returned Helen with both vehemence and indefiniteness.

And for the time, George Bascombe's ideas were a comfort to her. It was all nonsense about a God. Where was a God to be found who could and might help them? How were they to approach him? Or what could he do for them? She no longer saw any glimmer of hope but such as lay in George's theory of death. If there were no helper who could cleanse hearts and revive the light of life, then death would be welcome!

But might the curate help? Helen found herself wondering. Of one thing she was certain: he would tell them no more than he knew. Even George Bascombe, who did not believe one thing the curate said, considered Wingfold an honest man. Might she venture to consult him, putting the case as of a person who had done wrong—say, one who had stolen money or committed forgery or something? Might she not thus gather a little honey of comfort and bring hope to Leopold?

Thinking thus, she sat silent; and all the time the suffering eyes were fixed upon her face.

"Are you thinking about the sermon, Helen?" he asked. "Who preached it?"

"Mr. Wingfold," she answered listlessly.

"Who is Mr. Wingfold?"

"Our curate at the abbey."

"What sort of man is he?"

"Oh, a man somewhere about thirty—a straightforward, ordinary kind of man."

They both fell silent again for a few moments.

Helen realized she *must* speak to somebody. She would go mad otherwise. And why not Mr. Wingfold? She would try to see if she could approach the subject with him.

But how was she to see him? It would be awkward to call upon him at his lodgings. She would have to see him absolutely alone to dare even a whisper of what was troubling her mind.

At last she withdrew to the dressing room, laid herself on her bed, and began to plan how to meet the curate. By an innocent cunning she would wile from him on false pretenses what spiritual balm she might gain for the torn heart and conscience of her brother. But how was it to be done? She could see only one way. With some inconsistency, she resolved to cast herself upon his generosity, and yet she would not open up and trust him entirely.

She did not go downstairs again, but had her tea with her brother. In the evening her aunt went out to visit some of her pensioners. It was one of Mrs. Ramshorn's clerical duties to be kind to the poor—a good deal at their expense, I am afraid. Presently, George came to the door of the sickroom and asked Helen to come down and sing to him. Of course, in the house of a dean's wife, no music except sacred must be heard on a Sunday; but to have Helen sing it, George would condescend even to a hymn. And there was Handel, for whom he professed a great admiration. But she positively refused to gratify him this evening. She must stay with Leopold, she insisted.

Perhaps she could hardly have told herself why, but George perceived the lingering influence of the morning's sermon, and was more vexed than he had ever yet been with her. He could not endure her to cherish the least prejudice in favor of what he despised, and so he turned quickly, hurried downstairs, and left the house to overtake his aunt.

The moment he was gone, Helen went to the piano and began to sing, "Comfort Ye." When she came to "Come unto me," she broke down. But with sudden resolution she rose and opened every door between the piano and her brother. She raised the top of the piano, sat down, and then sang "Come unto me" as she had never sung in her life. She sang long and loud, but when George and her aunt returned, she was kneeling beside her brother.

21   A Meeting

Tuesday morning as Wingfold enjoyed his breakfast by an open window looking across the churchyard, he received a letter by the local post.

Dear Mr. Wingfold:

I am about to take an unheard of liberty, but my reasons are such as make me bold. The day may come when I shall be able to tell you them all. In the meantime, I hope you can help me. I want very much to ask your counsel about a certain matter, and I cannot ask you to call at the house, for my aunt knows nothing of it. Could you contrive a suitable way of meeting me? You may imagine my necessity when I ask you in this way. But I must have confidence in a man who spoke as you did yesterday morning. I am, dear Mr. Wingfold, sincerely yours,

Helen Lingard

P.S. I shall be walking along Pine Street from our end, at eleven o'clock tomorrow.

The curate was not taken with great surprise. But something like fear overshadowed him at finding his sermons coming back upon him. Was he, an unbelieving laborer, to go reaping with his blunt and broken sickle where the corn was ripest? But he had no time to think about that now. It was nearly ten o'clock, and she would be looking for her answer by eleven. He did not have to think long, however, before he arrived at what seemed to be a suitable plan; whereupon he wrote:

Dear Miss Lingard:

Of course I am entirely at your service. But I am doubtful if the only way that occurs to me will commend itself to you. I know what I am about to propose is safe, but you may not have confidence in my judgment to accept it as such.

Undoubtedly you have seen the two deformed persons, an uncle and niece named Polwarth, who keep the gate of Osterfield Park. I know them well, and, strange as it may seem, I must tell you that whatever change you may have observed in me is owing to the influence of those two, who have more faith in God than I have ever met with before. They are also of gentle blood as well as noble nature. With this introduction, I venture to propose that we should meet at their cottage. To them it would not appear at all strange that one of my congregation should wish to see me alone, and I know you may trust their discretion. But while I write thus with all confidence in you and in them, I must tell you that I have none in myself. I am perplexed that you should imagine any help in me. Of all, I am the poorest creature to give counsel. All I can say for myself is that whatever I see I will say. If I can see nothing to help you, I will be silent. And yet I may be able to direct you where you could find what I cannot give you. If you accept my plan, and will set the day and hour, I shall tell the Polwarths. Should you object to this plan, I shall try to think of another. I am, dear Miss Lingard, yours very truly,

Thomas Wingfold

He placed the letter between the pages of a pamphlet, took his hat and stick, and was walking down Pine Street as the abbey clock struck eleven. Midway he met Helen, shook hands with her, and after an indifferent word or two, gave her the pamphlet, and bade her good morning.

Helen hurried home. It had required all her self-command to look him in the face. Her heart beat almost painfully as she opened the letter.

By the next post the curate received a grateful answer, appointing the time, and expressing a perfect readiness to trust the Polwarths.

When the time came she was received at the cottage door by Rachel, who asked her to walk into the garden where Mr. Wingfold was expecting her. The curate led her to a seat overgrown with honeysuckle. It was some moments before either of them spoke, and it did not help Wingfold that she sat shrouded in a dark-colored veil.

At length he said, "You must not be afraid to trust me because I doubt my ability to help you. I can at least assure you of sympathy. The trouble I have had myself enables me to promise you that."

"Can you tell me," she inquired from behind more veils than the one of lace she was wearing, "how to get rid of a haunting idea?"

"That depends on the nature of the idea, I should imagine," answered the curate. "If it be a thought of something past and gone, for which nothing can be done, I think activity in one's daily work must be the best help."

"Oh, dear! oh, dear!" sighed Helen. "When one has no heart to go on and hates the very sunlight! —You wouldn't talk about work to a man dying of hunger, would you?"

"I'm not sure about that."

"He wouldn't heed you."

"Perhaps not."

"What would you do then?" pressed Helen, a deeper question hidden in her mind.

"Give him some food, and then try him again, I think," proposed Wingfold.

"Then give me some food—some hope, I mean, and try me again. Without that, I don't care about duty or life or anything."

"Tell me then what is the matter; I may be able to hint at some hope," said Wingfold very gently. "Do you call yourself a Christian?"

The question would to most people have sounded abrupt, inquisitorial; but to Helen it sounded not that way at all.

"No," she answered.

"Ah!" said the curate a little sadly, and went on. "Because then I could have said, 'You know where to go for comfort.' Might it not be well, however, to see if there is any comfort to be had from him that said, *'Come unto me and I will give you rest'*?"

"I can do nothing with that. I have tried and tried to pray, but it is of no use. There is such a weight on my heart that no power of mine can lift it up. I suppose it is because I cannot believe there is anyone hearing a word I say. Yesterday, when I got alone in the park, I prayed aloud; I thought that perhaps even if he might not be able to read what was in my heart, he might be able to hear my voice. I was even foolish enough to wish I knew Greek, because perhaps he would understand me better if I were to pray in Greek. But it is no use! There is no help anywhere!"

She tried hard but could not prevent a sob. And then followed a burst of tears.

"Will you not tell me something about it?" asked the curate, yet more gently. How gladly would he relieve her heart if he could! "Perhaps Jesus has begun to give you help, though you do not know it yet," he suggested. "His help may be on the way to you, or even with you, only you do not recognize it for what it is."

Helen's sobs ceased, but, to the curate at least, a long silence followed. At length she disclosed, with faltering voice: "Suppose it was a great wrong that had been done, and that was the unendurable thought? *Suppose*, I say, that was what made me most miserable?"

"Then you must of course make all possible reparation," answered Wingfold at once.

"But if none were possible—what then?"

Here the answer was not so plain and the curate had to think.

"At least," he said at length, "you could confess the wrong and ask forgiveness."

"But if that were also impossible," ventured Helen, shuddering inwardly to find how near she drew to the edge of the awful fact by her statements.

Again the curate took time to reply.

"I am trying to answer your questions as best I can," he responded; "but it is hard to deal with generalities. You see how useless my answers have been thus far. Still, I have something more to say. I hesitate only because it may imply more confidence than I dare profess, and of all things I dread untruth. But I am honest in this much at least: I desire with a true heart to find a God who will acknowledge me as his creature and make me his child, and if there be any God I am nearly certain he will do so. For surely there cannot be any other kind of God than the Father of Jesus Christ. In the strength of this truth I venture to say this: no crime can be committed against a creature without being committed also against the creator of that creature. Therefore, surely the first step for anyone who has committed such a deed must be to humble himself before God, confess the sin, and ask forgiveness and cleansing. If there is anything in religion at all, it must rest upon actual individual communication between God and the creature he has made. And if God heard the man's prayer and forgave him, then the man would certainly know it in his heart and be consoled—perhaps by the gift of humility."

"Then you think confession to God is all that is required?" probed Helen.

"If there is no one else wronged to whom confession can be made. If the case were mine—and sometimes I am afraid that in taking holy orders I have grievously sinned—I should then do just as I have done with regard to that: cry to the living power which I think originated me, to set the matter right."

"But if it could not be set right?"

"Then I would cry to him to forgive and console me."

"Alas! alas! that he will not hear of," Helen mourned. "He would rather be punished than consoled. I fear for his brain."

She had gone much further than she had intended; but the more doubtful help became, the more she was driven by the agony of a perishing hope to search the heart of Wingfold.

Again the curate pondered.

"Are you sure," he said at length, "that the person of whom you speak is not neglecting something he ought to do—perhaps something he knows?"

He had come back to the same answer with which he had begun.

Through her veil he saw her turn deadly white. Ever since Leopold had said the word *jury*, a ghastly fear had haunted Helen. She pressed her hand on her heart and made no answer.

"I speak from experience," the curate went on, "—from what

else could I speak? I know that so long as we shrink back from doing what conscience urges, there is no peace for us. I will not say our prayers are not heard, for Mr. Polwarth has taught me that the most precious answer prayer can have lies in the growing strength of the impulse toward the dreaded duty, and in the ever-sharper stings of the conscience. I think I asked already whether there were no relatives to whom restitution could be made?"

"Yes, yes," gasped Helen, "and I told you restitution was impossible."

Her voice had sunk almost to a groan.

"But at least confession—" began Wingfold—then started from his seat.

A stifled cry interrupted him at the word "confession." Helen was pressing her handkerchief to her mouth. She rose and ran from him. Wingfold stood alarmed and irresolute. She had not gone many steps, however, when her pace slowed, her knees gave way, and she crumpled on the grass. Wingfold ran to the house for water. Rachel hurried to her and Polwarth followed. It was some time before they succeeded in reviving her.

When at length the color began to return to her cheeks, Polwarth dropped on his knees at her feet and prayed, in his low, husky voice: "Life Eternal, this lady of thine hath a sore heart, and we cannot help her. Thou art Help, O Mighty Love. Speak to her; let her know thy will, and give her strength to do it, O Father of Jesus Christ! Amen."

When Helen opened her eyes, she saw only the dark leaves of an arbutus over her, and knew nothing beyond a sense of utter misery, mingled with an impulse to jump up and run. With an effort she moved her head a little, and then saw the three kneeling forms, the clergyman and the two dwarfs. She thought she was dead and they were kneeling about her corpse. Her head dropped with a weary sigh of relief, she lay passive, and heard the dwarf's prayer. Then she knew that she was not dead and was bitterly disappointed. But she thought of Leopold and was consoled. After a few minutes of quiet, they helped her into the house, and laid her on a sofa in the parlor.

"Don't be frightened, dear lady," said the little woman. "Nobody shall come near you. We will watch you as if you were the queen. I am going to get some tea for you."

But the moment she left the room, Helen got up. She could not remain a moment longer in the place. There was a demon at her brother's ear, whispering to him to confess his wrong, to rid himself of his torture by the aid of the law. She must rush home and drive it away. She took her hat in her hand, opened the door softly, and before Rachel could say a word, had flitted through the kitchen, and was among the trees on the opposite side of the road. Rachel ran to the garden to tell her father and Wingfold. They looked at each other for a moment in silence.

"I will follow her," offered Wingfold. "She may faint again. If she does, I shall whistle."

He kept her in sight until she was safe in her aunt's garden.

22   A Haunted Soul

Helen made her way to a little summer house in the garden. It had been her best retreat since she had given her room to her brother, and there she seated herself to regain breath and composure. She had sought the door of Paradise, and the door of hell had been opened to her! The frightful idea of confession had no doubt already suggested itself to Leopold. If he should now be encouraged, there lay nothing but madness before her! Infinitely would she rather poison herself and him. She must take care that that foolish, extravagant curate should not come near him! There was no knowing what he might persuade her brother to do. Poor Poldie was so easily led by anything that looked grand or self-sacrificing.

Helen had hoped that the man who had spoken in public so tenderly, and at the same time so powerfully, of the saving heart of the universe, would in private have spoken words of hope and consolation. She then could have carried them home in gladness to her sick-souled brother, to comfort and strengthen him and make him feel that after all there was yet a place for him in the universe, and that he was no outcast. But instead of such words of gentle might, like those of the man of whom he was so fond of talking, Wingfold had only spoken drearily of duty, hinting at a horror that would plunge the whole ancient family into a hell of dishonor and contempt! It did indeed prove what mere heartless windbags of sterile theology those priests were! This whole tragedy was all Poldie's mother's fault—the fault of her race—and of the horrible drug her people had taught him to take! And was he to go and confess it, and be tried for it, and be—? Great God!— And here was the priest actually counseling what was worse than any suicide?

Suddenly, however, it occurred to her that the curate possessed no knowledge of the facts of the case, and had therefore been forced to talk at random. It was impossible he could suspect the crime of which her brother had been guilty, and therefore could not know the frightful consequences of such a confession as he had counseled. Had she not better, then, tell him everything, and so gather from him some right and reasonable advice? But what security would she have that a man capable of such priestly severity would not himself betray the sufferer to the vengeance of justice? No; she could venture no further. Sooner would she go to George Bascombe—from whom she not only could look for no spiritual comfort, but whose theories were so cruel against culprits of all sorts! Alas! She was alone. But for a man to talk so of the tenderness of Jesus Christ and then serve her as the curate had done—it was indeed shameless. Jesus would never have treated a poor wretched woman like that!—And as she said thus to herself, again the words sounded in the ear of her heart: *"Come unto me, all you that labor and are heavy laden, and I will give you rest."*

Before she knew it, Helen fell on her knees, her head on the chair. She cried to the hearer of cries—possible or impossible being, she knew not in the least, but whose tender offer birthed in her a desperate cry to help her in her dire need.

Instead of any word or thought coming to her that might have been imagined an answer, she was frightened from her knees by an approaching step. The housekeeper was coming with the message from her aunt that Leopold was more restless than usual, not at all like himself, and she could do nothing with him.

With a heart of lead in her body, Helen rose and hastened to her brother.

She was shocked when she saw him; some change had passed on him since the morning! Was that eager look in his eyes a new onrush of the fever? Or was she but reading in his face the agony she had herself gone through that day?

"Helen! Helen," he cried as she entered the room, "come here, close to me."

She hastened to him, sat down on the bedside, and took his hand.

"Helen," he repeated, a strange expression in his voice, for it seemed that of hope, "I have been thinking all day of what you told me on Sunday!"

"What was that, Poldie?" asked Helen with a pang of fear.

"Why, those words of course—what else! You sang them to me afterward, you remember, '*Comfort Ye*.' Helen, I would like to see Mr. Wingfold. Don't you think he might be able to help in some way?"

"What sort of way, Poldie?" she faltered, growing sick at heart. *Was this what came of praying!* she thought bitterly.

"Something or other. Surely Mr. Wingfold could tell me something—comfort me somehow, if I were to tell him all about it. I could trust the man that said such things as those you told me. Oh! I wish I hadn't run away, but had let them take me and hang me."

Helen felt herself growing white and weak. She turned away and pretended to search for something she had dropped.

"I don't think he would be of the slightest use to you," she cautioned, still stooping.

"Not if I told him everything?"

"No, not if you told him everything," she answered, and felt like a judge condemning him to death.

"What is he there for, then?" sighed Leopold, and turned his face to the wall with a moan.

Helen had not yet thought of asking herself whether her love for her brother was true love, in no way mingled with selfishness—whether it was of him only she thought or whether possible shame to herself had not a share in her misery. As far as she was aware, she was quite honest in what she said about the curate. What attempts had he made to comfort even her? What had he done but utter commonplaces about duty? And who could tell but that he might bring the artillery of his fanaticism to bear upon her poor boy's wild temperament and persuade him to confess the terrible thing he had done? So Leopold lay and moaned, and she sat crushed and speechless, weighted with despairing misery.

All at once Leopold sat straight up, his eyes fixed and flaming, his face white. He looked like a corpse possessed by a spirit of fear and horror. Helen's heart swelled into her throat as with wide eyes she stared at him. Surely, she thought afterward, she must have been at that moment in the presence of something unearthly! How long it was before it relaxed its hold she could not tell; it could not have been long. Suddenly the light sank from Leopold's eyes, his muscles relaxed, he fell back motionless on the pillow, and she thought he was dead. The same moment she was free: the horror had departed from her too.

At length Leopold opened his eyes, gave a terrified glance around, held out his arms to her, and drew her to him.

"I saw her!" he groaned in a voice that sounded as if it came from the grave.

"Nonsense, dear Poldie! It was all fancy—nothing more," she returned, in a voice almost as hollow as his.

"Fancy!" he repeated. "I know what fancy is as well as any man or woman born. That was no fancy. She stood there, by the wardrobe—in the same dress—her face as white as her dress!"

His voice had risen to a strangled shriek, and he shook like a child on the point of yelling aloud in an agony of fear. Helen clasped his face between her hands, and gathering courage from despair, said: "Let her come then, Poldie! I am with you and I defy her! She shall know how strong is a sister's love. Say what you will, she had herself to blame, and I don't doubt she did twenty worse things than you did when you killed her."

But Leopold seemed not to hear a word she said, and lay with his face to the wall.

At length he turned his head suddenly and uttered decisively,

"Helen, if you don't let me see Mr. Wingfold, I shall go mad. Then *everything* will come out."

Helen flew to the dressing room to hide her dismay, and there threw herself on the bed. She had no choice but to yield. After a few moments she rose and returned to her brother.

"I am going to find Mr. Wingfold," she said in a hoarse voice, as she took her hat.

"Don't be long, Helen," returned Leopold. "I can't bear you out of my sight. And don't let Aunt come into the room. *She* might come again, you know, and then all would be out.—Bring him with you, Helen."

"I will," answered Helen, and went.

The curate might have returned home, so she would look for him first at his house. She cared nothing of what people thought now.

It was a dull afternoon. Clouds had gathered and the wind was chilly. It seemed to blow out of the church, which stood up cold and gray against the sky, filling the end of the street. What a wretched, horrible world it was! She entered the churchyard, hurried across it, and reached the house. But Mr. Wingfold had not yet returned, and she hurried back again to tell Leopold that she must go farther to find him.

The poor youth was already more composed: what the vaguest hope can do for a man! Helen told him she had seen the curate in the park when she was out in the morning, and he might be there, or she might meet him coming back. She left again and took the road to the lodge.

She did not meet him, and it was with repugnance that she approached the gate.

"Is Mr. Wingfold here?" she asked Rachel, as if she had never spoken to her before. Rachel answered that he was in the garden with her uncle, and went to call him.

The moment he appeared, she pleaded, "Will you come to my brother? He is very ill and wants to see you."

"Certainly," answered Wingfold. "I will go with you at once."

But in his heart he trembled at the thought of being looked to for consolation and counsel—and apparently in no ordinary kind of case. Most likely he would not know what to say or how to behave himself. How different it would be if with all his heart he believed the grand things of his profession! Still he must go and do his best.

They walked across the park to reach the house by the garden, and for some distance they walked in silence. At length Helen said: "You must not encourage my brother to talk much, and you must not mind what he says. He has had brain fever and sometimes talks strangely. But on the other hand, if he thinks you don't believe him, it will drive him wild—so you must take care—please?"

Her voice was like that of a soul trying to speak with untried lips.

"Miss Lingard," said Wingfold, slowly and quietly, and if his voice trembled, only he was aware of it, "I cannot see your face; therefore you must pardon me if I ask you—are you being altogether honest with me?"

Helen's first feeling was anger. She held her peace for a time. Then she said, "So, Mr. Wingfold! *That* is the way you help the helpless!"

"How can any man help without knowing what has to be helped?" returned the curate. "The very nature of his help depends upon his knowing the truth. It is very plain you do not trust me, and equally impossible I can be of service to you as long as such is the case."

Again Helen held her peace. Resentment and dislike toward him, combined with terror of his anticipated counsel, made her speechless.

Her silence lasted so long that Wingfold came to the resolution of making a venture that had occurred to him more than once that morning.

"Maybe this will help to satisfy you that, whatever my advice may be worth, at least my discretion may be trusted," he assured her.

They were at the moment passing through a little thicket in the park, where nobody could see them, and as he spoke he took the knife sheath from his pocket and held it out to her.

She started like a young horse seeing something dead. She had never seen it, but recognized it by the shape. She grew deathly pale and retreated a step. With a drawing back of her head and neck and a spreading of her nostrils, she stared for a moment, first at the sheath, then at the curate, gave a little moan, and bit her lower lip hard. She held out her hand—but as if she were afraid to touch the thing—and said, "What is it? Where did you find it?"

She would have taken it, but Wingfold held it tight.

"Give it to me," she demanded. "It is mine. I lost it."

"There is something dark on the lining of it," pointed out the curate, and looked straight into her eyes.

She let go her hold. But almost the same moment she snatched the sheath out of his hand, while her look of terror changed into one of defiance. Wingfold made no attempt to recover it. She put it in her pocket, and drew herself up.

"What do you mean?" she retorted, in a voice that was hard, yet trembled.

She felt like one that sees the vultures above him, and lifts a single movable finger in defiance. Then with sudden haughtiness both of gesture and word: "You have been playing the part of a spy, sir!"

"No," returned the curate quietly. "The sheath was committed to my care by another. Certain facts had come to his knowledge—certain words he overheard—"

He paused. She shook noticeably, but still would hold what little ground might yet be left to her.

"Why did you not give it to me before?" she asked.

"In the public street, or in your aunt's presence?"

"You are cruel!" she gasped. Her strength was going. "What do you know?"

"Nothing so well as that I want to serve you, and you may trust me," he answered her.

"What do you intend to do?"

"My best to help you and your brother."

"But to what end?"

"To the end that is right."

"But how? What would you tell him to do?"

"You must help me to discover what he ought to do."

"Not—" she cried and swallowed hard, "—you will not tell him to give himself up? Promise me you will not, and I will tell you everything. He shall do anything you please but that! Anything but that!"

Wingfold's heart was sore at the sight of her agony.

"I dare not promise anything," he cautioned. "I *must* do what I may see to be right. Believe me, I have no wish to force myself into your confidence, but you have let me see that you are in great trouble and in need of help. I should be unfaithful to my calling if I did not do my best to make you trust me."

A pause followed. They resumed their walk, and just as they reached the door in the fence which would let them out upon the meadow in sight of the Manor-house, she turned to him and said, "I will trust you, Mr. Wingfold. I mean, I will take you to my brother and he shall do as he thinks proper."

They passed through the door and walked across the meadow in silence. In the passage under the fence, as she turned from closing the door behind them, she stood and pressed her hand to her side.

"Oh, Mr. Wingfold," she cried, "he has no one but me! No one but me to be mother and sister to him all in one. He is *not* a bad boy, my poor darling!"

She caught the curate by the arm with a grasp which left its mark behind it, and gazed appealingly into his face.

"Save him from madness," she pleaded. "Save him from the remorse gnawing at his heart. But do not, *do not* counsel him to give himself up."

"Would it not be better you should tell me about it," advised the curate, "and save him the pain?"

"I will do so if he wishes it, not otherwise. Come; we must not stay longer. He can hardly bear me out of his sight. I will leave you for one moment in the library, and then come to you. If you should see my aunt, not a word of all this, please. All she knows is that he has had brain fever and is recovering very slowly. I have never given her even a hint of anything worse. In sincere honesty, Mr. Wingfold, I am not certain at all he did do what he will tell you. But there is his misery all the same. Do have pity on us, and don't be hard on him. He is but a boy—only twenty."

"May God be to me as I am to him," vowed Wingfold solemnly.

Helen released his arm, and they went up into the garden and entered the house.

Helen left him in the library, as she had said, and there he awaited her return in a kind of stupor, unable to think, and feeling as if he were lost in a strange and anxious nightmare.

23 In Confidence

"Come," beckoned Helen, reentering, and the curate rose and followed her.

The moment he turned the corner of the bed and saw the face on the pillow, he knew in his soul that Helen was right: this was no wicked youth who lay before him. Wingfold once had a brother, the only being in the world he had ever loved tenderly. He had died young, and a thin film of ice had since gathered over the well of Wingfold's affections. But now suddenly the ice broke and vanished, and his heart yearned over the suffering youth. Reading the gospel story had roused in his heart a reverence and a love for his kind which now first sprang awake in the feeling that drew him toward Leopold.

Softly he approached the bed, his face full of tenderness and strong pity. The lad, weak with illness and mental tortures, gave one look in his face, and stretched out his arms to him. The curate put his arms around him as if he had been a child.

"I knew you would come," sobbed Lingard.

"What else could I do but come?" returned Wingfold.

"I have seen you somewhere before," said Lingard, "—in one of my dreams, I suppose."

Then, his voice sinking to a whisper, he added: "Do you know you came right after *her*? She looked around and saw you, then vanished."

Wingfold did not even try to guess at his meaning.

"Hush, my dear fellow," he said. "I must not let you talk wildly, or the doctor might forbid my seeing you."

"I am not talking a bit wildly," returned Leopold.

Wingfold sat down on the side of the bed and took the thin, hot hand next to him in his own firm, cool one.

"Come now," he encouraged, "tell me all about it. Or shall your sister tell me? —Come here, please, Miss Lingard."

"No, no!" cried Leopold hastily. "I will tell you myself. My poor sister could not bear to tell it to you. It would kill her. But how am I to know you will not get up and walk out the moment you have a glimpse of what is coming?"

"I would as soon leave a child burning in the fire and go out and shut the door," assured Wingfold.

"You can go now, Helen," whispered Lingard very quietly. "Why should you be tortured over again? You needn't mind leaving me. Mr. Wingfold will take care of me."

Helen left the room, casting one anxious look at her brother as she went.

Without a moment's further delay, Leopold began, and in direct and unbroken narrative, told the sad, evil tale as he had formerly told it to his sister, only more quietly and in order. All the time he kept watching Wingfold's face, the expressions of which the curate felt those eyes were reading like a book. He was so well prepared, however, that no expression of surprise, no ghastly reflex met Leopold's gaze, and he went on to the end without even a pause. When he had finished, both sat silent, looking in each other's eyes, Wingfold's brimming with compassion, and Leopold's glimmering with doubtful, anxious inquiry and appeal.

At length Wingfold said: "And what do you think I can do for you?"

"I don't know. I thought you could tell me something. I cannot live like this! If I had but thought before I did it, and killed myself instead of her, it would have been so much better. Of course I should be in hell now, but that would be all right, and this is all wrong. I have no right to be lying here and Emmeline in her grave. I know I deserve to be miserable forever and ever, and I don't want not to be miserable—that is all right—but there is something in this wretchedness I cannot bear. Tell me something to make me able to endure my misery. That is what you can do for me. Worst

of all, I have made my sister miserable, and I can't bear to see it.
She is wasting away with it. And besides, I think she loves George
Bascombe—and who would marry the sister of a murderer? And
now she has begun to come again to me in the daytime—I mean
Emmeline!—or I have begun to see her again—I don't know
which. Perhaps she is always here, only I don't see her always—
and it doesn't matter much. Only if other people were to see
her!—While she is here, nothing could persuade me I do not see
her, but afterward I am not so sure that I did. And at night I keep
dreaming the horrible thing over and over again. And the agony
is to think I shall never rid myself of it, and never feel clean again.
To forever and ever be a murderer and people not know it is more
than I can bear."

Not seeing yet what he should say, the curate let the talk take
its natural course, and said the next thing that came to him.

"How do you feel when you think that you may yet be found
out?" he asked.

"At first I was more afraid of that than anything else. Then
after the danger seemed past, I was afraid of the life to come. That
fear left me next, and now it is the thing itself that is always haunting me. I often wish they would come and take me. It would be a
comfort to have it all known, and never need to be afraid again. If
it would annihilate the deed, or bring Emmeline back, I cannot tell
you how gladly I would be hanged. I would, indeed, Mr. Wingfold.
I hope you will believe me, though I don't deserve to have you do
so."

"I do believe you," assured the curate, and a silence followed.
"There is but one thing I can say with confidence at this moment,"
Wingfold resumed: "It is that I am your friend, and will stand by
you. But the first part of friendship sometimes is to confess poverty, and I want to tell you that the very things I ought to know
most about, I know least. I have but recently begun to search after
God myself, and I dare not say that I have found him. But I think
I know now where to find him. And I do think, if we could find
him, then we would find help. All I can do for you now is only to
be near you, and talk to you, and pray to God for you, so that
together we may wait for what light may come. Does anything
ever look to you as if it would make you feel better?"

"I have no right to feel better or take comfort from anything."

"I am not sure about that. Do you feel any better for having me come to see you?"

"Oh, yes! Indeed I do!"

"Well, there is no wrong in that, is there?"

"I don't know. My sister makes excuses for me, but the moment I begin to listen to them I only feel all the more horrid."

"I have said nothing of that kind to you."

"No, sir."

"And yet you like to have me here?"

"Yes, indeed, sir," he answered earnestly.

"And it does not make you think less your crime?"

"No. It makes me feel worse than ever to see you sitting there, a clean, strong, innocent man, and think what I might have been."

"Then the comfort you get from me does you no harm, at least. If I were to find that my company made you think less hatefully of your crime, I would go away that instant."

"Thank you," said Leopold humbly. He resumed after a little silence, "Oh, to think that never more to all eternity shall I be able to think of myself as I used to think."

"Perhaps you used to think too much of yourself," returned the curate. "For the greatest rascal in creation there is yet a worse condition, and that is not to know it, but to think oneself a respectable man. Though you would undoubtedly have laughed at the idea a day earlier, the event proves you were capable of committing a murder. You know what Jeremiah said, that the heart is desperately wicked—the heart of every man; mine is as wicked as yours or anyone else's. I have come to see—at least, I think I have—that except a man has God dwelling in him, he may be, or may become, capable of any crime within the compass of human nature."

"I don't know anything about God," confessed Leopold. "I thought I did before this happened—before I did it, I mean," he added in correction, "—but I know now that I never did."

"Ah, Leopold!" said the curate, "just think; if my coming to you comforts you, what would it be to have him who made you always with you!"

"What would be the good of it? I dare say he might forgive me if I were to do this and that, but where would be the good of it? It would not take the thing off me in the least?"

"Ah, now," returned Wingfold. "I am afraid you are thinking a little too much of your own disgrace and not about the bad you have done. Why should you not be ashamed? Would you have the shame taken off you? No, you must humbly consent to bear it. Perhaps your shame is the hand of love washing the defilement from you. Let us keep our shame, and be made clean from the filth."

"I don't know that I understand you. What do you mean by defilement? Isn't the deed the defilement?"

"Is it not rather to have that within you that makes you capable of doing it? If you had resisted and conquered, you would have been clean from it. And now, if you repent and God comes to you, you will yet be clean. Again I say, let us keep our shame and be made clean! Shame is not defilement, though pride persuades men that it is. On the contrary, the man who is honestly ashamed has begun to be clean."

"But what good would that do to Emmeline? It cannot bring her up out of the dark grave into the bright world."

"Emmeline is not in the dark grave."

"Where is she, then?"

"That I do not know. I only know that, if there is a God, she is in his hands," replied the curate.

The youth gazed in his face and made no answer. Wingfold saw that he had been wrong in trying to comfort him with the thought of God dwelling in him. How was such a poor, passionate creature to take that for a comfort? He would try another approach.

"Shall I tell you what sometimes seems to me the only thing I want to help me out of all my difficulties?"

"Yes, please," answered Leopold, as humbly as a child.

"I think sometimes, if I could but see Jesus for one moment—"

"Ah!" cried Leopold, and gave a great sigh.

"You would like to see him too, would you?"

"Oh, yes."

"What would you say to him if you saw him?"

"I don't know. I would fall down on my face and hold his feet so he wouldn't go away from me."

"Do you think then he could help you?"

"Yes. He could make Emmeline alive again. He could destroy what I had done."

"But still, as you say, the crime would remain."

"But, as you say, he could pardon that and make me so that I would never, never sin again."

"So you think the story about Jesus Christ is true?"

"Yes. Don't you?" said Leopold with an amazed, half-frightened look.

"Yes, indeed I do.—Then do you remember what he said to his disciples as he left them, 'I am with you always to the end of the world'? If that is true, then he can hear you just as well now as ever. And when he was in the world, he said, 'Come unto me, all you that labor and are heavy laden, and I will give you rest.' It is rest you want, my poor boy—not deliverance from danger or shame, but rest—such peace of mind as you had when you were a child. If he cannot give you that, I don't know where or how it is to be obtained. Do not waste time in asking yourself how he can do it; that is for him to understand, not you—until it is done. Ask him to forgive you and make you clean and set things right for you. If he will not do it, then he is not the Savior of men, and was wrongly named Jesus."

The curate rose. Leopold had hidden his face. When he looked again, Wingfold was gone.

As Wingfold came out of the room which was near the stair, Helen rose from the top of it. She had been sitting there all the time he had been with her brother. He closed the door gently behind him, and stepped softly along the landing. A human soul in guilt and agony is an awful presence, but there was more than that in the hush of the curate. He felt as if he had left the physician of souls behind him at the bedside. He was not aware that the tears stood in his eyes, but Helen saw them.

"You know all?" she said with a faltering voice.

"I do. Will you let me out by the garden door, please? I wish to be alone."

She led the way down the stairs and walked with him through the garden. Wingfold did not speak.

155

"You don't think very badly of my poor brother, do you, Mr. Wingfold?" said Helen meekly.

"It is a terrible fate," he returned. "I do hope his mind will soon be more composed. I think he knows the one place where he can find rest. I am well aware how foolish I sound to some minds, Miss Lingard; but when a man is overwhelmed by his own deeds, when he loathes himself and turns with sickness from his past, I know but one choice left, and that is between the death your friend Mr. Bascombe preaches and the life preached by Jesus."

"I am so glad you don't hate him."

"Hate him! Who could hate him?"

Helen lifted a grateful look from eyes that swam in tears. The terror of his possible counsel vanished for the moment.

"But as I told you, I am a poor scholar in these high matters," resumed the curate, "and I want to bring Mr. Polwarth to see him."

"The dwarf!" exclaimed Helen, shuddering at the remembrance of what she had gone through at the cottage.

"Yes. That man's soul is as grand and beautiful and patient as his body is insignificant and troubled. He is the wisest man I have ever known."

"I must ask Leopold," returned Helen. The better the man was represented, the more fearful she felt of the advice he might give. Her love and her conscience were not yet at one with each other.

They parted at the door from the garden and she returned to the sickroom.

She paused, hesitating to enter. All was still as the grave. She turned the handle softly and peeped in: could it be that Wingfold's bearing had communicated to her mind a shadow of the awe with which he had left the place where perhaps a soul was being born again? Leopold did not move. She stepped quickly in and around the screen to the side of his bed. There, to her glad surprise, he lay fast asleep, with the tears not yet dried upon his face. Her heart swelled with some sense unknown before: was it rudimentary thankfulness to the Father of her spirit?

As she stood gazing with the look of a mother over her sick child, he lifted his eyelids and smiled a sad smile.

"When did you come into the room?" he asked.

"A minute ago," she answered.

"I did not hear you," he returned.

"You were asleep."

"But Mr. Wingfold just left."

"I have already let him out on the meadow."

Leopold looked amazed.

"Did God make me sleep, then, Helen?"

She did not answer. The light of a new hope in his eye, as if the dawn had begun at last to break over the dark mountains, was already reflected from her heart.

"Oh, Helen!" Leopold exclaimed, "he is a good fellow."

A momentary pang of jealousy shot to her heart. "You will be able to do without me now," she sighed sadly.

"I am hardly likely to forget you for Mr. Wingfold, good and kind and strong as he is," replied Leopold. "But neither you nor I can do without Mr. Wingfold anymore. I wish you liked him better—but you will in time. Only you see—"

"Only you see, Poldie," interrupted Helen with a smile, rare thing between them, "you seem to know all about him, though you never saw him before a few minutes ago."

"That is true," returned Leopold. "But then he came to me with his door open, and let me walk in. It doesn't take long to know a man like that. He hasn't got a secret to hide like us, Helen."

"What did he say to you?"

"Much that he said to you from the pulpit the other day, I imagine. He is coming again tomorrow. And then perhaps he will tell me more, and help me on a bit."

"Did he tell you he wants to bring a friend with him?"

"No."

"I can't see the good of taking more people into our confidence."

"Why should he not do what he thinks best, Helen? You don't interfere with the doctor, why should you with him? When a man is going to the bottom as fast as he can, and another comes diving after him, it isn't for me to say how he is to take hold of me. No, Helen; when I trust, I trust all the way."

24 Divine Service

The next day the curate called again on Leopold. Helen happened to be otherwise engaged and Mrs. Ramshorn was in the sickroom when the servant brought his name. With her jealousy of Wingfold's teaching, she would not have admitted him, but Leopold made such a loud protest and insisted on seeing him that she had to give in and tell the maid to show him up. Little conversation therefore was possible. Still the face of his new friend was a comfort to Leopold, and before he left him they had managed to fix a time for the next day when they would not be thus foiled of their talk.

Later that afternoon Wingfold took the draper to see Polwarth. The dwarf allowed Wingfold to help him in getting tea, and the conversation, as will be the case where all are in earnest, quickly found the right channel.

It is not often in life that such conversations occur. In most discussions, each man has some point to maintain and his object is to justify his own thesis and disprove his neighbor's. He may have originally adopted his thesis because of some sign of truth in it, but his mode of supporting it is generally to block up every cranny in his soul at which more truth might enter. In the present case, unusual as it is for as many as three truth-loving men to come together on the face of this planet, here were three simply set on uttering truth they had seen, and gaining sight of truth as yet hidden from them.

I shall attempt only a general impression of the result of their evening's discussion.

"I have been trying hard to follow you, Mr. Polwarth," acknowledged the draper, after his host had for a while had the talk to himself, "but I cannot get hold of it. Would you tell me what you mean by divine service? I think you use the phrase in some different sense from what I have been accustomed to."

"When I use the phrase *divine service*," explained Polwarth, "I mean nothing whatever about the church or its observance. I mean simply serving God. Shall I make the church a temple of idolatrous worship by supposing that it exists for the sake of supplying some need that God has, or of gratifying some taste in him, that I there listen to his Word, say prayers to him, and sing his praises for his benefit? Shall I degrade the sanctity of the closet, hallowed in the words of Jesus, by shutting myself behind its door in the vain fancy of doing something there that God requires of me as a sacred *observance*? Shall I foolishly imagine that to exercise the highest and loveliest privilege of my existence, that of pouring forth my whole heart in prayer into the heart of him who is accountable for me, who has glorified me with his own image—in my soul, gentlemen, sadly disfigured as it is in my body!—shall I call *that* serving God?"

"But," interjected Drew, "is not God pleased that a man should pour out his soul to him?"

"Yes, doubtless. But is the child who sits by his father's knee and looks up into his father's face *serving* that father because the heart of the father delights to look down upon the child? And shall the moment of my deepest repose, the moment when I serve myself with the life of the universe, be called serving my God? What would you think of a child who said, 'I am very useful to my father, for when I ask him for something, or tell him I love him, it gives him such pleasure'? When my child would serve me, he sees some need I have, jumps from his seat at my knee, finds that which will meet my need, and is my eager, happy servant; he has done something for his father. His seat by my knee is love, delight, well-being, peace—not service, however pleasing in my eyes. Do not talk of public worship as divine service. Search the prophets and you will find observances, fasts and sacrifices and solemn feasts of the temple were regarded by God's holy men with loathing and scorn just because by the people they were regarded as *divine service*."

"But," speculated Mr. Drew, "I can't help thinking that if the phrase ever was used in that sense, there is no meaning of that kind attached to it now: service stands merely for the forms of public worship."

"If there were no such thing as *divine service* in the true sense of the word, then it would scarcely be worthwhile to quarrel with its misapplication. But I believe that true and genuine service may be given to the living God. And for the development of the divine nature in man, it is necessary that he should do something for God. And it is not hard to discover how, for God is in every creature and in their needs. Therefore, Jesus says that whatever is done to one of his little ones is done to him. And if the soul of a believer be the temple of the Spirit, then is not the place of that man's labor—his shop, his bank, his laboratory, his school, his factory—the temple of Jesus Christ, where the spirit of the man is at work? Mr. Drew, your shop is the temple of your service where the Lord Christ ought to be throned. Your counter ought to be his altar, and everything laid on it with intent of doing as you can for your neighbor, in the name of Christ Jesus."

The little prophet's face glowed as he stopped. But neither of his companions spoke.

Polwarth went on, "You will not become a rich man, but by so doing you will be saved from growing too rich and you will be a fellow worker with God for the salvation of his world."

"I must live; I cannot give my goods away," murmured Mr. Drew, thinking about all he had heard.

"Giving them away would be easy," added Polwarth. "No, a harder task is yours, Mr. Drew—to make your business profitable to you, and at the same time to be not only just, but interested in, and careful of, and caring for your neighbor—as a servant of the God of bounty who gives to all men liberally. Your calling is to do the best for your neighbor that you reasonably can."

"But who is to determine what is reasonable?" asked Drew.

"The man himself, thinking in the presence of Jesus Christ. There is a holy moderation which is of God, and he will gladly reveal it to you."

"There won't be many fortunes made by that rule, Mr. Polwarth."

"Very few," admitted the dwarf.

"Then do you say that no great fortunes have been righteously made?"

"I will not judge. That is for the conscience of the man himself, not for his neighbor. Why should I be judged by another man's conscience? But you see, Mr. Drew—and this is what I was driving at—you have it in your power to *serve* God through the needs of his children all the working day, from morning to night, so long as there is a customer in your shop."

"I do think you are right," concluded the linendraper. "I had a glimpse of the same thing the other night myself. And yet it seems as though you are speaking of a purely ideal state—one that could not be realized in this world."

"Purely ideal or not, one thing is certain: it will never be reached by one who is so indifferent to it as to believe it impossible. Whether it may be reached in this world or not, that is a question of less consequence. Whether a man has begun to reach after it is of the utmost importance. And if it be ideal, what else but the ideal should the followers of the ideal strive toward?"

"Can a man attain to anything ideal before he has God dwelling in him, filling every cranny of his soul?" asked the curate.

"No," answered Polwarth. "It is not until a man throws his door wide open to the Father of his spirit, when his individual being is thus filled with the individuality that originated it, that the man becomes a whole, healthy, complete existence. Then indeed, and then only, will he do no wrong, think no wrong, and love perfectly. Then will he hardly think of praying, because God dwells in every thought. Then he will forgive and endure, and pour out his soul for the beloved who yet grope along their way in doubt. Then every man will be dear and precious to him; for in all others also lies an unknown yearning after the same peace wherein he rests and loves."

He sat down suddenly and a deep silence filled the room.

"Tell them your vision of the shops in heaven, Uncle," said Rachel after a long silence.

"Oh, no, Rachel," said Polwarth.

"I know the gentlemen would like to hear it."

"That we should," insisted both men at once.

"I venture my objections are not likely to stand in this company," returned Polwarth with a smile. "Agreed, then. This was no dream, Mr. Wingfold. It is something I have thought out many times. But the only form I could find for it was that of a vision."

He stopped, took a deep breath while the others waited expectantly. Then he began.

" 'And now,' said my guide to me, 'I will take you to the city of the righteous, and show you how they buy and sell in the kingdom of heaven.' So we journeyed on and on and I was weary before we arrived. After I had refreshed my soul, my conductor led me into a large place that we would call a shop here, although the arrangements were different and an air of stateliness dwelt in and around the place. It was filled with the loveliest silk and woolens—all types and colors, a thousand delights.

"I stood in the midst of the place in silence and watched those that bought and sold. On the faces of those that sold I saw only expressions of a calm and concentrated ministration. As soon as one buyer was contented, they turned graciously to another and listened until they perfectly understood what he had come seeking. And once they had provided what the customer had desired, such a look of satisfaction lingered on their faces, as of having just had a great success.

"When I turned to watch the faces of those who bought, in like manner I saw complete humility—yet it was not humility because they sought a favor, for with their humility was mingled the total confidence of receiving all that they sought. It was truly a pleasure to see how everyone knew what his desire was, and then made his choice readily and with decision. I perceived also that everyone spoke not merely respectfully, but gratefully, to him who served him. And the kindly greetings and partings made me wonder how every inhabitant of such a huge city would know every other. But I soon saw that it came not of individual knowledge, but of universal love.

"And as I stood watching, suddenly it came to me that I had yet to see a single coin passed. So I began to keep my eyes on those who were buying. A certain woman was picking out a large quantity of silk, but when she had made her purchase, she simply took it in her arms and carried it out of the shop and did not pay. So I turned to watch another, but when he carried away his goods he paid no money either. I said to myself, 'These must be well-known persons who trade here often. The shopkeeper knows them and will bill them at a later time.' So I turned to another, but he did not pay either! Then I began to observe that those who were selling were writing nothing down concerning each sale. They were making no record of each purchase or keeping track of what was owed them.

"So I turned to my guide and said, 'How lovely is this honesty.

I see that every man and woman keeps track of his own debts in his mind so that time is not wasted in paying small sums or in keeping accounts. But those that buy count up their purchases and undoubtedly when the day of reckoning comes, they each come and pay the merchant what is owed, and both are satisfied.'

"Then my conductor smiled and said, 'Watch a little longer.'

"And I did as he said and stood and watched. And the same thing went on everywhere. Suddenly at my side a man dropped on his knees and bowed his head. And there arose a sound as of soft thunder, and everyone in the place dropped upon his knees and spread out his hands before him. Every voice and every noise was hushed and every movement had ceased.

"Then I whispered in his ear, 'It is the hour of prayer; shouldn't we kneel also?' And my guide answered, 'No man in the city kneels because another does, and no man is judged if he does not kneel.'

"For a few moments all was utter stillness—every man and woman was kneeling with hands outstretched, except him who had first kneeled, and his hands hung by his sides and his head was still bowed to the earth. At length he rose up, and his face was wet with tears, and all the others rose also. The man gave a bow to those around him, which they returned with reverence, and then, with downcast eyes, he walked slowly from the shop. The moment he was gone the business of the place began again as before.

"I went out at last with my guide and we seated ourselves under a tree on the bank of a quiet stream and I began to question him. 'Tell me, sir,' I said, 'the meaning of what I have seen. I do not yet understand how these happy people do their business without passing a single coin.' And he answered, 'Where greed and ambition and self-love rule, there must be money; where there is neither greed nor ambition nor self-love, money is useless.' And I asked, 'Is it by barter that they go about their affairs? For I saw no exchange of any sort.' 'No,' answered my guide, 'if you had gone into any shop in the city, you would have seen the same thing. Where no greed, ambition, or selfishness exists, need and desire can have free rein, for they can work no evil. Here men can give freely to whoever asks of him without thought of return, because all his own needs will be likewise supplied by others. By giving, each also receives. There are no advantages to be gained or sought. The sole desire is to more greatly serve. This world is contrary to your world. Everything here is upside down. The man here that does the greatest service, that helps others the most in the obtaining of their honest desires, is the man who stands in the highest regard with the Lord of the place, and his great reward and honor is to be enabled to spend himself yet more for the good of his fellows. There is even now a rumor among us that before long one shall be ripe to be enabled to carry a message from the King to the spirits that are in prison. That is indeed a strong incentive to stir up thought and energy to find things that will serve and minister to others, that will please their eyes and cheer their brains and gladden their hearts. So when one man asks, "Give me, friend, of your loaves of bread," the baker or shopkeeper may answer, "Take of them, friend, as many as you need." That is indeed a potent motive toward diligence. It is much stronger than the desire to hoard or excel or accumulate passing wealth. What a greater incentive it is to share the bliss of God who hoards nothing but always gives liberally. The joy of a man here is to give away what he has made, to make glad the heart of another and in so doing, grow. This doctrine appears strange and unbelievable to the man in whom the well of life is yet sealed. There have never been many at a time in the old world who could thus enter into the joy of their Lord. Surely you know of a few in your world who are thus in their hearts, who would willingly consent to be as nothing, so to give life to their fellows. In this city so it is with everyone.'

"And I said, 'Tell me one thing: how much may a man have for the asking?' 'What he wants. What he can well use.' 'But what if he should turn to greed and begin to hoard?' 'Did you not see today the man because of whom all business ceased for a time? To that man had come the thought of accumulation instead of growth, and he dropped on his knees in shame and terror. And you saw how immediately all business stopped and immediately that shop was made what below they call a church. For everyone hastened to the poor man's help. The air was filled with praying and the atmosphere of God-loving souls surrounded him, and the foul thought fled and the man went forth glad and humble, and tomorrow he will return for that which he needed. If you should be present then, you will see him all the more tenderly ministered unto.' 'Now I think I know and understand,' I answered, and we rose and went further."

"Could it be?" wondered the curate, breaking the silence that followed.

"Not in this world," asserted the draper.

"To doubt that it *could* be," declared the gatekeeper, "would be to doubt whether the kingdom of heaven be but a foolish fancy or a divine idea."

25   Polwarth and Lingard

The morning after Wingfold's second visit, Lingard—much to his sister's surprise, partly to her pleasure, and somewhat to her consternation—asked for his clothes. He wanted to get up.

It took him a long time to dress, but he had resolved to do it himself, and at length called Helen. She found he looked worse in his clothes—fearfully worn and white. Ah, what a sad ghost he was of his former sunny self!

"Will you get me something to eat, Helen?" he said. "Mr. Wingfold will be here, and I want to be able to talk to him."

It was the first time he had asked for food, though he had seldom refused to take what she brought him. She made him lie on the couch and gave orders that if Mr. Wingfold called, he should be shown up at once. Leopold's face brightened; he actually looked pleased when his soup came. When Wingfold was announced, Helen received him respectfully, but not altogether cordially.

"Would your brother like to see Mr. Polwarth?" asked the curate.

"I will see anyone you would like me to see, Mr. Wingfold," answered Lingard for himself, with a decision that strongly indicated returning strength.

"But, Leopold, you know that it is hardly to be desired," suggested Helen, "that more persons—"

"I *don't* know that," interrupted Leopold, with strange expression.

"Perhaps it will encourage you, Miss Lingard," added the curate, "that it was Mr. Polwarth who found the thing I gave you. After your visit, he could not fail to put things together. I repeat in your brother's hearing what I said to you, that he is the wisest man I have ever known. I left him in the meadow at the foot of the garden. If you will allow me, I will go and bring him in."

"Please do," insisted Leopold. "Just think, Helen. If he is the wisest man Mr. Wingfold has ever known, tell him where to find the key!"

"I will go myself," she offered, yielding to the inevitable.

When she opened the door, there was the little man seated a few yards off on the grass. He had plucked a cowslip and was staring into it so intently that he neither heard nor saw her.

"Mr. Polwarth!" called Helen.

He lifted his eyes, rose, and, taking off his hat, said with a smile, "How is your brother, Miss Lingard?"

Helen answered with cold politeness, then led the way up the garden with considerably more stateliness of demeanor than was necessary.

"This is Mr. Polwarth, Leopold," announced the curate, rising respectfully. "You may speak to him as freely as to me, and he is far more able to give you counsel than I am."

"Would you mind shaking hands with me, Mr. Polwarth?" asked Leopold, holding out his thin, shadowy hand.

Polwarth took it, with the kindest of smiles, and held it a moment in his.

"You think me an odd-looking creature, don't you?" he said matter-of-factly. Without waiting for a response, he continued, "Because God has allowed me to be so, I have been compelled to think about things I might otherwise have forgotten, and that is why Mr. Wingfold would have me come to see you."

The curate placed a chair for him, and the gatekeeper sat down. Helen seated herself a little way off, pretending—hardly more—to hem a handkerchief. Leopold's big eyes went wandering from one to the other of the two men.

"I am sorry to hear that you suffer so much," said Leopold

kindly, for he heard the labored breath of the little man and saw the heaving of his chest.

"It does not trouble me greatly," returned Polwarth. "It is not my fault, you see," he added with a smile, "—at least I don't think it is."

"You are happy to suffer without fault," concluded Leopold. "What I mean is that my punishment seems greater than I can bear."

"You need God's forgiveness in your soul."

"I don't see how that should do anything for me."

"I do not mean it would take away your suffering, but it would make you able to bear it. It would be fresh life in you."

"I can't see why it should. I can't feel that I have wronged God. I have been trying to feel it, Mr. Wingfold, ever since you talked to me. But I don't know God, and I only feel what I have done to Emmeline. If I said to God, 'Pardon me,' and he said to me, 'I do pardon you,' I would feel just the same. What could that do to set anything right that I have done?"

He hid his face in his hands.

What use can it be to torture the poor boy so? Helen thought to herself.

The two men sat silent. Then Polwarth said, "I doubt if there is any use in *trying* to feel a certain way. And no amount of trying could enable you to imagine what God's forgiveness is like to those who have it in them. Tell me something more about how you do feel, Mr. Lingard."

"I feel that I could kill myself in order to bring her back to life."

"That is, you would kindly make amends for the wrong you have done her."

"I would give my life, my soul, to do it."

"And there is nothing you can do to make amends?" inquired Polwarth.

Helen began to tremble. She feared what could come of this.

"What is there that *can* be done?" answered Leopold. "It does seem hard that a man should be made capable of doing things that he is not made capable of undoing again."

"It is indeed a terrible thought! Even the smallest wrong is, perhaps, too awful a thing for created beings ever to set right again."

"You mean it takes God to do that?"

"I do," affirmed the dwarf.

"I don't see how he could ever set things right."

"He would not be God if he could not or would not do for his creature what his creature cannot do for himself, something the creature must have done in his behalf or lose his life."

"Then he isn't God, for he can't help me."

"Because you don't see what can be done, you say God can do nothing—which is like saying there cannot be more within his scope than there is within yours. One thing is clear: if he saw no more than lies within your sight, he could not be God. The very impossibility you see in the thing points to the region God works in."

"I don't understand you. But it doesn't matter. It's all a horrible mess. I wish I were dead." Leopold hung his head.

"God takes our sins on himself," the gatekeeper went on, "so that he may clear them out of the universe. How could he say that he took our sins upon himself if he could not make amends for those we had hurt?"

"Ah," cried Leopold, with a profound sigh, "if that could be! If he could really do that!"

"Why, of course he can do that!" avowed Polwarth. "What sort of watchmaker would he be who could not set right the watches and clocks he himself made?"

"But the hearts of men and women—"

"Is there not the might of love, and all eternity for it to work in, to set things right?" concluded Polwarth.

"O God!" cried Leopold, "if that might be true! That would be a gift indeed—the power to make up for the wrong I have done!"

To Helen this sounded like mere raving madness, and she thought how wrong she had been to allow such fanatics to hold out such false hope to her poor Leopold.

"Mr. Wingfold," Leopold declared, "I want to ask you one more favor. Will you take me to the nearest magistrate? I want to give myself up."

Helen started up and came forward, paler than the sick man.

"Mr. Wingfold! Mr. Polwarth!" she blurted, turning from the one to the other, "the boy is not himself. You will never allow him to do such a mad thing!"

"It may be the right thing to do," advised the curate to Leopold, "but we must not act without consideration."

"And not without prayer at how the thing should best be done," interjected Polwarth.

"I have considered and considered it for days—for weeks," returned Leopold. "But until this moment I have not had the courage to resolve even the plainest of duties. Helen, if I were to go to the throne of God and say to him, 'Against you, and you only, I have sinned,' I would be false, for I have sinned against every man, woman, and child in England at least, and I will repudiate myself. To the throne of God I want to go, and there is no way but through the gate of the law."

"Leopold!" pleaded Helen, "what good can it do to send another life after the one that is gone? It cannot bring it back or heal a single sorrow."

"Except, perhaps, my own," uttered Leopold in a feeble voice, but not the less in a determined tone.

"Live till God sends for you," persisted Helen, heedless of his words. "You can give your life to make up for the wrong you have done in a thousand better ways."

Leopold sank on the couch.

"I am sitting down again, Helen, only because I am not able to stand," he said. "I *will* go. Don't talk to me about doing good! Whatever I touched I should but smear with blood. I want the responsibility of my own life taken off me. For this reason is my strength given back to me, and I am once more able to will and to resolve. You will find I can act too. Helen, if you are indeed my true sister, you must not prevent me now. I know I am dragging your life down with mine, but I cannot help it. If I don't confess, I shall but pass out of one madness into another. Mr. Polwarth, is it not my duty to give myself up? Then I shall be able to die and go to God and see what he can do for me."

"Why should you put it off till then?" answered Polwarth. "Why not go to him at once and tell him everything?"

As if it had been Samuel at the command of Eli, Leopold rose and crept feebly across the floor to the dressing room. He entered it and closed the door.

Then Helen turned upon Wingfold with a face white as a sheet and eyes flashing with fierce wrath. The tigress mother swelled in her heart.

"Is this then your religion?" she cried with quivering nostril. "Would he you dare call your master play upon the weakness of a poor lad suffering from brain fever? What is it to you whether he confesses his sins or not? If he confesses them to him you say is your God, is not that enough?"

She ceased and stood trembling—a human thundercloud. Neither of the men cared to assert innocence. Although they had not advised the step, they entirely approved of it, knowing confession to be the first step on the road to forgiveness and healing.

A moment more and her anger suddenly went out. She burst into tears and fell on her knees before the curate. It was terrible for Wingfold to see a woman in such agony. In vain he sought to raise her.

"If you do not save Leopold, I will kill myself!" she cried, "and my blood will be on your head."

"The only way to save your brother is to strengthen him to do his duty, whatever that may be."

The hot fit of her mental labor returned. She sprang to her feet and her face turned again, almost like that of a corpse, with pale wrath.

"Leave the house!" she ordered, turning sharply upon Polwarth, who stood solemn and calm at Wingfold's side a step behind.

"If my friend goes, I go too," declared Wingfold. "But I must first tell your brother why."

He made a step toward the dressing room.

But another change of mood suddenly came upon Helen. She darted between him and the door and stood there with such a look of humble entreaty that it penetrated his very heart. But not even her tears could turn Wingfold from what seemed his duty. They could only bring answering tears from the depths of a tender heart. She saw he would not flinch.

"Then may God do to you as you have done to me and my family!" she cried.

"Amen!" returned Wingfold and Polwarth together.

The door of the dressing room opened and out came Leopold, his white face shining.

"God has heard me!" he cried.

"How do you know that?" demanded his sister in unbelieving despair.

"Because he has made me strong to do my duty. He has reminded me that another man may be accused of my crime, and that now to conceal myself would only make my crime that much worse."

"You can think about that when there is a need for it. What you imagine might never happen," objected Helen in the same unnatural voice.

"How could I just wait," cried Leopold, "until an innocent man shall suffer the torture and shame of a false accusation so that a guilty man may a little longer act the hypocrite! No, Helen, I have not fallen so low as that yet." But as he spoke, the light died out of his face, and before they could reach him, he had fallen heavily on the floor.

"You have killed him!" cried Helen, stifling her shriek, for all the time she had never forgotten that her aunt might hear.

"Go, I beg of you," she pleaded, "before my aunt comes. She must have heard the fall. I hear the key to the door below."

The men obeyed and left the house in silence.

It was some time before Leopold returned to consciousness. He made no resistance when Helen put him to bed again, where he lay in extreme exhaustion.

26 Wingfold and Helen

The day after that was Saturday, and George Bascombe visited as usual. The sound of his step in the hall made Helen's dying hope once more flutter its wings. Having lost her confidence in the parson, from whom she had never expected much, she turned in her despair to her cousin, from whom she had never looked for anything. What was she to say to him? Nothing yet, she resolved. But she would take him to see Leopold. She was not sure this was the right thing to do, but she would do it. And if she left them together, possibly George might drop some good *practical* advice. *George is such a healthy nature and such a sound thinker!* was her desperate conclusion.

Leopold was better, and willing enough to see him, saying, "Only I wish it were Mr. Wingfold."

George's entrance brought with it a waft of breezy health and a show of bodily vigor, pleasant and refreshing to the heart of the invalid. Kindness shone in his eyes, and his large, handsome hand was extended as usual while he was yet yards away. It swallowed up that of poor Leopold and held it fast.

"Come, come, old fellow! what's the meaning of this?" he said heartily. "You ought to be ashamed of yourself—lying in bed like this in such weather! Why aren't you riding in the park with Helen instead of moping in this dark room? We must see what we can do to get you up!"

Thus he talked on for some time, in expostulatory rattle, the very high priest of social morality, before Leopold could get a word in. But when he did, it turned the current of the conversation into quite another channel.

An hour passed, and George reappeared in the drawing room where Helen was waiting for him. He looked very grave.

"I am afraid matters are worse with poor Leopold than I had imagined," he remarked sagely.

Helen gave a sad nod of agreement.

"He's quite out of his head," continued George, "—telling me such a cock-and-bull story with the greatest seriousness! He insists that he is a murderer—the murderer of that very girl I was telling you about, you remember—"

"Yes, yes! I know," replied Helen, as a faint gleam of reviving hope shot through her. George took the whole thing for a sick fancy, and who was likely to know better than he—a lawyer skilled in evidence? Not a word would she say to interfere with such an opinion!

"I hope you set him straight," she said.

"Of course I did," he answered, "but it was of no use. He gave me a full and circumstantial account of the affair, filling in all the gaps, it is true, but going no further than the skeleton of facts which the newspapers supplied. How he got away, for instance, he could not tell me. And now he insists nothing will do but that he confess it all! The moment I saw him I read madness in his eye. What's to be done now?"

"George, I look to you," pleaded Helen. "Poor Aunt is no use. Just think what will become of her if the unhappy boy should attempt to give himself up! We would be the talk of the whole neighborhood—of the whole country!"

"Why didn't you tell me of this before, Helen? It must have been coming on for some time."

"George, I didn't know what to do. And I had heard you say such terrible things about the duty of punishing crime."

"Good gracious! Helen. What has crime to do with it? Anyone with half an eye can see the boy is mad!"

Helen wondered if she had made a slip in mentioning the possibility of Leopold turning himself in. She held her peace, and George went on.

"He ought to be put away somewhere."

"No! no!" Helen almost screamed, covering her face with her hands.

"I've done my best to persuade him. But I will have another try. That a fellow is out of his mind is no reason why he shouldn't be able to be persuaded by good, sound logic."

"But he is set upon it, George," Helen insisted. "I don't know what is to be done."

George got up, went back to Leopold, and plied him with the very best of arguments. But they were of no avail. There was but one door out of hell, Leopold insisted, and that was the door of confession—no matter what might lie on the other side of it.

George was silent. He found himself in that rare condition for him—perplexity. It would be most awkward if the thing came to be talked about. Some would even be fools enough to believe the story! Leopold's account was so circumstantial—and therefore plausible. There was no doubt most magistrates would be ready at once to commit him for trial—and then there would be no end to the embarrassments.

Thus George reflected uneasily. But at length an idea struck him.

"Well," he said lightly, "if you will, you will. We must try to make it as easy for you as we can. I will manage it, and go with you. I know all about such things, you know. If you are quiet to-day—let me see: tomorrow is Sunday—and if you still feel the same way on Monday, I will take you to Mr. Hooker—he's one of the county judges—and you shall make your statement to him."

"Thank you. I would like Mr. Wingfold to go too."

So! muttered George to himself. "By all means," he answered. "We can take him with us."

He went again to Helen.

"Keep your mind easy, Helen," he encouraged her. "I'll see what I can do. But what's the meaning of his wanting that fellow Wingfold to go with him? I shouldn't wonder a bit if it all came of some of his nonsense!—to save his soul, of course! How did he come to see him?"

"The poor boy insisted upon it."

"What made him think of the curate in the first place?"

Helen held her peace. She saw George suspected the truth.

"Well, no matter," replied George. "But one never knows what may come of things. You had better go lie down a while, Helen. You don't seem quite yourself. I will take care of Leopold."

Helen's strength had been sorely tried. She had borne up bravely, but now that she could do no more, her strength had begun to give way. And almost for the first time in her life, she longed to go to bed during the daytime. Let George, or Wingfold, or whoever wanted to, see to the willful boy; she had done what she could.

She gladly yielded to George's suggestion, went to an unoccupied room, locked the door, and threw herself on the bed.

George went again to Leopold's room and sat down beside him. He was asleep. George sat at his bedside for a while, then rose and went to get a book from the library. On the stair he met the butler; Mr. Wingfold had called to see Mr. Lingard, he said.

"He can't see him today; he is much too exhausted," informed Bascombe.

The curate left the house thoughtful and sorry. He walked away along the street toward the church with downbent head, seeing no one. Before long he found himself thinking how the soul of Helen rather than of Leopold was in the graver danger. Poor Leopold had the serpent of his crime to sting him into life, but Helen had the vampire of an imperfect love to fan her asleep with the airs of a false devotion. It was Helen more than Leopold he had to be anxious about.

After a walk through the churchyard, he turned and walked back to the house.

"May I see Miss Lingard?" he asked.

It was a maid who opened the door this time. She showed him into the library and went to inquire.

When Helen had lain down, she tried to sleep, but she could not even lie still. For all her preference of George and his counsel, and her hope in the view he took of Leopold's case, the mere knowledge that in the next room her cousin sat by her brother made her anxious and restless.

At first it was the mere feeling that they were together—the thing she had for so long taken such pains to prevent. Next came the fear that Leopold should succeed in persuading George that he really was guilty—in which case only the thought of what the self-righteous George might counsel was terrible indeed. And last and worse of all, what hope of peace lay in any of his counsel? Would it not be better that Leopold should die believing Mr. Wingfold and not George? If then there were nothing behind the veil of death, he would be nothing the worse; if there were, the curate might have in some way prepared him for it.

And now for the first time she began to feel that she was a little afraid of her cousin—perhaps she had yielded too much to his influence. He was a very good fellow, but was he one fit to rule her life? Would her nature consent to always look up to him if she were to marry him? But the thought only flitted like a cloud across the surface of her mind.

All these feelings together had combined to form her mood when her maid came to the door with the message that Mr. Wingfold was in the library. She resolved at once to see him.

The curate's heart trembled a little as he waited for her. He was not quite sure that it was his business to tell her her duty, yet something seemed to drive him to it. It is no easy matter for one man to confront another with his duty in the simplest relations of life. Here was a man, naturally shy, daring to rebuke and instruct a woman whose presence was mighty upon him, and whose influence was ten times heightened by the suffering that softened her beauty!

She entered the room, troubled, yet stately; doubtful, yet with a kind of half-trust in her demeanor; white and blue-eyed, with pained mouth and a droop of weariness and suffering in her eyelids.

Thomas Wingfold's nature was more than usually bent toward helpfulness, but his early years, his lack of friends, of confidence, of convictions had all prevented the development of that tendency. But now, like discharging water which, having found a way, gathers force momentarily, the pent-up ministration of his soul was asserting itself. Now that he understood more of the human heart, and recognized in this and that human countenance the bars of a cage through which looked an imprisoned life, his own heart burned in him with the love of the helpless. For Wingfold lived in the presence of the face of Jesus Christ more and more from day to day, without even knowing it.

The best help a woman can get is from a right man; equally true is the converse. But let the man who ventures take heed. Unless he is able to counsel a woman to do the hardest thing that bears the name of duty, let him not dare give advice even if she asks for it.

Helen, however, had not come to ask advice of Wingfold. She was in no such mood. She was indeed weary of a losing battle and except for a glimmer of possible help from her cousin, saw inevitable ruin before her. This revival of hope in George had roused anew her indignation at the intrusion of Wingfold with what she chose to consider unsought counsel. At the same time, through all the indignation, terror, and dismay, something within her murmured that the curate and not her cousin was the guide who could lead her brother into peace. It was therefore with a sense of bewilderment, discord, and uncertainty that she now entered the library.

Wingfold rose, bowed, and advanced a step or two. He would not offer a hand that might not be welcome, and Helen did not offer hers. She bent her neck graciously, and motioned him to be seated.

"I hope Mr. Lingard is not worse," he offered.

"No. Why should he be worse?" she answered. "Have they told you anything?"

"I have heard nothing. Only, as I was not allowed to see him, I thought—"

"I left him with Mr. Bascombe half an hour ago," she interrupted, escaping the implication that it had been she who had refused him admittance.

Wingfold gave an involuntary sigh.

"You do not think that gentleman's company desirable for my brother, I presume," she said, with a smile so void of feeling that it seemed bitter. "He won't do him any harm—at least I think you need not fear it."

"No one in my profession can think his opinions harmless, and certainly he will not suppress them."

"And you are worried my cousin will be unable to lighten my brother's burden?"

"A man with such a weight on his soul as your brother carries will not think it lightened by having lumps of lead thrown upon it. An easy mind may take a shroud on its shoulders for wings, but when trouble comes and it wants to fly, then it knows the difference. Leopold will not be misled by Mr. Bascombe. No, I am not worried."

Helen grew paler. She would rather have him misled than to betray himself.

"I am far more afraid of *your* influence than his," added the curate cautiously.

"What bad influence do you suppose me likely to exercise?" asked Helen with a cold smile.

"The bad influence of wishing him to act upon *your* conscience instead of his own."

"Is my conscience a worse one than Leopold's?" she asked.

"It is not his, and that is enough. His own, and no other, can tell him what to do."

"Why not leave it to him, then?" she asked bitterly.

"That is what I want of you, Miss Lingard. I would have you not touch the life of the poor youth."

"Touch his life! I would give him mine to save it. *You* counsel him to throw it away!"

"What different meanings we put on the word! You call the few years he may have to live in this world his life; while I—"

"While you count the millions of years which you know nothing about—somewhere from which no one has ever returned to bring any news!—a wretched life at best, if it be such as you say."

"Pardon me, that is merely what you suppose I mean by the word. But I do not mean that. I mean something altogether different. When I spoke of his life, I thought nothing about here or there, now or then. You will see what I mean if you recall how the life came back to his eye and the color to his cheek the moment he had made up his mind to do what had long seemed to him to be his duty. A demon-haunted existence had begun to change to a morning of spring; the life of well-being, of law and order, and peace, had begun to dawn in obedience and self-renunciation. His resurrection was at hand. But you would stop this resurrection; you would seat yourself upon his gravestone to keep him down. And why? So that you and your family will not be disgraced by letting him out of his grave to tell the truth."

"Sir!" cried Helen indignantly, drawing herself to her full height and even a little more.

Wingfold took one step nearer to her. "My calling is to speak the truth," he admonished gently, "and I am bound to warn you that you will never be at peace in your own soul until you love your brother with a right love."

"Love my brother!" Helen almost screamed. "I would die for him!"

"Then at least let your pride die for him," responded Wingfold.

Helen left the room, and Wingfold the house.

She had hardly shut the door and fallen again upon the bed when she began to know in her heart that the curate was right. But the more she knew it, the less would she confess it even to herself. It was unendurable.

27 Who Is the Sinner?

When the curate stood up in the pulpit the following morning, his eyes sought Mrs. Ramshorn's pew as under their own will. There sat Helen, with a look that revealed more of determination and less of suffering. Her aunt was by her side, cold and glaring. Bascombe was not visible, and that was a relief. Wingfold tried hard to forget the faces and by the time he came to the sermon, was thinking of nothing but human hearts and him who came to call them to himself.

" 'I came not to call the righteous, but sinners to repentance,' " he began. "If our Lord were to come again visibly now, which do you think would come crowding around him in greater numbers— the respectable churchgoers, or the people from the slums? I do not know. I dare not judge. But the fact that the church draws so few of those whom Jesus drew and to whom he most expressly came gives ground for question as to how much the church is like her Lord. Certainly many would find their way to the feet of the Master from whom the respectable churchgoer, the Pharisee of our time, would draw back with disgust. And doubtless it would be in the religious world that a man like Jesus would meet with the chief opponents of his doctrine and life. After all, he taught without a professional education and early training, uttering hardly a phrase endorsed by the clerical system, or a word of the religious cant of the day."

Thus began Wingfold to preach. And as he went, he opened the Scriptures to his hearers concerning man's universal sinfulness and our crying need for repentance and forgiveness so that we might live more like him who came to save us, and thereby partake of the life he came to give us. By the time the curate reached his conclusion, his eyes shone with the fervor instilled by the inspiring texts.

"Come then at the call of the Waker, the Healer, the Giver of repentance and light, the Friend of sinners, all you on whom lies

179

the weight of a sin or the gathered heap of a thousand crimes. He came to call such as you that he might make you clean. He cannot bear that you should live in such misery, such blackness of darkness. He wants to give you your life again, the bliss of your being. He will not speak to you one word of reproach, except you should try to justify yourself by accusing your neighbor. He will leave it to those who cherish the same sins in their hearts to cast stones at you: he who has not sin casts no stones. Heartily he loves you, heartily he hates the evil in you. The rest of you, keep aloof, if you will, until you shall have done some deed that compels you to cry out for deliverance. But you that already know yourselves to be sinners, come to him that he may work in you his perfect work, for he came not to call the righteous, but sinners—us, you and me—to repentance."

As the sermon drew to a close, and the mist of his emotion began to disperse, individual faces of his audience again focused in the preacher's vision. Mr. Drew's head was down. As I have already said, certain things he had been taught in his youth and had practiced in his manhood had now become repugnant to him. He had been doing his best to banish them from his business, and yet they were a painful presence to his spirit. No one in the abbey church of Glaston that morning would have suspected that the well-known successful man of business was weeping. Who could have imagined another reason for the laying down of his round, good-humored, and contented face on his hymnbook than pure drowsiness? Yet there was a human soul crying out after its birthright. Oh! to be clean as a mountain river! clean as the air above the clouds or on the seas!

While Wingfold had been speaking in general terms, he had yet thought more of one soul, with its intolerable burden, than of all the rest. Leopold was ever present to him, though he was not among the congregation. At times, in fact, he felt as if he were speaking to him and to him alone. Then again, he felt as if he were comforting the sister in holding out for her brother the mighty hope of a restored purity. And when once more his mind beheld the faces before him, he saw upon Helen's the warm sunrise of a rapt attention. It was already fading away, but the eyes had wept and the glow yet hung about her cheek and forehead. By the time

Helen had walked home with her aunt, the glow had sunk from her soul, and a gray, wintry mist had settled down upon her spirit. And she said to herself that if this last hope in George should fail her, she would not allow the matter to trouble her any further. Leopold had chosen other counselors, and after all she had done for the love of him, had turned away from her. She was a free woman. She would put money in her purse, set out for France or Italy, and leave him to the fate, whatever it might be, which his new advisors and his own obstinacy might bring upon him.

When she went into Leopold's room, he knew that a cloud had come between them; and that after all she had borne and done for him, he and his sister were far apart. His eyes followed her as she walked across to the dressing room. The tears rose and filled them, but he said nothing. And the sister, who all the time of the sermon had been filled with wave upon wave of wishing that Poldie could hear this or that, could have such a thought to comfort him or such a lovely word to drive the horror from his soul, now cast on him a chilly glance. She said not a word of the things to which she had listened with such heavings of her emotions, for she felt that they would but strengthen him in his determination to do whatever the teacher of them might approve.

To the friend who joined her at the church door, Mrs. Ramshorn remarked that the curate was certainly a most dangerous man. He so confounded all the ordinary principles of right and wrong, representing the honest man as no better than the thief, and the murderer as no worse than anybody else—teaching people that the best thing they could do was to commit some terrible crime in order to attain a better innocence than could ever be theirs otherwise. How far she misunderstood, or how far she knew or suspected that she spoke falsely, I will not pretend to know. But although she spoke as she did, there was something, either in the curate or in the sermon, that had quieted her a little, and she was less contemptuous in her condemnation of him than usual.

Happily, both for himself and others, the curate was not one of those who cripple the truth by trying to worry about every scruple and judgment of their listeners. To try to explain truth to him who loves it not is but to give him more plentiful material for misinterpretation. Let a man have truth in the inward parts, and out of the abundance of his heart let his mouth speak.

George Bascombe had been absent. After an early breakfast that morning, he had mounted Helen's mare and set out to call on Mr. Hooker before he left for church. Helen expected him back for dinner and was anxiously looking for him. So was Leopold, but the hopes of the two were quite different.

At length the mare's hoofs echoed through all Glaston and presently George rode up. The groom took his horse in the street, and he came into the drawing room. Helen hastened to meet him.

"Well, George?" she asked anxiously.

"Oh, it's all right!—It will be at least, I am sure. I will tell you all about it in the garden after dinner. Aunt has the good sense never to interrupt us there," he added. "I'll just run up and look in for a moment on Leopold. He must not suspect that I am playing him false. Not that it is false, you know! Two negatives make a positive, and to fool a madman is to give him fair play."

The words jarred sorely on Helen's ear.

Bascombe hurried to Leopold and informed him that he had seen Mr. Hooker, and that everything was arranged for taking him over to his place on Tuesday morning, if by that time he was up for the journey.

"Why not tomorrow?" suggested Leopold. "I am quite able."

"Oh, I told him you were not very strong. And he wanted a chase with the hounds tomorrow. So we thought it would be better to put it off till Tuesday."

Leopold gave a sigh, and said no more.

After dinner the cousins went to the summerhouse, and there George gave Helen his report, revealing his plan for Leopold.

"Such fancies must be humored, you know, Helen. There is nothing to be gained by opposing them," he said.

Helen looked at him with keen eyes, and he returned the gaze. The confidence between them was not perfect; each was doubtful as to the thought of the other, and neither asked what it was.

"Mr. Hooker is a fine old fellow," said George; "a jolly, good-natured churchman, as simple as a baby, and took everything I told him without a hint of doubt or objection—just the sort of man I expected to find him. When I mentioned my name he recalled that he had known my father, and that gave me a good opening. I explained the thing, saying it was a very delicate case in which were concerned the children of a man of whom he had at one time known something—General Lingard. 'To be sure!' he cried; 'I knew him very well—a fine fellow, but hasty in his temper!' I said I had never known him myself, but one of his children was my cousin; the other was the child of his second wife, and it was about him I presumed to trouble him. Then I plunged into the matter at once, telling him that Leopold had suffered a violent brain fever, brought on by a horrible drug he had begun using in India. Although he had recovered from the fever, I said, it was doubtful if he would ever recover from the consequences of it. He had become the victim of a fixed idea, the hard deposit from a heated imagination. 'And what is the idea?' he asked. 'That he is a murderer,' I answered. 'God bless me!' he cried, somewhat to my alarm, for I had been making all this introduction to prejudice the old gentleman in the right direction. I echoed the spirit of his exclamation and told him the rest of Leopold's story. Finally, I said that nothing would serve the lad but that he give himself up and meet his fate on the gallows, 'in the hope, my dear sir,' I said, 'of finding her in the other world, and there making it up with her!' 'God bless me!' he cried again, in a tone of absolute horror.

"I went on to remark that whatever hint the newspapers had given, Leopold had expanded and connected with every other, but that at one part of the story I had found him entirely in error: he could not tell what he did or where he went after the deed was done. He confessed all after that to be a blank until he found himself in bed. But when I told him something he had not seen— namely, the testimony of the coastguardsman about the fishing boat with the two men in it—but I have lost the thread of my sentence. Well, never mind. But then I told him something I have not told you yet, Helen—that when I alluded to that portion of the story, Leopold started up with flashing eyes, and exclaimed, 'Now I remember! It all comes back to me as clear as day. I remember running down the hill, and jumping into the boat just as they shoved off. I was exhausted and fell down in the stern. When I came to myself, the two men were in the front. I saw their legs beneath the sails. I thought they would be sure to give me up, and at once I slipped overboard. The water revived me, but when I reached the shore I fell down again, and lay there I don't know how long. Indeed, I don't remember anything more.' That is what Leopold said, and what I now told Mr. Hooker. Then at last I confided in him as to why I ventured to ask his assistance. I requested that he would allow me to bring Leopold and would let him go through the form of giving himself up to justice. Especially I asked that he would listen to all he had to say, and give no sign that he doubted his story. 'And then, sir,' I concluded, 'I would leave it to you to do what we cannot—reconcile him to going home instead of to prison.'

"He sat with his head on his hand for a while, as if pondering some weighty question of law. Then he said, 'I will think the matter over. You may rely on me. Will you take a seat in church with us, and come to dinner afterward?' I excused myself on the ground that I must return at once to poor Leopold, who was anxiously looking for me. And you must forgive me, Helen, for I yielded to the temptation of a little longer ride once I got out into the open countryside."

Helen assured him with grateful eyes that she knew her mare was as safe with him as with herself. She felt such a rush of gratitude following the revival of hope that she was nearer being in love with her cousin than ever before. Her gratitude inwardly delighted George, and he thought the light in her blue eyes lovelier than ever. Although strongly tempted, he judged it better to delay a formal confession of his intentions toward her until circumstances should be more comfortable.

28 The Confession

All that day and the next Leopold was in wonderful spirits. But on Monday night there came a considerable reaction: he was dejected, worn, and weary. Twelve o'clock the next day was the hour set for their visit to Mr. Hooker, and at eleven he was dressed and ready—restless, agitated, and very pale, but not a whit less determined than at first. A drive was the pretext for borrowing Mrs. Ramshorn's carriage.

"Why is Mr. Wingfold not coming?" asked Lingard anxiously, when it began to move.

"I am sure we shall be quite as comfortable without him, Poldie," answered Helen. "Did you expect him?"

"He promised to go with me. But he hasn't called since the time was set." Here Helen looked out of the window. "I can't think why. I can do my duty without him, though," continued Leopold, "and perhaps it is just as well. Do you know, George, since I made up my mind I have seen her but once, and that was last night, and only in a dream."

"A state of irresolution leaves one peculiarly open to unhealthy visions," returned George good-naturedly.

Leopold turned from him to his sister.

"The strange thing, Helen," he remarked, "was that I did not feel the least afraid of her, or even ashamed. 'Be at peace,' I told her, 'I am coming and you shall do to me what you will.' And then— O my God!—She smiled one of her old smiles—only sad, too, very sad—and vanished. I woke, and she seemed only to have just left the room, for there was a stir in the darkness.—Do you believe in ghosts, George?"

Leopold was not one of George's initiated, I need hardly say.

"No," answered Bascombe.

"I don't wonder. I can't blame you, for neither did I once. But just wait till you have met one, George!"

"God forbid!" exclaimed Bascombe, forgetting his own denial of such a being.

"Amen!" returned Leopold, "for after that there's no help but to become a ghost yourself, you know."

If he would only talk like that to old Hooker! thought George. *It would go a long way to prevent any possible misconception of the case.*

"I can't think why Mr. Wingfold did not come yesterday," resumed Leopold.

"Now, Poldie, you mustn't talk," insisted Helen, "or you'll be exhausted before we get to Mr. Hooker's."

She did not wish the nonappearance of the curate on Monday to be closely asked about. His company at the magistrate's was to be avoided by all possible means.

When they arrived at Mr. Hooker's house, George easily persuaded Helen—more easily than he had expected—to wait for them in the carriage. The two men were shown into the library where the magistrate joined them. He would have shaken hands with Leopold as well as George, but the conscious felon drew back.

"No, sir; excuse me," he said. "Hear what I have to tell you first. If after that you want to shake hands with me, it will be a kindness indeed."

Worthy Mr. Hooker was overwhelmed with pity at the sight of the worn face with the great eyes. He found every appearance to confirm the tale with which Bascombe had filled and prejudiced every fiber of his judgment. He listened in the kindest way while the poor boy forced the words of his confession from his throat. When he at last ended, Leopold sat silent, in the posture of one whose wrists are already clasped by the double bracelet of steel.

Now, Mr. Hooker had thought the thing out in church on the Sunday, and after a hard run at the tail of a strong fox over rough country on the Monday, and a good sleep well into Tuesday morning, could see no better way. His device was simple.

"My dear young gentleman," he replied. "I am very sorry for you, but I must do my duty."

"That, sir, is what I came to you for," answered Leopold humbly.

"Then you must consider yourself my prisoner. The moment you are gone, I shall make notes of your deposition, and proceed to arrange for the necessary formalities. As a mere matter of form, I shall set your bail at a thousand pounds, to be surrendered when called upon."

"But I am not of age, and haven't got a thousand pounds," answered Leopold.

"Perhaps Mr. Hooker will accept my recognizance in lieu of the cash amount," suggested Bascombe.

"Certainly," answered Mr. Hooker, and wrote something which Bascombe signed.

"You are very good, George," said Leopold. "But you know I

can't run away even if I would," he added, with a pitiful attempt at a smile.

"You must keep yourself ready," reminded the magistrate, "to give yourself up at any moment. And remember, I shall call upon you when I please, every week perhaps, or oftener, to see that you are safe. Your aunt is an old friend of mine, and there will be no need of explanations. This turns out to be no common case, and after hearing the whole of it, I do not hesitate to offer you my hand."

Leopold was overcome by his kindness, and withdrew speechless, but greatly relieved.

Several times during the course of his narrative, its apparent truthfulness nearly staggered Mr. Hooker into believing it. But a glance at Bascombe's face with its half-amused smile instantly set him right again, and he thought with dismay how near he had been to letting himself be fooled by a madman.

In the carriage Leopold laid his head on Helen's shoulder, and looked up in her face with such a smile as she had never seen on his before. Certainly there was something in confession—if only enthusiasts like Mr. Wingfold would not spoil it all by pushing him to further extremes!

Leopold was yet such a child and had little concerned himself with society's normal operations. He was so entirely unacquainted with the modes of criminal procedure that the conduct of the magistrate never struck him as strange, not to say illegal. And so strongly did he feel the good man's kindness and sympathy that his comfort from making a clean breast of it was even greater than he had expected. Before they reached home he was fast asleep. When laid on his couch, he fell asleep almost instantly, and Helen saw him smile as he slept.

But although George Bascombe had declared Leopold innocent, and proven as much by their visit to the judge, he could not keep away the flickering doubt which had shown itself when he first listened to the story. Amid all the wildness of the tale there was yet a certain quality about it that was not to be questioned—not the truthfulness in the narrator, but of likelihood in the narration. Leopold's air of conviction also had its force, though George persistently pooh-poohed him. The vanity he would himself have denied had made him unfit for perceiving this truth, possibly other truth also. Nor do I know how much difference there is between accepting what is untrue and refusing what is true.

The second time he had listened to Leopold's continuous narrative, the doubt returned with more clearness and less flicker. Might he not be taking himself in with his own incredulity? Ought he not to apply some test to see whether the story *could* be true? And did Leopold's story offer any means of doing so? One thing, he then discovered, had been dimly haunting his thoughts ever since he heard it: Leopold said he had thrown his cloak and mask down an old mine-shaft pit near the place of the murder. If there was such a shaft, could it be searched? Recurring doubt at length so worked on his mind that he resolved to make his holiday excursion to that neighborhood, and there try to gain what assurance might be had. What end beyond his own possible satisfaction the inquiry was to answer, he did not ask himself. The restless spirit of the detective was at work in him. But that was not all; he had to know the facts, if possible, of anything concerning Helen. He would not marry into the unknown.

———

The house where the terrible thing took place was not far from a little moorland village. There Bascombe found a small inn, where he took up his quarters, pretending to be a geologist out for a holiday. He soon came upon the abandoned mine.

Later that evening, he visited the local inn which was frequented a good deal by the coal miners of the district—a rough crowd. But they were not beyond Bascombe's influences of self-assertion and good fellowship, for he had almost immediately perceived that among them he might find the assistance he wanted. In the course of conversation, he mentioned the shaft on which he pretended to have stumbled on one of his walks about the area. He remarked on the danger of such places, and learned that this particular one served for ventilation, and was still accessible below from other workings of the mine. Therefore he asked permission to go down one of the pits on the pretext of examining the coal strata and managed to secure a guide as well, one of the most intelligent of those whose acquaintance he had made at the inn.

When they made their little journey the following day, Bascombe asked to be shown to the bottom of the shaft he had seen from above. When at last he raised his head, wearily bent beneath the low roofs of the passages, and looked upwards, there appeared a star looking down at him—the faint gleam from the opening far above, which was in reality the sky of day. But George never wasted time in staring at what was above his head, and so he began instantly to search about as if examining the strata by use of the faint torch they had brought with them. Was it possible! Could it be? There was a piece of black something that was not coal and seemed like cloth! It was a half-mask, for there were the eyeholes in it! He picked it up and put it into his bag—but not so quickly that his movement set his guide to speculating. Giving out proper expressions of incredulity about the various rock formations to conceal his true intent, Bascombe saw nevertheless that his actions were noted. The man afterward offered to carry his bag, but George would not allow it.

The next morning he left the place and returned to London, taking Glaston as a detour on his way. A few questions to Leopold drew from him a description of the mask he had worn, corresponding completely with the one George had found. At length he was satisfied that there was indeed truth in Leopold's confession. It was not his business, however, to set judges right, he now said to himself. True, he had set Mr. Hooker wrong in the first place, but he had done it in good faith, and how could he now turn traitor to Helen and her brother? At the same time, Leopold's eagerness to confess might yet drive the matter further, and if so, it might become awkward for him. He might be looked to act the part of defense counsel. Were he not certain his guide had noticed his concealment of what he had picked up, he might have ventured to undertake it, for certainly it would offer a rare chance for a display of the forensic talent he so thoroughly believed himself to possess. But as it was, the moment he was called to the bar—which would be within two weeks—he would go abroad, say to Paris, and there, for twelve months or so, await events to see what would happen. It could become too ticklish and he did not want to get any more involved.

When George disclosed to Helen his evil success in the coal

pit, it was but the merest film of a remaining hope that it destroyed, for she had known her brother was guilty. George and she now felt that they were linked by the possession of a common secret.

But the cloak had been found a short time before, and was in the possession of Emmeline's mother. She was a woman of strong passions and determined character. The first shock of the catastrophe over, her grief had been supplanted by a rage for vengeance, and she vowed herself to discovery and revenge as the one business of her life.

In the neighborhood her mind was well known, and many found their advantage in supplying her passion with the fuel of hope. Any hint of evidence, however small, the remotest suggestion even toward discovery, they would take at once to her. For she was a generous woman, and in such cases would give profusely. It had therefore occurred to a certain miner to make his way to the bottom of the shaft, on the chance—hardly of finding, but of being enabled to invent something worth reporting; and there, to his great surprise, he had found the cloak.

The mother had been over to Holland, where she had set in motion unavailing inquiries in the villages along the coast and had been home but a few days when the cloak was brought to her. In her mind it immediately associated itself with the costumes of the horrible ball, and at once she sought the lists of the guests who had been in attendance. In fact, she sat perusing the list at the very moment when the man who had been Bascombe's guide sent in to request an interview. Their talk turned her attention for the time in another direction: who could the visitor to the mine have been?

Little was to be gathered in the neighborhood beyond the facts that the letters "G B" were on his carpetbag, and that a scrap of torn envelope bore what seemed to be the letters "mbe." She dispatched the poor indications to a detective office in London to see what they might turn up.

29 The Curate and the Doctor

The day after his confession to Mr. Hooker, a considerable change took place in Leopold. He did not leave his bed and lay exhausted all day. He said he had caught a cold. He coughed a little, wondered why Mr. Wingfold did not come to see him, dozed a good deal, and often woke with a start. The following day Mr. Hooker called and went up to see him. There he said all he could think of to make him comfortable. He repeated that certain preliminaries had to be gone through before the commencement of the prosecution, and said that it was better he should be in his sister's care than in prison, where he most probably would die before the trial could begin. He ended by saying that he was sure the judge at the time of the trial would consider the provocation he had undergone, only he would have to satisfy the jury that there had been no premeditation.

"I will not utter a word to excuse myself, Mr. Hooker," replied Leopold.

The worthy magistrate smiled sadly and went away more convinced than ever of the poor lad's insanity.

The visit helped Leopold over that day, but when the next also passed, and neither did Wingfold appear nor any explanation of his absence reach him, he made up his mind to act for himself.

The cause of the curate's apparent neglect, though hard to find, was not far to seek.

On Monday the curate had, upon some pretext or other, been turned away. On Tuesday he had been told Mr. Lingard was out for a drive. On Wednesday, that he was much too tired to be seen. Thereupon Thomas had judged it better to leave things to themselves. If Leopold did not want to see him, it would be of no use to force his way to him by persistence. But on the other hand, if he did want to see him, he felt convinced the poor fellow would manage to have his way somehow.

The next morning Leopold said he was better, and got up and

dressed. He then lay on the sofa and waited as quietly as he could until Helen went out; Mr. Faber had insisted she should do so every day for her own health. He put his slippers on his feet, crept unseen from the house, and headed in the direction of the abbey. But when crossing the churchyard to the curate's lodging, suddenly his brain seemed to go swimming away from before him. He attempted to seat himself on a gravestone, but lost consciousness and fainted.

When Helen returned, she was horrified to find that he was gone—when or where nobody knew; no one had missed him. Her first fear was the river, but her conscience reminded her of the curate. She immediately left for the abbey. In her haste she passed him where he lay a little way off the path.

Shown into the curate's study, she gave a hurried glance around, and her anxiety became terror again.

"Oh, Mr. Wingfold!" she cried. "Where is Leopold?"

"I have not seen him," replied the curate, turning pale.

"Then he has thrown himself in the river!" cried Helen, and sank on a chair.

The curate grabbed his hat.

"You wait here," he instructed. "I will go and look for him."

But Helen rose, and without another word they set off together, and again entered the churchyard. As they hurried across it, the curate caught sight of something on the ground. He ran forward and found Leopold.

"He is dead!" cried Helen in agony, when she saw him stop and stoop down.

The curate lifted him out of the damp shadow and laid him on the sun-warmed stone with his head on Helen's lap. He then ran to order the carriage and hurried back with brandy. They got a little into his mouth, but he could not swallow it. Still it seemed to do him good, for presently he gave a deep sigh. Just then they heard the carriage stop at the gate. Wingfold picked him up and carried him to it. The curate got him in by holding him in his arms, and there held him on his knees until they reached the manor house, where he carried him upstairs and laid him on the sofa. When they had brought him round a little, Wingfold undressed him and put him to bed.

"Do not leave me," murmured Leopold to the curate just as Helen entered the room.

Wingfold looked to her for the answer he was to make. Her bearing was much altered; she was both ashamed and humbled.

"Yes, Leopold," she reassured him, "Mr. Wingfold will, I am sure, stay with you as long as he can."

"Indeed I will," assented the curate. "But I must run for Mr. Faber first."

"How did I get here?" asked Leopold, opening his large eyes on Helen after swallowing a spoonful of the broth she held to his lips. But before she could answer him he turned sick, and by the time the doctor came he was very feverish. Faber gave the necessary directions, and Wingfold walked back with him to get the prescription made up.

"There is something strange about that young man's illness," declared Faber, as soon as they had left the house. "I imagine you know more than you can tell. And if so, then I have committed no indiscretion in saying as much."

"Perhaps it might be an indiscretion to acknowledge as much, however," replied the curate with a smile.

"You are right. I have not been in Glaston long," returned Faber, "and you have had no opportunity of testing me. But I am honest as well as you, though I don't go along with you in everything."

"People would have me believe you don't go along with me in anything."

"They say as much, do they?" returned Faber, with some annoyance. "Well, I know nothing about God and all that kind of thing; however, though I don't think I'm a coward, I know I would like to have your pluck."

"I haven't got any pluck," said the curate.

"I wouldn't dare go and say what I think or don't think in the bedroom of my least orthodox patient, while you go on saying what you believe Sunday after Sunday. How you can believe it I don't know, and it's no business of mine."

"Oh, yes it is!" returned Wingfold. "But as to the pluck, it is nothing but my conscience."

"It's a damned fine thing to have anyhow, whatever name you put on it!" said Faber.

"Excuse me if I find your oath more amusing than apt," said Wingfold laughing.

"You are quite right," said Faber. "I apologize for speaking so."

"As to the pluck again," Wingfold continued, "if you think of this one fact: that my whole desire is to believe in God, and that the only thing I can be sure of sometimes is that, if there be a God, nothing but an honest man will ever find him: you will not then say there is much pluck in my speaking the truth."

"I don't see how that makes it a hair easier in the face of such a set of gaping noodles as—"

"I beg your pardon. There is more lack of conscience than of brains in the abbey on a Sunday, I fear."

"Well, all I have to say is that I can't for the life of me see what you want to believe in a God for! It seems to me the world would go on rather better without any such fancy. Look here; there is young Spenser—out there at Horwood—a patient of mine. His wife died yesterday—one of the loveliest young creatures you ever saw. The poor fellow is in agony about it. Well, he's one of your sort and said to me just the other day, 'It's the will of God,' he said, 'and we must hold our peace.' 'Don't talk to me about God,' I said, for I couldn't stand it. 'Do you mean to tell me that if there was a God, he would have taken such a lovely girl as that away from her husband and her helpless baby at the age of twenty-two? I scorn to believe it.'"

"What did he say?"

"He turned white as death and never said a word."

"Ah, you forgot that you were taking from him his only hope of seeing her again."

"I certainly did not think of that," admitted Faber.

"Even then," resumed Wingfold, "I should not say you were wrong if you had searched every possible region of existence and had found no God. Or if you had tried every theory man had invented, or even that you were able to invent yourself, and had found none of them consistent with the being of a God. I do not say that then you would be right in your judgment. I only say that if that were the case, I would not blame you for saying what you did. But you must admit it a very serious thing to assert that there is no God without any such grounds."

The doctor was silent.

"I don't doubt you spoke in a burst of indignation. But it seems to me you speak rather positively about things you haven't thought much about."

"You are wrong there," returned Faber, "for I was brought up in the strictest sect of the Pharisees, and know what I am saying."

"The strictest sect of the Pharisees can hardly be the school in which to gather an idea of God."

"They profess to know," asserted Faber.

"What does that matter, they and their opinions being what they are? If there be a God, do you imagine he would choose such a sect to be his interpreters?"

"But the question is not of the idea of a God, but of the existence of God. And if he exists, he must be such as the human heart could never accept as God because of the cruelty he permits."

"I grant that argument a certain amount of force, and that very thing has troubled me at times, but I am coming to see it in a different light. I heard some children the other day saying that Dr. Faber was a very cruel man, for he pulled out nurse's tooth, and gave poor little baby such a nasty, nasty powder."

"Is that a fair parallel?" asked Faber.

"I think it is. What you do is often unpleasant, sometimes most painful, but it does not follow that you are a cruel man, one that hurts rather than heals."

"I think there is fault in the analogy," objected Faber. "I am nothing but a slave to laws already existing, and compelled to work according to them. It is not my fault, therefore, that the remedies I have to use are unpleasant. But if there be a God, he has the matter in his own hands."

"But suppose," suggested the curate, "that the design of God involved the perfecting of men as the children of God. Suppose his grand idea could not be content with creatures perfect only by his gift but also involved in partaking of God's individuality and free will and choice of good. And suppose that suffering were the only way through which the individual soul could be set, in separate and self-individuality, so far apart from God that it might *will* and

so become a partaker of his singleness and freedom. And suppose
that God saw the seed of a pure affection, say in your friend and
his wife, but saw also that it was a seed so imperfect and weak
that it could not encounter the coming frosts and winds of the
world without loss and decay. Yet, if they were parted now for a
few years, it would grow and strengthen and expand to the certainty of an infinitely higher and deeper and keener love through
the endless ages to follow—so that by suffering should come, in
place of contented decline, abortion, and death, a troubled birth of
joyous result in health and immortality—suppose all this, what
then?"

Faber was silent a moment, and then answered, "Your theory
has but one fault; it is too good to be true."

"My theory leaves plenty of difficulty, but has no such fault as
that. Why, what sort of a God would content you, Mr. Faber? The
one idea is too bad to be true, the other too good. Must you expand
and trim until you get one exactly to the measure of yourself before you can accept it as thinkable or possible? Why, a God like
that would not rest your soul a week. The only possibility of believing in a God seems to me in finding an idea of God large
enough, grand enough, pure enough, lovely enough to be fit to believe in."

"And have you found such, may I ask?"

"I think I am finding such," confessed Wingfold.

"Where?"

"In the man of the New Testament. I have pondered a little
more about these things, I imagine, than you have, Mr. Faber, and
I may come to be sure of something in the end. I don't see how a
man can ever be sure of nothing."

"Come in with me, and I will make up the medicine myself,"
said Mr. Faber as they reached his door. "It will save time. Don't
suppose me quite dumbfounded, though I can't answer all your
arguments," he resumed in his office. "But about this poor fellow
Lingard; Glaston gossip says he is out of his mind."

"If I were you, Mr. Faber, I would not take pains to contradict
it. He is not out of his mind, but has such trouble in it as might
well drive him out. Don't even hint at that, though."

"I understand," acknowledged Faber.

"If doctor and minister did understand each other better and work together," said Wingfold, "I fancy a good deal more might be done."

"I don't doubt it. What sort of fellow is that cousin of theirs—Bascombe is his name I believe?"

"A man to suit you, I should think," answered the curate, "a man with a most tremendous power of believing in nothing."

"Come, come!" returned the doctor. "You don't know half enough about me to tell what sort of man I should like or dislike."

"Well, all I will say about Bascombe is that if he were not conceited, he would be honest. And if he were as honest as he believes himself, he would not be so ready to judge everyone dishonest who does not agree with him."

"I hope we may have another talk soon," said the doctor, searching for a cork. "Someday I may tell you a few things that may stagger you."

"Likely enough. I am only learning to walk yet," admitted Wingfold. "But a man may stagger and not fall, and I am ready to hear anything you choose to tell me."

Faber handed him the bottle and he took his leave.

Before the morning, Leopold lay in the net of a low fever, almost as ill as ever. However, his mind was far less troubled, and even his most restless dreams no longer scared him awake. And yet many a time, as she watched by his side, it was excruciatingly plain to Helen that the stuff of which his dreams were made was the last process toward the final execution of the law. Sometimes he would murmur prayers, and sometimes it seemed to Helen that he must be dreaming of himself talking face-to-face with Jesus, for the look of trustful awe upon his countenance was amazing.

Helen herself was subject to a host of changing emotions. At one time she bitterly accused herself of having been the cause of the return of his illness. The next moment a gush of gladness would swell her heart at the thought that now she had him at least safer for a while, and that he might die and so escape the whole gamut of horrible possibilities. For George's manipulation of the magistrate could delay the disclosure of the truth. Even if no discovery were made, Leopold would eventually suspect a trick and that would at once drive him to new action.

It became more and more plain to her that she had taken the evil part against the one she loved best in the world. She had stood almost bodily in the way to turn him from the path of peace. Whether the path he had sought to follow was the only one or not, it was the only one he knew. But she, in order to avoid shame and pity for the sake of the family, as she had convinced herself, had followed a course which would have resulted in shutting him up in a madhouse with his own inborn horrors, with vain remorse. Her conscience, now that her mind was quieter, had begun speaking louder. And she listened, but still with one question: why might he not receive the consolations of the gospel without committing the suicide of surrender? She could not see that confession was the very door of refuge and safety toward which he must press.

George's absence was now again a relief, and while she shrank from the severity of Wingfold, she could not help an indescribable sense of safety in his presence—at least so long as Leopold was too ill to talk.

For the curate, he became more and more interested in the woman who could love so strongly and yet not entirely. The desire to help her grew in him, although he could see no way of reaching her. But what a man dares not say to another individually, he can say open-faced before the whole congregation, and the person in need of it may hear without offense. Would that all our pulpits were in the power of similar men, who by suffering know the human, and by obedience the divine heart!

Therefore, when Wingfold was in the pulpit, he could speak as from the secret to the secret. Elsewhere he felt, with regard to Helen, like a transport ship filled with troops, which had to go sailing around the shores of an invaded ally, frustrated in search for a landing. *Oh! to help that woman that the light of life might rise in her heart and her cheek bloom again with the rose of peace!*

The tenderness of the curate's service, the heart that showed itself in everything he did, even in the turn and expression of the ministering hand, was a kind of revelation to Helen. For while his intellect was blocking the door, asking questions, and uneasily shifting hither and thither in its perplexities, the spirit of the Master had passed by it unrecognized and entered into the chamber of his heart.

After preaching the sermon last recorded, there came a reaction of doubt and depression on the mind of the curate, greater
than usual. Had he not ventured further than he had a right to go?
Had he not implied more conviction than was actually his? He consoled himself with the thought that he had no such intention. If he
had not been untrue to himself, no harm would follow. Was a man
never to be carried beyond himself and the regions of his knowledge?

Difficulties went on presenting themselves to him; at times he
would be overwhelmed by the tossing waves of contradiction and
impossibility. But with every fresh conflict, every fresh gleam of
doubtful victory, the essential idea of the Master looked more and
more lovely. And he began to see the working of his doubts on the
growth of his heart and soul—preventing it from becoming faith
in an *idea* of God instead of in the living God.

He had much time for reflection as he sat silent by the bedside
of Leopold. Sometimes Helen would be sitting near; though generally when he arrived, she went out for her walk. But nothing
ever came to him that he could say to her.

Mrs. Ramshorn had become at least reconciled to the frequent
presence of the curate, partly from the testimony of Helen, partly
from the witness of her own eyes to the quality of his ministra-
tions. She was by no means one of the loveliest among women, yet
she had a heart, and could appreciate some kinds of goodness
which the arrogance of her relation to the church did not interfere
to hide—for nothing is so deadening to the divine as a habitual
dealing with the outsides of holy things. She became half friendly
and quite courteous when she met the curate on the stair, and now
and then, when she thought of it, would bring him a glass of wine
as he sat by Leopold's bedside.

30 A Visit

The acquaintance between the draper and the gatekeeper rapidly ripened into friendship. Very generally, as soon as he had shut his shop, Drew would walk to the park gate to see Polwarth; and at least three times a week the curate was one of the party. Much was then talked, more was thought, and, I venture to say, more yet was understood.

One evening the curate went earlier than usual and had tea with the Polwarths.

"Do you remember," he asked of his host, "once putting the question to me, what our Lord came into this world for?"

"I do," answered Polwarth.

"And you remember I answered you wrong: I said it was to save the world?"

"I do. But remember, I specified *primarily*; for of course he did come to save the world."

"Yes, just so you put it. Well, I think I can answer the question correctly now; and in learning the true answer I have learned much. Did he not come first of all to do the will of his Father? Was not his Father first with him always and his fellowmen next; for they were his Father's?"

"I need hardly say it at this point—for you know you are right. Jesus is ten times more real a person to you, is he not, since you discovered that truth?"

"I think so; I hope so. It does seem as if a grand yet simple reality has begun to dawn upon me out of the fog," admitted the curate.

"And now, may I ask, are you able to accept the miracles, things so improbable in themselves?"

"If we suppose the question settled as to whether the man was what he said, then all that remains is to ask whether the works reported of him are consistent with what you can see of his character."

"And to you they seem—?" probed the dwarf.

"Some consistent, others not. Concerning the latter, I continue to look for more light."

"In the meantime, let me ask you a question about them: what was the main object of the miracles?"

"One thing at least I have learned, Mr. Polwarth, and that is not to answer any question of yours in a hurry," replied Wingfold with a smile. "I will, if you please, take this one home with me and hold the light to it."

"Do," urged Polwarth, "and you will find it will return the light to you three times over. One word more before Mr. Drew comes: are you still thinking of giving up your curacy?"

"I had almost forgotten I ever thought of such a thing. Whatever energies I may or may not have, I know one thing for certain: I could not devote them to anything else worth doing. Indeed, nothing seems interesting enough but telling my fellowmen about the one man who is the truth. Even if there be no hereafter, I would live my time believing in a grand thing that ought to be true if it is not. No facts can take the place of truths: and if these be not truths, then is the loftiest part of our nature a waste? I will go further, Polwarth, and say I would rather die believing as Jesus believed than live forever believing as those that deny him. If there be no God, then this existence is but a chaos of contradictions from which can emerge nothing worthy to be called a truth, nothing worth living for.—No, I will not give up my curacy. I will teach that which is good, even if there should be no God to make a fact of it. I will spend my life on it in the growing hope, which may become assurance, that there is indeed a perfect God worthy of being the father of Jesus Christ."

"I thank God to hear you say so. And I have confidence you will not remain there, for further growth and insights always follow the search of an open heart, which you have shown yours to be," said Polwarth. "—But here comes Mr. Drew."

"How goes business?" inquired Polwarth, when the newcomer had seated himself.

"That is hardly a question I look for from you," returned the draper, smiling all over his round face. "For me, I am glad to leave it behind me in the shop."

"True business can never be left in any shop."

"That is a fact," responded Drew. "But I have encountered a new rush of doubts since I saw you last, Mr. Polwarth, and I find myself altogether unfit to tackle them. I have no weapons—not a single argument. I wonder if it be a law of nature that no sooner shall a man get into a muddle with one thing than a thousand other muddles shall come pouring in upon him. Here I am just beginning to get a little start in more honest ways when up comes the ugly head of doubt telling me that after this world there is nothing more for us. The flowers bloom again in the spring and the corn ripens in the autumn, but they aren't the same flowers or the same corn. They're just as different as the new generations of men."

"There's no false claim that we come back either. We only say we don't go into the ground but away somewhere else."

"You can't prove that," challenged Drew.

"No."

"And you don't know anything about it."

"Not much—but enough I think, from the tale of one who rose again and brought his body with him."

"Yes; but Jesus was only one!"

"Except two or three whom, they say, he brought to life."

"Still there are but three or four."

"To tell you the truth, I do not much care to argue the point with you. It is by no means a matter of the *first* importance whether we live forever or not."

"Mr. Polwarth!" exclaimed the draper, in such astonishment mingled with horror which proved he was not in immediate danger of becoming an advocate of the doctrine of extinction.

The gatekeeper smiled what might have been called a knowing smile.

"Suppose a thing were in itself not worth having," he went on, "would it be the gift to give it to someone forever? Most people think it a fine thing to have a bit of land to call their own and leave to their children. But suppose it was a stinking and undrainable swamp, full of foul springs?"

The draper only stared, but his stare was a thorough one. The curate sat waiting with both amusement and interest, for he saw the direction in which the little man was driving.

"You astonish me!" exclaimed Mr. Drew, recovering his mental breath. "How can you compare God's gift to such a horrible thing? Where would we be without eternal life?"

Rachel burst out laughing and the curate could not help joining her. "Mr. Drew," said Polwarth half merrily, "are you going to help me drag my chain out to its weary length, or are you too much shocked at the doubtful condition of its first links to touch them? I promise you the last shall be of bright gold."

"I beg your pardon," said the draper, "I might have known you didn't mean it."

"On the contrary, I mean everything I say. Perhaps I don't mean everything you fancy I mean. Tell me, then, would life be worth having on any and every possible condition?"

"Certainly not."

"You know some, I dare say, who would be glad to be rid of life such as it is, and such as they suppose it must continue?"

"Occasionally you meet someone like that."

"I repeat then, that to prove life endless is not a matter of the *first* importance. It follows that there is something of prior importance, and greater importance, than the possession of mere immortality. What do you suppose that something is?"

"I imagine that the immortality itself should be worth possessing," reasoned the draper.

"Yes, if the life should be of such quality that one could enjoy it forever. And what if it is not?"

"The question then would be whether or not it could not be made such."

"You are right. And wherein consists the essential inherent worthiness of a life as life? The only perfect idea of life is God, the only one. That a man should complete himself by taking into himself that origin, and with his whole being commit himself to will the will of God in himself—that is the highest possible condition of a man. Then he has completed his cycle. This is the essence of life—the rounding, recreating, unifying of the man."

"And then," said Mr. Drew with some eagerness, "lawfully comes the question, 'Shall I or shall I not live forever?'"

"Pardon me," returned the little prophet. "I think rather we have done away with the question. The man with life so in himself—that quality of life we spoke of—will not dream of asking whether he shall live forever. It is only in the twilight of a half life that the doubtful anxiety of immortality can arise."

When the rest of their conversation was past and the visit nearly over, Wingfold took his leave. But Drew soon overtook him and they walked together into Glaston.

"That man certainly has been blessed with God's wisdom, has he not?" said Drew.

"Indeed," replied Wingfold, "has not God chosen what seems the weak things of the world to confound the mighty?"

They parted at the shop and the curate went on.

He stopped at the manor house to ask about Leopold, for it was still only beginning to be late. Helen received him with her usual coldness—a manner which she assumed partly for self-protection, for in his presence she always felt rebuked, and this had the effect of raising a veil between them.

Wingfold's interest in Helen deepened and deepened. He could not help admiring her strength of character even when he saw it spent for worse than nothing; and the longing of the curate to help her continued to grow. But as the hours and days and weeks passed, and the longing found no outlet, it turned to an almost hopeless brooding upon the face of the woman until before long he loved her with the passion of a man mingled with the compassion of a prophet. He saw plainly that something had to be done *in* her—perhaps some saving shock in the guise of ruin had to visit her; some door had to be burst open, some roof blown away, some rock blasted, that light and air might have free entry into her soul's house. Without this her soul could never grow stately like the house it inhabited. Whatever might be destined to cause this, he would watch in silence and self-restraint for the chance of giving aid, lest he should breathe frost instead of balm upon the buds of her delaying spring. If he might but be allowed to minister when at length the sleeping soul should stir! If its waking glance— ah! if it might fall on him!

He accused himself of mingling earthly motives and feelings with the unselfish and true. And was not Bascombe already the favored of her heart? The thought of her marriage to such a guide into the desert of denial and chosen godlessness threatened sometimes to upset the whole fabric of his growing faith. That such a thing should be possible seemed to bear more against the existence of a God than all the other grounds of the question together. Then a shudder would go to the very depths of his heart, and he would go out for a walk in the pine woods. There, where the somber green boughs were upheld by a hundred slender columns, he bowed his heart before the Eternal, gathered together all the might of his being, and groaned forth in deepest effort of a struggling will: "Thy will be done, not mine."

Sometimes he was sorely perplexed to think how the weakness, as he called it, had begun, and how this unfamiliar feeling for a woman had stolen upon him. He could not say it was his doing. Did not the whole thing spring out of his nature, a nature that was not of his design, and was beyond him and his control? And if it was born of God, then let that God look to it, for surely that which belonged to his nature could not be evil. But he could not settle his mind about it. Did his love spring from the God-will or the man-will? He was greatly unnerved by the question, and the marvel was that he was able to go on preaching, and even with some sense of honesty and joy in his work.

Amidst this trouble, Wingfold felt more than ever that if there were no God, his soul was adrift in nothing but a chaotic universe. Often he would rush through the dark, as it were, crying for God; but he would always emerge from it with some tiny piece of the light, enough to keep him alive and send him to his work. And there in her own seat, Sunday after Sunday, sat the woman whom he had seen ten times during the week by the bedside of her brother, yet to whom only now, in the open secrecy of the pulpit, did he dare speak the words he would so have liked to pour directly into her suffering heart. And Sunday after Sunday, the face he loved bore witness to the trouble of the heart he loved yet more; that heart was not yet redeemed! Oh, might it be granted him to set some little wind blowing for its revival and hope! As often as he stood up to preach, his heart swelled with the message he bore, and he spoke with the freedom and dignity of a prophet. But when he saw her afterward, he scarcely dared let his eyes rest a moment on her face. He would only pluck the flower of a glance, or steal it at such moments when he thought she would not notice. She caught his glance, however, far oftener than he knew, and was sometimes aware of it without seeing it. And there was something in the curate's behavior, in his absolute avoidance of self-assertion, or the least possible intrusion upon her mental privacy during all the time of his simple ministration to her brother which the nobility of the woman could not fail to note, and seek to understand.

It was altogether a time of great struggle with Wingfold. He seemed to be assailed in every direction and to feel the strong house of life giving way, and yet he held on.

31   The Lawn

Leopold had begun to cough, and the fever continued. His talk was excited and mostly about his coming trial. To Helen it was painful, and she confessed to herself that if it were not for Wingfold she would have given way. Leopold insisted on seeing Mr. Hooker every time he called, and every time told him he must not allow pity for his weak state to prevent him from applying the severe remedy of the law. But in truth, it began to appear that the disease would run a race with the law for his life, even if the latter should at once proceed to justify a claim. Faber doubted if he would ever recover, and it soon became evident that more than his lungs were affected. His cough increased and he began to lose what little flesh he had.

The duty of Wingfold's conscience concerning Leopold's crime, in light of his clerical position and the boy's trusting in the confessional of his ears, was a question that plagued the curate above all his other troubles. His duty as God's servant was primarily to offer what peace he could to the tormented soul. Beyond that, he was perplexed to discern what his obligations might be. It was a question, however, which Leopold's sickness removed from the curate's shoulders.

One day Faber expressed his conviction to Wingfold that he

was fighting the disease at the great disadvantage of having an unknown enemy to contend with.

"The fellow is unhappy," he pointed out, "and if that lasts another month I shall throw in the sponge. His vitality is yielding, and within another month he will be in a raging consumption."

Leopold, however, seemed to have no idea of his condition, and the curate wondered what he would think or do were he to learn that he was dying. Would he insist on completing his confession and urging on a trial? He had told Wingfold all that had happened with the magistrate, and was doubtful at times whether all was as it seemed. The curate was not deceived. He had been present during a visit from Mr. Hooker, and nothing could be plainer than the impression of Leopold's madness which the good man held. Nor could Wingfold fail to suspect the cunning deception in the guise of kindness from George Bascombe in the affair. But the poor boy had done as much as lay in him in the direction of duty, and was daily becoming more and more unfit either to originate or carry out any further action.

Faber urged him to leave the country for some warmer southern climate, but he would not hear of it. Indeed, he was not in a condition to be moved. Also the weather had recently grown colder, and he was sensitive to atmospheric changes.

But after two weeks, when it was now the middle of the autumn, it grew quite warm again. He revived and made such progress that they were able to carry him into the garden every day. He sat in a chair on the lawn, his feet on a sheepskin and a fur cloak about him. And for all the pain in his heart, the sunshine was yet pleasing in his eyes. The soft breathing of the wind was pleasant to his cheek, even while he cursed himself for the pleasure it gave him. The few flowers that were left looked up at him mournfully. He let them look and did not turn his eyes away but let the tears gather and flow. The first agonies of the encounter of life and death were over and life was slowly wasting away.

One hot noon Wingfold lay beside him on the grass. Neither had spoken for some time when the curate plucked a pale red pimpernel and handed it up over his head to Leopold. The youth looked at it for a moment and burst into tears. The curate rose hastily.

"It is so heartless of me," sighed Leopold, "to take pleasure in such innocence as this."

"It merely shows," returned the curate, laying his hand gently on his shoulder, "that even in these lowly things, there is a something that has its root deeper than your pain. All about us in earth and air, wherever eye or ear can reach, there is a power ever breathing itself forth in signs. Now it shows itself in a daisy, now in a waft of wind, a cloud, a sunset, and this power holds constant relation with the dark and silent world within us. The same God who is in us, and upon whose tree we are the buds, also is all about us—inside, the Spirit; outside, the Word. And the two are ever trying to meet in us; and when they meet, then the sign without and the longing within become one. The man no more walks in darkness, but in light, knowing where he is going."

As he ended, the curate bent over and looked at Leopold. But the poor boy had not listened to a word he said. Something in his tone had soothed him, but the moment he stopped, the vein of his grief burst out bleeding afresh. He clasped his thin hands together, and looked up in an agony of hopeless appeal to the blue sky. The sky had now grown paler as in fear of the coming cold, though still the air was warm and sweet, and he cried, "Oh, if God would unmake me, and let the darkness cover me! Yet even then my deed would remain! Not even my annihilation could make up for my sin, or rid it out of the universe."

"True, Leopold," acknowledged the curate. "Nothing but the burning love of God can rid sin out of anywhere. But are you not forgetting him who surely knew what he undertook when he would save the world? You can no more tell what the love of God is, or what it can do for you, than you could have set that sun flaming overhead. Few men have such a cry to raise to the Father as you, such a claim of sin and helplessness to heave up before him. Cry to him, Leopold, my dear boy! Cry to him again and yet again, for he himself said that men ought always to pray and not to faint. God does hear and will answer although he might seem long about it."

Leopold did not answer, and the shadow lay deep on his face for a while. But at length it began to thin, and at last a feeble quivering smile broke through the cloud, and he wept soft tears of refreshing.

On days such as this, Wingfold found that nothing calmed and brightened Leopold like talking about Jesus. He would begin thinking aloud on some part of the gospel story, that which was most in his mind at the time—talking with himself, as it were, all about it. Now and then, but not often, Leopold would interrupt him and turn the monologue into dialogue. But even then Wingfold would hardly ever look at him. He would not disturb Leopold with more of his presence than he could help, or allow the truth to be flavored with more of his individuality than was unavoidable. It was like hatching a sermon in the sun instead of in the oven. Occasionally, he looked up and found his pupil fast asleep—sometimes with a smile, sometimes with a tear on his face. The sight would satisfy him well. Calm upon such a tormented sea must be the gift of God. And the curate would sometimes fall asleep himself—to start awake at the first far-off sound of Helen's dress sweeping over the grass toward them. By this time all the old tenderness of her ministration to her brother had returned, and she no longer seemed jealous of Wingfold's.

One day she came up behind them as they talked. Since the grass had been mown that morning, and also since she happened to be dressed in her riding habit and had gathered up the skirt over her arm, on this occasion she made no sound of sweet approach. Wingfold had been in one of his rambling monologues, and he and Leopold were talking about the women Jesus had spoken to. They discussed the women in the seventh chapter of John—Mary his mother, Mary Magdalene, and the Gentile from Syrophoenicia. Their talk went on a long time, and all the while Helen listened entranced as the curate told Leopold how one could see how much Jesus loved women by the way he talked to them.

Then at the end he said: "How any woman can help casting herself heart and soul at the feet of such a man, I cannot imagine. You do not once read of a woman being against him—except his own mother when she thought he was going astray and forgetting his high mission. The divine love in him toward his Father in heaven and his brethren was ever melting down his conscious individuality in sweetest showers upon individual hearts. He came down like rain upon the mown grass, like showers that water the earth. No woman, no man surely ever saw him as he was and did not worship him!"

Helen turned and glided silently back into the house, and neither knew she had been there.

It became clearer every week that Leopold was withering away; the roots of his being were being torn away from the soil of the world. Before long, symptoms appeared which no one could mistake, and Lingard himself knew he was dying.

"They say," said Leopold to his friend one day, "that God accepts the will the same as the deed—do you think so?"

"Certainly, if it be a true genuine will."

"I know I meant to give myself up," stated Leopold. "I had not the slightest idea they were fooling me. I know it now, but what can I do? I am so weak. I would only die on the way."

He tried to rise but fell back in the chair.

"Oh," he sighed, "isn't it good of God to let me die? Who knows what he may do for me on the other side! Who can tell what the bounty of a God like Jesus may be!"

It shot a terrible pang to Helen's heart when she learned that her darling must die. The same evening of the day on which the doctor's final announcement had come, Leopold insisted on dictating his confession to the curate, which he signed, making Wingfold and Helen witness the signature. Wingfold took charge of the document, promising to make the right use of it, whatever he should conclude that to be. After this, Leopold's mind seemed at ease.

His sufferings from cough and weakness and fever grew; and it was plain, from the light in his eye and the far-off look, that hope and expectation were high in him. The prospect of coming deliverance strengthened him.

"I wish it was over," he said once.

"So do I," returned the curate. "But be of good courage. I think nothing will be given you to bear that you will not be able to bear."

"I can bear a great deal more than I have had to yet. I don't think I shall ever complain. That would be to take myself out of his hands, and I have no hope anywhere else.—Are you any surer about him now than you used to be?"

"At least I hope in him far more," answered Wingfold.

"Is that enough?"

"No, I want more."

"I wish I could come back and tell you that I am alive and all is true."

"I would rather have the natural way of it, and get the good of not knowing first."

"But if I could tell you I had found God, then that would make you sure."

Wingfold could not help but smile—as if any assurance from such a simple soul could settle the questions that tossed his troubled spirit.

"I think I shall find all I want in Jesus Christ," he responded.

"But you can't see him, you know."

"Perhaps I can do better. In any event, I can wait," replied the curate. "Even if he would let me, I would not see him one moment before he thought it best. I would not be out of a doubt or difficulty an hour sooner than he would take me."

Leopold gazed at him and said no more.

32 The Meadow

As the disease advanced, Leopold's desire for fresh air grew. One hot day the fancy seized him to venture out of the garden into the meadow beyond. There a red cow was switching her tail as she gathered her milk from the world, and looking as if all was well. He liked the look of the cow and the open meadow, and wanted to share in it. Helen, with the anxiety of a careful nurse, feared it might hurt him.

"What does it matter?" he returned. "Is life so sweet that every moment more of it is a precious blessing?"

Helen let him have his will and they prepared a sort of litter, and the curate and the coachman prepared to carry him. Hearing what they were about, Mrs. Ramshorn hurried into the garden to protest, but in vain. So she joined the little procession, walking with Helen like a second mourner after the bier. They crossed the lawn and, through a double row of small cypresses, went winding down to the underground passage and then out into the sun and air. They set him down in the middle of the field in a low chair—not far from a small clump of trees. Mrs. Ramshorn sent for her knitting. Helen sat down at her brother's feet, and Wingfold, taking a book from his pocket, withdrew to the trees.

He had not read long, sitting within sight and call of the group, when Helen came to him.

"Leopold seems inclined to go to sleep," she said. "Perhaps if you would read something, it would send him off."

"I will with pleasure," he offered, and returning with her, sat down on the grass.

"May I read you a few verses I came upon the other day, Leopold?" he asked.

"Please do," answered the invalid rather sleepily.

Leopold smiled as Wingfold read, and before the reading was over was fast asleep.

"What can the little object want here?" asked Mrs. Ramshorn.

Wingfold looked up and seeing who it was approaching them, said, "Oh, that is Mr. Polwarth, who keeps the park gate."

"Nobody can mistake him," returned Mrs. Ramshorn. "Everybody knows the creature."

"Few people really *know* him," remarked Wingfold.

"I *have* heard that he is an oddity in mind as well as in body," returned Mrs. Ramshorn.

"He is a friend of mine," rejoined the curate. "I will go and meet him. He undoubtedly wants to know how Leopold is."

"Keep your seat, Mr. Wingfold. I don't in the least mind him," responded Mrs. Ramshorn. "Any 'friend' of yours, as you are kind enough to call him, will be welcome. Clergymen come to know—indeed, it is their duty to be acquainted with—all sorts of people. The late Dean of Halystone would stop and speak to any pauper."

The curate did however go to meet Polwarth, and returning with him presented him to Mrs. Ramshorn, who received him with perfect condescension and a most gracious bow. The little man turned from them, and for a moment stood looking on the face of the sleeping youth; he had not seen the poor lad since Helen ordered him to leave the house. A great tenderness came over his face, and his lips moved softly. "The Lord of thy life keep it for thee, my son!" he murmured, gazed a moment longer, then rejoined Wingfold. They walked aside a few paces and seated themselves on the grass.

"Please be seated," said Mrs. Ramshorn, without looking up from her knitting—the seat she offered being the wide meadow.

But they had already done so, and presently were deep in a gentle talk. At length certain words that had been foolhardy enough to wander within her range attracted the notice of Mrs. Ramshorn, and she began to listen. But she could not hear distinctly. She fancied, from certain obscure associations in her own mind, that they were speaking against persons of low origin, who might wish to enter the church for the sake of *bettering themselves*. Holding as she did that no church position should be obtained except by persons of good family and position, she was gratified to hear, as she supposed, the same sentiments from the mouth of such an illiterate person as she imagined Polwarth to be. Therefore, she proceeded to patronize him a little.

"I quite agree with you," she announced. "None but such as you describe should presume to set foot within the sacred precincts of the profession."

Polwarth was not desirous of pursuing the conversation with Mrs. Ramshorn, especially since she clearly had misinterpreted the words she had chanced to hear. But he felt he had to reply.

"Yes," he agreed, "the great evil in the church has always been the presence in it of persons unsuited for the work required of them there. One very simple sifting rule would be, that no one should be admitted to the clergy who had not first proved himself capable of making a better living in some other calling."

"I cannot go with you so far as that—so few careers are open to gentlemen," rejoined Mrs. Ramshorn. "But it would not be a bad rule that everyone, for admission to holy orders, should possess property sufficient at least to live on. With that for a foundation, he would occupy the superior position every clergyman ought to have."

"I was thinking," responded Polwarth, "mainly of the experience in life he would gather by having to make his own living. Behind the counter or the plough, or in the workshop, he would come to know men and their struggles and their thoughts—"

"Good heavens!" exclaimed Mrs. Ramshorn. "But it is not possible that you can be speaking of the *church*—of the clerical *profession*. The moment she is brought within reach of such people as you describe, that moment the church sinks to such a low level!"

"Say, rather, to the level of Jeremy Taylor," returned Polwarth, "who was the son of a barber; which is another point I was just making to Mr. Wingfold. I would have no one ordained till after forty, by which time he would know whether he had any real call or only a temptation to the church from the hope of an easy living."

By this time Mrs. Ramshorn had heard more than enough. The man was a leveller, a chartist, a positivist—a despiser of dignities!

"Mr.—Mr.—I don't know your name—you will oblige me by uttering no more such slanders in my company. You are talking about what you do not in the least understand. I am astonished, Mr. Wingfold, at your allowing a member of your congregation to speak with so little regard for the feelings of the clergy. You forget, sir, who said the laborer was worthy of his hire."

"I hope not, madam," responded Polwarth. "I only suggest that though the laborer is worthy of his hire, not every man is worthy of the labor."

Wingfold was highly amused at the turn things had taken. Polwarth looked annoyed at having allowed himself to be beguiled into such an utterly useless beating of the air.

"My friend *has* some rather unusual notions, Mrs. Ramshorn," interjected the curate. "But you must admit that it was your approval that encouraged him to go on."

"My husband used to say that very few of the clergy realized how they were envied by the lower classes. To low human nature the truth has always been unpalatable."

What precisely she meant by "the truth" it would be hard to say, but if the visual embodiment of it was not a departed dean, in her mind at least, it was always associated with a cathedral choir and a portly person in silk stockings.

Here happily Leopold woke, and his eyes fell upon the gate-keeper.

"Ah, Mr. Polwarth. I am so glad to see you!" he exclaimed. "I am getting on, you see. It will be over soon."

"I see," replied Polwarth, going up to him and taking the youth's offered hand in both his. "I could almost envy you for having got so near the end of your troubles."

While they spoke Mrs. Ramshorn beckoned to the curate from where she sat a few yards on the other side of Leopold. A little ashamed of having lost her temper, when the curate went up to her, she asked with an attempt at gaiety: "Is your odd little friend, as you call him, all—" And she tapped her lace cap carefully with her finger.

"Rather more so than most people," answered Wingfold. "He is a very remarkable man."

"He speaks as if he had seen better days—though where he can have gathered such notions, I can't imagine."

"He is a man of education, as you see," pointed out the curate.

"You don't mean he has been to Oxford or Cambridge?"

"No. His education has been of a much higher sort than is generally found there. He knows ten times as much as most university men."

"Ah, yes; but that means nothing, he hasn't the standing. And his manners! To speak of the clergy as he did in the hearing of one whose whole history is bound up with the church!"

She meant herself, not Wingfold.

"Nothing but a gatekeeper," she went on, "and to talk like that about bishops and what not. People that are crooked in body are always crooked in mind too.—A gatekeeper indeed!"

"Wasn't it something like that King David wanted to be?" reminded the curate.

"Mr. Wingfold, I never allow such foolish jests in my hearing. It was a doorkeeper the Psalmist said—and to the house of God, not a nobleman's park," retorted the dean's widow, and drew herself up.

The curate accepted his dismissal, and joined the little man by Leopold's chair.

"I wish you two could be with me when I am dying," said Leopold.

"If you will let your sister know your wish, you may easily have it," replied the curate.

"It will be just like saying goodbye at the pier, and pushing off alone—you can't get more than one into the boat. Out, out alone, into the infinite ocean of nobody knows what or where," said Leopold.

"Except those that are there already, and they will be waiting to receive you," replied Polwarth. "You may well hope, if you have friends to see you off, that you will have friends to welcome you too. But I think it's not so much like setting off from the pier as it is landing at the pier, where your friends are all standing waiting for you."

"Well, I don't know," said Leopold with a sigh of weariness. "I only want to stop coughing and aching and go to sleep."

"Jesus was glad to give up his spirit into his Father's hands."

"Thank you. Thank you. I have him. He is somewhere. You can't mention his name but it brings me something to live and hope for. If he is there, all will be well."

He closed his eyes.

"I want to go to bed," he whispered.

They all rose, and the men, except for the dwarf who returned to the park, carried him into the house.

Every day after this, so long as the weather continued warm, it was Leopold's desire to be carried out to the meadow. Regularly too, every day, about one o'clock, the gnome-like figure of the gate-keeper would come from the little door in the park fence, and march across the grass toward Leopold's chair, which was set near the small clump of trees. The curate was almost always there, not talking much to the invalid, but letting him know every now and then by some little attention or word, or merely by showing himself, that he was near. He would generally be thinking out what he wanted to say to his people the next Sunday. His mind was much occupied with Helen, but his faith in God was all the time growing through what seemed a succession of interruptions.

Nothing is so ruinous to progress in which effort is needed as satisfaction with apparent achievement. That always brings

216

growth to a halt. Fortunately, Wingfold's experience had been that no sooner did he set his foot on the lowest hill toward the higher ground than some new difficulty came along, and he rose in the strength of the necessity. He sought to deepen and broaden his foundations that he might build higher and trust farther. He was gradually learning that his faith must be an absolute one, claiming from God everything the love of a perfect Father could give. He learned that he could not even love Helen aright—simply, perfectly, unselfishly—except through the presence of the originating Love.

One day Polwarth did not appear, but soon after his usual time the still more gnome-like form of his little niece came scrambling rather than walking over the meadow. Gently and modestly, almost shyly, she came up to Helen, made her a curtsy like a village schoolgirl, and said while she glanced at Leopold now and then with an ocean of tenderness in her large, clear woman eyes: "My uncle is sorry, Miss Lingard, that he cannot come to see your brother today, since he is laid up with an attack of asthma. He wished Mr. Lingard to know that he was thinking of him. Shall I tell you just what he said?"

Helen did not feel much interest in the matter. But Leopold answered, "Every word of such a man is precious: tell me, please."

Rachel turned to him with the flush of a white rose on her face.

"I asked him, sir, 'Shall I tell him you are praying for him?' and he said, 'No. I am not exactly praying for him, but I am thinking of God and him together.'"

The tears rose in Leopold's eyes. Rachel lifted her baby-hand and stroked the dusky long-fingered one that lay upon the arm of the chair.

"Dear Mr. Lingard," she murmured, "I could well wish, if it pleased God, that I was as near home as you."

Leopold took her hand in his.

"Do you suffer then?" he asked.

"Just look at me!" she answered, with a smile, "—shut up all my life in this deformity. I'm not grumbling, but you can't imagine how tired I often get of it."

"Mr. Wingfold was telling me yesterday that some people think

St. Paul was little and misshapen, and that was his thorn in the flesh."

"I don't see how that could be true, or he would never have compared his body to a tabernacle. But I'm ashamed of complaining like this. It just came of my wanting to tell you I can't be sorry you are going."

"And I would gladly stay a while if my conscience was clean like yours," said Leopold smiling. "Do you know about God the same way your uncle does, Miss Polwarth?"

"I hope I do—a little. I doubt if anybody knows as much as he does," she returned very seriously. "But God knows about us all the same, and he doesn't limit his goodness to us by our knowledge of him. It's so wonderful that he is capable of being all to everybody!"

What an odd creature! thought Helen, who understood next to nothing of their talk. *I dare say they are both out of their minds. Poor things!*

"I beg your pardon for talking so much," concluded Rachel, and, with a curtsy first to the one then to the other, she turned and walked back the way she had come.

33   The Bloodhound

I need not recount the steps by which the detective office was able to enlighten the mother of Emmeline concerning the recent visitor to the deserted mine shaft. She had now come to the area in pursuit of yet additional discovery concerning him. She had no plan in her mind except finding out more about this unknown man, Bascombe, who had led her, through the circuitous means, to the town of Glaston. She knew nothing of his connection with the family of Lingard. Her only design was to go to the village church and anywhere else in the area where people congregated in the hope of something turning up. Not a suspicion of Leopold had ever crossed her path. She had been but barely acquainted with him and did not even know that he had a sister in Glaston, for Emmeline's friends had not all been on intimate terms with her parents.

On the morning after her arrival, she went out early to take a walk and think about the vengeance she sought. Finding her way into the park, she wandered about in it for some time. At length she left it by another gate and made her way back to Glaston by another footpath through the fields. As she walked she came to a stile, and being weary with her long walk, she sat down on it to rest. The day was a grand autumnal one. But nature had no charms for her.

Leopold was asleep in the meadow in his chair. Wingfold was seated in the shade of the trees, but Helen had returned to the house for a moment. Just then the curate saw Polwarth coming from the little door in the fence and he went to meet him. When he turned back, to his surprise he saw a lady standing beside the sleeping youth and gazing at him with a strange intentness. Polwarth had seen her come from the clump of trees and supposed her a friend of the family. The curate walked hastily back, fearing Leopold might wake and be startled at the sight of the stranger. So intent was the gazing lady that he was within a few yards of her before she heard him. She started, gave one glance at the curate, and hurried away toward the town. There was an agitation in her movements that Wingfold did not like. A suspicion crossed his mind and he decided to follow her. He turned over his charge of Leopold to Polwarth, and set off after the lady.

The moment the eyes of Emmeline's mother fell on the face of Leopold, whom she recognized at once despite the changes his suffering had caused, the suspicion awoke in her that here was the murderer of her daughter. His poor condition only confirmed the likelihood of it. Her first idea was to wake him and see the effect of her sudden presence. Finding he was attended, she hurried away to inquire in the town and discover all she could about him.

A few moments later, Polwarth had taken charge of him, and while he stood looking on him tenderly, the youth woke with a start.

"Where is Helen?" he asked.

"I have not seen her. Ah, here she comes."

"Did you find me alone, then?"

"Mr. Wingfold was with you. He gave you up to me, because he had to go into the town."

He looked questioningly at his sister as she walked up, and she looked the same way at Polwarth.

"I feel as if I had been lying all alone in this wide field," said Leopold, "and as if Emmeline had been by me, though I didn't see her."

Polwarth looked after the two diminishing forms, which were now almost at the end of the meadow and about to come out on the high road, then turned to Leopold and began to comfort him with conversation.

Helen followed Polwarth's look with hers. A sense of danger seized her. When she had recovered herself after a few moments, she came and took her usual seat by her brother's side. She cast an anxious glance now and then into Polwarth's face, but dared not ask him anything.

Emmeline's mother had not gone far before she became aware that she was being followed. This was a turning of the tables she did not relish. A certain feeling of undefined terror came upon her and it was all the more oppressive because she did not choose to turn and face her pursuer. The fate of her daughter rose before her in association with herself. Perhaps this man pressing on her heels in the solitary meadow, and not the poor youth who lay dying there in the chair, was the murderer of Emmeline! Unconsciously she accelerated her pace until it was almost a run, beginning to fear for her life. But by so doing she did not widen by a single yard the distance between herself and the curate.

When she came out on the high road, she gave a glance in each direction, and avoiding the country, made for the houses. A short lane led her into Pine Street. There she felt safe. It was market day and a good many people were about. She slowed down, thinking her pursuer, whoever he was, would give up the chase. But she was disappointed, for several glances over her shoulder confirmed that he still kept the same distance behind her. She saw also that he was well known, for several were greeting and saluting him as he came. What could it mean? It must be the "G B" she had been seeking—who else? Should she stop and challenge his pursuit? No, she must elude him instead. But she did not know a single person in the place, or one house where she could seek refuge. Debating thus with herself, she hurried along the pavement of Pine Street, with the abbey church in front of her.

The footsteps grew louder and quicker; the man had made up his mind and was increasing his speed to catch her! Who could tell, he might be mad!

On came the footsteps, for the curate had indeed made up his mind to speak to her, and either remove or confirm his apprehensions. Nearer and nearer he came. Her courage and strength were giving way. Quickly she darted into a shop for refuge, sank on a chair by the counter, and asked for a glass of water. A young woman ran to fetch it, while Mr. Drew—for it was his shop she had entered—went up the stairs for a glass of wine. Returning with it he came from behind the counter and approached the lady where she sat leaning her head upon her hands.

In the meantime the curate had also entered the shop. He had placed himself where, unseen by her, he might await her departure, for he did not want to speak to her there. He watched as Mr. Drew went up to her.

"Do me the favor, madam, of taking but a sip," he said—but said no more. For at the sound of his voice, the lady gave a violent start, and raising her head looked at him. The wine glass dropped from his hand and broke on the floor. She gave a half-choked cry, and ran from the shop.

The curate sprang after her when he was stopped by the look on the face of the draper. Drew stood transfixed where she had left him, white and trembling, as if he had seen a ghost. Wingfold went up to him, and whispered gently:

"Who is she?"

"Mrs.—Mrs. Drew," answered his friend in an empty voice, and the next moment the curate was again after her like a greyhound.

A little crowd of the shop people had gathered.

"Pick up those pieces of glass, and call Jacob to wipe the floor," he said—then walked to the door and stood staring after the curate as Wingfold all but ran to overtake the swiftly gliding figure.

The woman, unaware that her pursuer was again on her track,

and hardly any longer caring where she went, hurried blindly toward the churchyard. Presently the curate relaxed his speed, hoping this would provide him a fit place to talk with her. "She must be Emmeline's mother," he said to himself. The moment he caught sight of the face lifted from its gaze at the sleeping youth, he had suspected the fact. He had not had time to analyze its expression, but there was something dreadful in it. A bold question would answer his suspicion.

She entered the churchyard, saw the abbey door open and hastened to it. She was in a state of bewilderment and terror that would have crazed a weaker woman. In the entryway she cast a glance behind her; there again was her pursuer! She sprang into the church. A woman was dusting a pew not far from the door.

"Who is that coming?" she asked with a tone and a look of fear that appalled Mrs. Jenkins.

She looked through the door and said, "Why, it be only the parson, ma'am."

"Then I shall hide myself over there, and you must tell him I went out by that other door. Here's a sovereign for you."

"I thank you, ma'am," replied Mrs. Jenkins looking wistfully at the coin, which was a great sum of money to a sexton's wife with children, then instantly went on with her dusting. "But it ain't no use tryin' tricks with our parson. He ain't one to be fooled. A man as don't play no tricks with hisself, as I heard a gentleman say, it ain't no use tryin' no tricks with *him*."

Almost while she spoke the curate entered. The lady drew herself up and tried to look both dignified and injured.

"Would you oblige me by walking this way for a moment?" he said, coming straight to her.

Without a word she followed him a long way into the church where they would not be heard. He asked her to be seated on a small flight of steps. Again she obeyed, and Wingfold sat down near her.

"Are you Emmeline's mother?" he asked.

The gasp, the expression of eye and cheek, and whole startled response of the woman, revealed that he had struck the truth. But she made no answer.

"You had better be open with me," he insisted, "for I mean to be very open with you."

She stared at him, but either could not, or would not speak. Probably it was caution; she must hear more before she would reveal herself.

The curate was already in a state of excitement, and I fear now got a little angry, for the look on the woman's face was not pleasant to his eyes.

"I want to tell you," he said, "that the poor youth whom your daughter's behavior made a murderer of—"

She gave a cry and turned ashen. The curate was ashamed of himself.

"Forgive me for sounding cruel," he added. "I am grievously sorry for what has happened, and for you in your loss of Emmeline. But the lad is now dying—will be gone in but a few weeks. The same blow killed both, only one has taken longer to die."

"And that is to excuse the evil he has done!" she cried, speaking at last.

"Nothing can excuse the dreadful wrong he has done. But that is between his God—and Emmeline—and him. No end can be served by now attempting to bring him to trial and judgment. If ever a man had repented for his crime—"

"And what is that to me, sir?" cried the avenging mother, becoming arrogant. "Will his sorrow bring back my child? The villain took her precious life without giving her a moment to prepare for eternity, and you ask me—her mother—to let him go free! I will not. I have vowed vengeance, and I will have it."

"Allow me to say that if you die in that same spirit of bitterness, you will be far worse prepared for eternity than I trust your poor daughter was."

"What is that to you? If I choose to run the risk, it is my business. I tell you I will not rest until I see the wretch brought to the gallows."

"But he cannot live to reach it. The necessary preliminaries would waste all that is left of his life."

"Justice must be done. There must be retribution for his crime!"

"Were he to live I would perhaps find it my duty to agree with you," replied the curate. "But his condition as it is, my responsibility is only to offer him what little I can to allow him to die in peace. We must forgive our enemies, you know. And *your* responsibility is to forgive him—for vengeance and retribution and justice can come only from the hand of the Lord. But indeed he is not even your enemy."

"No *enemy* of mine! The man who murdered my child no enemy of mine! Well, I promise you that he will find me his enemy. If I cannot bring him to the gallows, I can at least make every man and woman in the country point the finger of scorn and hatred at him. I can bring disgrace and ruin to his family. Their pride indeed! I am in my rights and I will have justice. My poor lovely innocent! I will have justice on the foul villain. We shall see if they are all too grand and proud to have a nephew hanged."

Her lips were white and her teeth set. She rose with the slow movement of one in a passion, and turned to leave the church.

"I warn you," declared the curate after her, "that such hatred will consume and destroy you. The only true justice to be found will come when you lay your bitter thirst for revenge on the same altar on which Leopold has offered the evil in his own heart—the altar of God's love and forgiveness."

"Don't talk to me of forgiveness!" she spat as she wheeled around to face him. "What do you know of forgiveness? Have you lost a daughter to a murderer? I will destroy him, I tell you, and his family with him!"

Again she turned and would have sped from the abbey in a silent fit of smoldering rage.

"It might hamper your proceedings a little," warned Wingfold, "if in the meantime a charge of bigamy were brought against yourself, *Mrs. Drew.*"

Her back was toward the curate, and for a moment she stopped and stood like a pillar of salt. Then she began to tremble and laid hold of the carved top of a bench. But her strength failed her completely. She sank on her knees and fell on the floor with a moan.

The curate called Mrs. Jenkins and sent her for water. With some difficulty they brought the visitor to herself.

She rose, shuddered, drew her shawl about her, and said to the woman, "I am sorry to give you so much trouble. When does the next train start for London?"

"Within an hour," answered the curate. "I will see you to it."

"I prefer going alone."

"That I cannot permit."

"I must go to my lodgings first."

"I will go with you," insisted Wingfold.

She cast on him a look of questioning hate, yielded, and laid two fingers on his offered arm.

They walked out of the church and to the place where she had lodged. There he left her for half an hour. When he returned he said, "Before I go with you to the train, you must give me your word to leave young Lingard unmolested. I know my friend Mr. Drew has no desire to trouble you, but I am equally confident he will do whatever I ask."

She sat silently with cold gleaming eyes, for a time, then spoke, "How am I to know this is not some trick to save his life?"

"You saw him; you could see he is dying. I do not think he can live a month. He must go with the first of the cold weather."

She could not help believing him.

"I promise," she said. "But you are cruel to compel a mother to forgive the villain that stabbed her daughter to the heart."

"If the poor lad were not dying I should see that he gave himself up, as indeed he set out to do some weeks ago but was frustrated by his friends. He is dying for love of her. I believe I say so with truth. His friends did not favor my visits, because I encouraged him to surrender, but he got out of the house alone to come to me. He fainted in the churchyard and lay on the damp earth for the better part of an hour, and will now never recover from the combined effects of the exposure and his grief. I have offered what spiritual help has been within my power and I do believe he is prepared to meet both Emmeline and his Maker. Now, my good woman, as painful as it may be for your flesh to hear, as you hope someday to be forgiven, you must forgive him."

He held out his hand to her. She was a little softened, and gave him hers.

"Allow me one word more," added the curate, "and then we shall go. Our crimes are friends that will hunt us either to the bosom of God or the pit of hell. We are all equally guilty before God—some of us for our sins of the heart, just as much as Leopold with his sin of deed. You and I have an equal need to lay our sinful selves in repentance before him that he may heal and cleanse and forgive us, as he is now beginning to do with Leopold. Sin is a matter of kind, not degree."

She looked down, but her look was still sullen and proud.

The curate rose and picked up her bag. He went with her to the station, got her ticket, and saw her off.

Then he hastened back to Drew and told him the whole story.

"Poor woman!" sighed her husband. "But God only knows how much *I* am to blame for all this. If I had behaved better to her she might have never left me, and your poor young friend would now be well and happy."

"Or perhaps consuming his soul to a cinder with that odious drug," added Wingfold. "It is so true, as the Book says, that all things work together for our good, even our sins and vices. He takes our sins on himself, and while he drives them out of us with a whip of scorpions, he will yet make them work his good ends. He defeats our sins, makes them prisoners, forces them into the service of good, and chains them like galley slaves to the rowing benches of the gospel ship. He makes them work toward salvation for us. No, poor Leopold might never have come to know the wide extent of God's forgiveness without such a mighty sin pressing on his heart. Who can tell how God will use this for the purifying of Leopold's heart in ways that might not have been able to come otherwise? and in Emmeline's mother? Not to mention in my heart, and yours, and Helen's. God's ways are indeed too large for us to fathom."

"Poor woman!" sighed Drew again, who for once had been inattentive to the curate. "Well, she is sorely punished too."

"She will have it still worse yet," replied the curate, "if I can read the signs of character. She is not repentant yet—though I did seem to catch a momentary glimpse of softening. But it's the repentant heart God is after, no matter what it takes. God will strive to achieve it in each of us."

"It is an awful retribution," admitted the draper, "and I may yet have to bear my share—God help me!"

"I suspect it is the weight of her own sin that makes her so fierce to avenge her daughter. I doubt if anything makes one so unforgiving as unrepentant guilt. And, as I told her, if there is one lesson to be gained from all this, it is that in God's eyes all sin is equally abhorrent—whether it be Leopold's killing, my reading of another's sermons, your business practices, or your wife's hateful unforgiveness. All sin, whatever the degree, is equal in its capacity to separate us from God's heart of love. Therefore, it all equally needs to be repented of and forgiven by him whose heart is forgiveness. You remember the scripture in Mark 7 in which the Lord listed the sins of the heart, naming the greater sins side by side with the lesser. He equated greed, envy, and pride with murder and adultery. In God's sight, the self-contented pride which characterized my life up till a few months ago was a sin equal to Leopold's in its capacity to keep my heart from him. To wake my spirit, the Lord chose a pointed question by an unbeliever; to wake you, he chose one of my sermons; to wake your wife, he chose the loss of a daughter; and to wake Leopold, he chose the stain of a beloved's blood on his own hand."

"Well, I am sure you are right. But right now my own heart is full with what responsibility may yet rest on my shoulders. I must try to find out where she is and keep an eye on her."

"That should be easy enough. But why?"

"Because, if, as you say, there is still more heartache in store for her, I may yet have it in my power to do her some good. I wonder if Mr. Polwarth would call that *divine service?*" he added with one of his sunny smiles.

"Undoubtedly he would," answered the curate.

34   The Bedside

When George Bascombe went to Paris he had no thought of deserting Helen. He had feared that it might be ruinous both to Lingard and himself to undertake his defense. From Paris he wrote often to Helen, and she replied—not so often, yet often enough to satisfy him. As soon as she was convinced that Leopold could not recover, she let George know, whereupon he instantly began his preparations for returning.

Before he came the weather had changed once more. It was now cold, and the cold had begun at once to weigh upon the invalid. There are some natures to which cold—moral, spiritual, or physical—is lethal. Lingard was of this class. When the dying leaves began to shiver in the breath of the coming winter, the very brightness of the sun to look gleamy, and nature to put on the unfriendly aspect of a world not made for living in, but for shutting out—when all things took the turn of reminding man that his life lay not in them, Leopold began to shrink and withdraw. He could not face the ghastly persistence of the winter.

His sufferings were now considerable, but he never complained. Restless and fevered and sick at heart, he was easy to take care of, though more from a lovely nature than from any virtue of his will. He was always gently grateful, and would have been far more thankful had he not believed that the object of the kindnesses was so unworthy. Next to Wingfold's and his sister's, the face he always welcomed most was that of the gatekeeper. Polwarth was like a father in Christ to him and came every day.

"I am getting so stupid, Mr. Polwarth," he confessed one day. "I hardly seem to care about anything. I would rather hear a simple children's story even than the New Testament—something I don't have to think about. All my past life seems to be gone from me. I don't care about it. Even my crime looks like something done ages ago. I know it is mine, and I would rather it were not mine, but it is as if a great cloud had come and swept away the world in which it took place."

This was a long speech for him to make, and he had spoken slowly and with frequent pauses. Polwarth did not once interrupt him, feeling that a dying man must be allowed to ease his mind however he can. Helen and Wingfold would both have told him that he must not tire himself, but Polwarth never did. The dying should not have their utterances checked, or the feeling of not having finished. They will have plenty of that feeling naturally, without more of it being forced upon them by overly cautious attendants.

A fit of coughing compelled Leopold to stop, and when it was over he lay panting and weary, but with his large eyes questioning the face of Polwarth. Then the little man spoke.

"He must give us every sort of opportunity for trusting him," he said. "The one he now gives you is this dullness that has come over you. Trust him through it, submitting to it and yet trusting against it, and you will get the good of it. In your present condition you cannot even try to force your mind into some higher state, but you can say to God something like this: 'See, Lord, I am dull and stupid. Take care of everything for me, heart and mind and all. I leave it in your hands. Don't let me shrink from new life and thought and duty, or be unready to come out of the shell of my sickness when you send for me. I wait for your will.'"

"Ah!" cried Leopold, "there you have touched it! How can you know so well what I feel?"

"Because I have often had to fight hard to keep death to his own dominion and not let him cross over into my spirit."

"Alas! I am not fighting at all; I am only letting things go," sighed Leopold.

"You are fighting more than you know, I suspect, for you are enduring, and patiently. Suppose Jesus were to knock at the door now, and there was no one in the room to open it for him. Suppose you were as weak as you are now. What would you do?"

"What else but get up and open it?" answered Leopold.

"Would you not be tempted to lie still and wait till someone else came?"

"No."

"So you see, you do care about him, perhaps more than you

might have thought a minute ago. There are many feelings in us that are not able to get upstairs the moment we call them. Be as dull as it pleases God to let you be, and do not trouble yourself about it. Just ask him to be with you all the same."

The little man dropped on his knees by the bedside and prayed, "O Lord Jesus, be near when it seems that our Father has forsaken us. Even you, who were mighty in death, needed the presence of your Father to make you able to endure. Do not forget us, the work of your hands, the labor of your heart and spirit. Ah, Lord! We know you will never leave us. You can do nothing else but care for us, for whether we be glad or sorry, slow of heart or full of faith all the same we are the children of your Father. Give us repentance and humility and love and faith that we may indeed become the children of your Father who is in heaven. Amen."

While Polwarth was praying, the door opened gently behind him. Helen, not knowing he was there, had entered with Bascombe. He neither heard their entrance, nor saw the face of disgust that George made behind his back. What was in Bascombe's deepest soul, who shall tell? Of that region he himself knew nothing. It was a silent, empty place into which he had never yet entered—lonely and deserted as the top of Sinai after the cloud had departed. In what he called and imagined his deepest soul, all he was now aware of was a loathing of the superstition so fitly embodied before him. The prayer of the kneeling absurdity audaciously mocked the laws of nature. He felt it both sad and ludicrous to see the poor dwarf kneeling by the bedside of the dying murderer to pray some comfort into his passing soul. At the same time, a cold shudder of disgust ran through Helen at the familiarity and irreverence of the little spiritual prig.

Polwarth rose from his knees, unaware of a hostile presence.

"Leopold," he comforted, taking his hand, "I would gladly walk with you through the shadow if I might. But the heart of all hearts will be with you. Rest in your tent a little while longer, which is indeed the hollow of the Father's hand turned over you. Your strong brother is carefully watching the door. Your imagination cannot go beyond the truth of him who is the Father of lights, or of him who is the Elder Brother of men."

Leopold answered only with his eyes. Polwarth turned to go

and saw the onlookers. They stood between him and the door, but parted and made room for him to pass. Neither spoke. He made a bow first to one and then to the other, looking up in the face of each, unabashed by a smile of scorn or a blush of annoyance. George ignored him and walked straight to the bed the moment the way was clear. Helen's conscience, or her heart, smote her. Returning his bow, she opened the door for her brother's friend. He thanked her and went his way.

"Poor dear fellow!" said George kindly, stroking the thin hand laid in his. "Can I do anything for you?"

"Nothing but be good to Helen when I am gone, and tell her now and then that I am not dead, but living in the hope of seeing her again one day before long. She might forget sometimes—not me, but that—you know."

"Yes, yes, I'll see to it," answered George, in the evil tone of one who faithfully promises a child an impossibility. Of course there was no more harm in lying to a man who was on the verge of being a man no more, than there had been in lying to him when he supposed him a madman.

"Do you suffer much?" asked George.

"Yes—a good deal."

"Pain?"

"Not so much—sometimes. The weakness is the worst, but it doesn't matter—God is with me."

"What good does that do you?" asked George, forgetting himself, half in contempt, half in curiosity.

But Leopold took it in good faith and answered. "It sets everything right and makes me able to be patient."

George laid down the hand he held and turned sadly to Helen, but said nothing.

The next moment Wingfold entered. Helen kissed the dying hand, and left the room with George.

Tenderly he led her into the garden. To Helen it all looked like a graveyard. The day was a cold, leaden one that would have rained if it could, to get rid of the deadness at its heart; but no tears came.

Neither spoke for some time.

"Poor Leopold!" said George at length, and took Helen's hand. She burst into tears, and again for some time neither spoke.

"George, I can't bear it!" she said finally.

"It is very sad," answered George. "But he had a happy life, I don't doubt, up to—to—"

"What does that matter now? It's all a horrible mess. To begin so lovely and end so cold and miserable!"

George did not like to say what he thought, namely, that it was Leopold's own doing.

"It *is* horrible," he admitted. "But what can we do? What's done is done and nobody can help it."

"There should be somebody to help it," sighed Helen.

"Ah, perhaps there should be," answered George. "Well, it's a comfort it will be over soon."

"Is it?" returned Helen almost sharply. "He's not your brother, and you don't know what it will be to lose him! Oh, how desolate the world will be!"

Again the tears came to her eyes.

"I will do all I can to make up for the loss, dearest Helen," assured George.

"Oh, George!" she cried, "is there *no* hope? I don't mean of his getting better, but is there no hope of *sometime* seeing him again? We know so little about it. *Might* there not possibly be some life—you know—after all—?"

But George was too self-assured and too true to his principles to pretend anything to Helen. Hers was an altogether different case from Leopold's. Here was a young woman full of health and vitality. He could not lie to her of a hope beyond the grave.

But if George could not lie, it was not necessary for him to speak the truth—silence was enough. A moment of it was all Helen could endure. She rose hastily, left the bench where George still sat, and walked back toward the house. George followed a few paces behind, so far quenched that he did not overtake her to walk by her side. The nearest George came to belief in a saving power was to console himself with the thought that *time* would do everything for Helen.

———

As Leopold slowly departed, he seemed to his sister to draw along with him all that was precious in her life. She felt herself grow dull and indifferent. Her feelings appeared to be dying with him who had drawn them forth more than any other. The battle was ending without even the poor pomp and circumstance of torn banners and wailful music.

Leopold said very little during the last few days. His coughing fits grew more frequent, and in the pauses he had neither strength nor desire to speak. When Helen came to his bedside, he would put out his hand to her, and she would sit down by him and hold it warm in hers. Finally, the hand of his sister was the touchpoint of the planet from which the spirit of the youth took its departure—when he let that go he was gone. But he died asleep, as so many do, and imagined, I presume, that he was waking into his old life when he woke into his new one.

Wingfold stood on the other side of the bed with Polwarth beside him, for Leopold had wished it so. While he yet lingered, one of Helen's listless, straying glances was stopped by the countenance of the gatekeeper. It was so still and so rapt that she thought he must be seeing within the veil and regarding what things were awaiting her brother on the other side. In fact, Polwarth saw no more than she, but he was standing in the presence of him who is not the God of the dead but of the living.

Wingfold's anxiety was all for Helen. He could do no more for Leopold, nor did Leopold need more from man. Concerning many of the things that puzzled him most, he was on his way to knowing more. But there was his sister, about to be left behind him without his hopes. For her, dreary days were at hand. The curate prayed the God of comfort and consolation to visit her.

Mrs. Ramshorn would now and then look in at the noiseless door of the chamber of death, but she rightly felt that her presence was not desired and though ready to help did not enter. Neither did George—not from heartlessness, but he judged it better to leave the priests of falsehood undisturbed in the exercise of their miserable office. What did it matter how many comforting lies were told to a dying man? What *could* it matter? There was small danger of their foolish prayers and superstitious ceremonies evoking a deity from the well-ordered universe of natural law. But let them tell the dying man their lies and utter their silly incantations. Aloof he stood on the shore, ready to reach the rescuing hand to

Helen the moment she should turn her eyes to him for help. Certainly he would rather not leave her unprotected against such subtle and insinuating influences. But he did not fear for the curate's power over her. She would eventually come back to his way of thinking. But the soft hand of time must first draw together the edges of her heart's wound.

But the deadness of Helen's feelings seemed in some vague way, yet unacknowledged by her, subtly associated with George Bascombe. That very morning when he had come into the breakfast room so quietly, she had not heard him. Looking up and seeing him unexpectedly, he seemed for a moment the dull fountain of all the miserable feeling which was pressing her heart flat in her bosom. The next moment she accused herself of a great injustice, for was not George the only true friend she had ever had? If she lost him she would be very lonely indeed. Yet the feeling lingered regardless.

At the same time she shrank from Wingfold as hard and unsympathetic. True, he had been most kind to her brother. But to her he had shown the rough side of her nature, going farther than any gentleman ought to go in criticizing her conduct, even if he was a clergyman.

The outside weather, although she was far past paying any attention to that, was in harmony with her soul's weather. A dull, dark, gray fog hung from the sky and obscured the sun. The air was very cold. There was neither joy nor hope anywhere. The bushes were leafless and budless, the summer gone, the spring not worth hoping for, because it also would go. Spring after spring came—for nothing but to go again. Things were so empty. The world around her, yes, all her life, all herself, was but the cold dead body of a summer world. And Leopold was going to be buried with the summer. His smiles had all gone with the flower. The weeds of his troubles were going also, for they would die with him. But he would not know it and be glad any more than she—she who was left caring for neither summer nor winter, joy nor sorrow, love nor hate, the past nor the future.

Many such thoughts wandered hazily through her mind as she now sat holding the hand of him who was fast sleeping away from her into death. Her eyes were fixed on the window through which he had entered that terrible night, but she saw nothing beyond it.

"He is gone," said Polwarth softly, in a voice that sounded unknown to the ears of Helen, and as he spoke he kneeled.

She started up with a cry, and looked in her brother's face. She had never seen anyone die, yet she saw that he was dead.

35   New Friends

How slowly the terrible time passed until it brought the funeral. Indeed, it was terrible for its very dullness. Helen's weary heart felt as a bare, blank wasteland. The days were all one, outside and inside. Her heart was but a lonely, narrow bay to the sea of cold, immovable fog. No one tried to help, no one indeed knew her trouble. Everyone took it for grief at the loss of her brother; to herself it was the oppression of a life that had not even the interest of pain. The curate had of course called to ask about her, but he had not been invited to enter. George had been everywhere with help, but he had no word to speak which could offer hope to the sickness in her heart.

The day of the funeral came, robed in thin fog and dull cold. The few friends gathered. The body was taken to the abbey. The curate received it at the gate in the name of the church—which takes our children in its arms and our bodies into its garden. Wingfold read the lovely words from the Scriptures, and earth was given back to earth, to mingle with the rest of the stuff the great workman uses to do his work. Cold was Helen's heart, cold her body, cold her very being. The earth, the air, the mist, the very light was cold. The past was cold, the future was yet colder. Her life seemed withering away from her like an autumn flower in the frosts of winter, and she hardly seemed to care. What was life worth when she could not even desire it to continue? Heartless she returned from the grave, careless of George's attentions, not even scornful of her aunt's shallow wail over the uncertainty of life and all things human—so indifferent to the whole misery that Helen walked straight up to the room, hers once more, from which the body had just been carried, and which for so many weary weeks had been the center of loving pain.

She shed her cloak and hat and laid them on the bed. Stepping to the window, she sat down and gazed, hardly seeing, out on the cold garden with its sodden earth, its leafless shrubs, and perennial trees of darkness and mourning. The meadow lay beyond, and there she saw the red cow busily feeding. Beyond the meadow stood the trees, with the park behind them. And yet farther behind lay the hollow with the awful house below, its dismal haunted lake, and its ruined garden. But nothing moved her. *Poldie is dead.* She would die soon herself: what did that or anything else matter?

There she sat until she was summoned to dinner—early for the sake of the friends who lived far away. She ate and drank and took her share in the talk as a matter of course. But only the frost of an unknown despair choked back the tears in her sad eyes.

No sooner was she free again than she sought her room, not consciously from love for her brother who had died there, but because the deadness of her heart chose a fitting loneliness. Again she seated herself at the window.

The dreary day was drawing to a close, and the night, drearier it could not be, was at hand. The gray had grown darker, and she sat waiting for the night like one waiting for a monster coming to claim its own and swallow her up.

Something caused her to lift her eyes. In the west the clouds had cleared a little. No sun came forth: she was already down; but a canopy of faint amber grew visible and stretched across the sky. The soul of the faint remaining sunset was so still, so resigned, so sad, so forsaken that she who had thought her heart gone from her suddenly felt its wells were filling, and soon they overflowed. She wept. But at what? A color in the sky! Was there then a God who knew sadness—was this his sign of comfort to her? Or was it but an accidental dance of the atoms of color, as George would have said.

Helen's doubts did not stop her weeping, as doubt generally does. For the sky with its sweet sadness was in front of her, and deep in her heart a lake of tears, now that it had begun to flow, would not be stopped. She did not know why she wept, but she wept and wept until her heart began to stir, and her tears came cooler and freer.

"Oh, Poldie! My own Poldie!" she cried, and fell upon her knees—not to pray, not for any reason she was aware of.

But in a moment she grew restless. There was no Poldie! She rose and walked about the room. Her brother's memory came back to her. She had stood between him and the only poor remnant of peace, consolation, and hope that it was possible he should have. And in the end through those friends whom she had treated with such distance and unkindness, he had received strength with which to die. Then out rushed from the chamber of her memory the vision of a small, dark, nervous, wild-looking Indian boy, who gazed at her but for one questioning moment, then ran into her arms and nestled close to her. What had she done to justify that childlike faith he had placed in her? She had received and sheltered him, yet when it came to the test, she had loved herself better than him, and would have doomed him to agony rather than herself to disgrace. *Oh, Poldie! Poldie!* But he could not hear! Never again would she be able to utter to him a word of sorrow or repentance. Never could she ask his forgiveness or let him know that now she knew better and had risen above such selfishness!

She stopped and looked sadly from the window. The sky was now cloudless overhead. She turned hastily to the bed where lay her cloak and hat, put them on with trembling hands, and went out into the garden. In a few moments she was crossing the meadow through the cold, frosty twilight air, now clear of its fog. Somehow the chill seemed to comfort, uplift, and strengthen her. The red cow was still feeding there. She stopped and talked to her a little. She seemed one of Poldie's friends, and Poldie had come back to her heart if he might never more to her arms.

She knew she must make this little journey to one of Poldie's best friends, whom he had loved even better than she. She had not honored Poldie's friends as they deserved or as Poldie must have desired. To get near them would be to get nearer to Poldie. At least she would be with those whom he had loved and who, she did not doubt, still loved him, believing him still alive. She could not go to the curate, but she could go to the Polwarths. No one would blame her for that—except, indeed, George. But even George would not come between her and what little communion with the memory of Poldie was left her! She would keep her freedom—she would rather break with George than lose her power to choose for herself.

She opened the door in the fence and entered the park, recovering strength with every step she took toward Poldie's friends. It was almost dark when she reached the lodge door and knocked.

No one answered. She repeated her knock, but still no answer came. Her heart began to fail her, but she heard voices. What if they were talking about Leopold? Finally, after knocking four or five times, she heard the step as of a child coming down a stair, but it passed the door. Clearly no one had heard her. She knocked again, and immediately the door was opened by Rachel. The pleasured surprise that shone in her face when she saw Helen was lovely to see. Rachel's sweet smile came like a sunrise of humanity on Helen's miserable isolation. She forgot her pride and in simple gratitude for the voiceless yet eloquent welcome, bent down and kissed the dwarf. The little arms were flung about her neck and the kiss returned with a gentle warmth and sweetness. Then Rachel took her by the hand and led her into the kitchen, placed a chair for her near the fire, and said, "I am sorry there is no fire in the parlor. The gentlemen are in my uncle's room. Oh, Miss Lingard, I do wish you could have heard how they have been talking!"

"Have they been saying anything about my brother?" asked Helen.

"It's all about him," she replied.

"May I ask who the gentlemen are?" said Helen doubtfully.

"Mr. Wingfold and Mr. Drew. They are here often."

"Is it—do you mean Mr. Drew the draper?"

"Yes. He is one of Mr. Wingfold's best pupils. Mr. Wingfold brought him to my uncle, and he has come often ever since."

"I never heard that—Mr. Wingfold—took pupils. I am afraid I do not quite understand you."

"I would have said *disciples*," returned Rachel smiling, "but that is such a sacred word. It would say best what I mean though, for there are people in Glaston that are actually mending their ways because of Mr. Wingfold's teaching, and Mr. Drew was the first of them. It is a long time since any such thing was heard of in the abbey. It never was in my time."

Helen sighed. She wished that she also could become one of Mr. Wingfold's pupils, but how could she now when she had learned that his teachings were at best only a lovely fantasy. George could explain the whole matter: religion invariably excited the imagination and weakened the conscience. Alas, she could not be a pupil of Mr. Wingfold! She could not deceive herself with such comfort. And yet!—*"Come unto me . . . and I will give you rest."*

"I do wish I could hear them," she said.

"And why not?" returned Rachel. "There is not one of them who would not be delighted to see you. I know that."

"I am afraid I would just hinder their talk. Would they speak just as freely as if I were not there? You know how the presence of a stranger—"

"You are no stranger to Mr. Wingfold or my uncle," replied Rachel. "And I am sure you know Mr. Drew."

"To tell you the truth, Miss Polwarth, I have not behaved as I should either to your uncle or Mr. Wingfold. I did not realize that until my brother was gone. They were so good to him! I feel now as if I had been possessed with an evil spirit. I could not bear them to be more to him than I was. Oh, how I should like to hear what they are saying! I feel as if I could almost get a glimpse of Leopold. But I couldn't face them all together."

Rachel was silent for a moment, thinking. Then she said: "I'll tell you what then. You don't have to go into the room with them. Between my uncle's room and mine there's a little closet where you could sit and hear every word."

"That would hardly be honorable though—would it?"

"I will answer for it. I shall tell my uncle afterward. There may be cases where the motive makes the right or wrong in a certain thing. It's not as if you were listening to find out secrets. I shall be in the room and that will be a connecting link, you know. Come now. We don't know what we may be losing."

The desire to hear Leopold's best friends talk about him was strong in Helen, but her heart had misgivings. Was it not an unbecoming thing to do? She would be in terror of discovery the whole time. In the middle of the stairway she drew Rachel back and whispered, "I dare not do it."

"Come on," insisted Rachel. "Hear what I shall say to them first. After that you shall do as you please." Her response was so quick, evidently her thoughts had been going in the same direction as Helen's. "Thank you for trusting me," she added, as Helen again followed her.

They arrived at the top of the stair. Helen stood trembling, while Rachel went into the room.

"Uncle," interjected Rachel, "I have a friend in the house who is very anxious to hear you and our friends speak your minds to each other, but for reasons does not wish to appear. Will you allow my friend to listen without being seen?"

"Is it your wish, Rachel, or are you only conveying the request of another?" asked her uncle.

"It is my wish," answered Rachel. "I really desire it—if you do not mind."

She looked from one to another as she spoke. The curate and the draper both nodded their full approval.

"Do you know quite what you are doing, Rachel?" asked Polwarth.

"Perfectly, Uncle," she answered. "There is no reason why you should not talk as freely as if you were talking only to me. I will put my friend in the closet, and you need never think that anyone is in the house but ourselves."

"Then I have no objections," returned her uncle with a smile. "Your *friend*, whoever he or she may be, is heartily welcome."

Rachel rejoined Helen, who had already drawn nearer to the door of the closet, and now seated herself in the midst of an atmosphere of apples and herbs. Already the talk was going on just as before. At first, each of the friends did now and then remember that there was a listener unseen, but when the conversation came to a close, each found that he had for a long time forgotten it.

Although satisfied after what Rachel had said to the men, Helen nevertheless felt oddly uncomfortable at first. But soon she fancied that she was listening at the door of the other world hoping to catch news of her Leopold, and that made her forget herself and put her at peace. For some time, however, the conversation was absolutely unintelligible to her. She understood the words and phrases, and even some of the sentences, but she had no clue to their meaning. Thus, understanding them was like attempting to realize the span of a rainbow from a foot or two of it appearing now and then vanishing again. It was chiefly Polwarth, often Wingfold, and now and then Drew that spoke, Rachel contributing only an occasional word. At length something of a dawn broke over the seeming chaos. The light which first reached Helen flowed from the words of the draper.

"I still can't grasp it, despite what you say," he confessed. "Why, if there is life beyond the grave—and most sincerely I trust there is—I don't see why we should know so little about it. Confess now, Mr. Polwarth! Mr. Wingfold!" he insisted, "does it not seem strange to you? Our dearest friends go on living somewhere else; yet the moment they cease to breathe, they pass away from us utterly—so completely that from that moment no hint or trace of their existence ever reaches us. Nature, the Bible, God himself says nothing about how they exist or where they are, or why they are so silent; and here we are left with aching hearts staring into a silent and awful blank."

The gatekeeper and curate exchanged a pleased look of surprise at the draper's eloquence, but Polwarth instantly took up his answer.

"I grant you it would look strange indeed if there were no good reason for it," he admitted.

"Then do you say," asked Wingfold, "that because of that darkness, we are at liberty to remain in doubt as to whether there is any life after death?"

"I would say so," answered Polwarth, "if it were not for the story of Jesus. If we accept his story, we can surely be satisfied as to a good reason for the mystery that overshadows Leopold's new life, whether we have found one or not."

"Are we forbidden to seek such a reason?" inquired the curate.

The draper glanced from the one to the other with keen interest.

"Certainly not," returned the gatekeeper. "God gave us our minds to use. He wants us to seek reasons for our faith at every turn—good, logical, soundly intellectual reasons why we believe. Why else are our imaginations given us but to help us discover good reasons to believe as we do?"

"Can you imagine any good reason, then," argued Drew, "why we should be kept in such absolute ignorance of everything that comes to the departed spirit from the moment of death when it leaves its life with us?"

"I think I know one," answered Polwarth. "I have sometimes imagined it might be because no true idea of their condition could possibly be grasped by those who remain living in these earthly bodies of ours. To understand their condition we must first be clothed in our new bodies too—which are to the old as a house is to a tent. I doubt if there are any human words in which more facts of a life beyond could be imparted to our knowledge. The facts themselves are no doubt beyond the reach of any of the senses we now possess. I expect to find my new body provided with new and completely different senses beyond what I now possess.

"But I do not care to dwell on this kind of speculation, so I will give you my reason in answer to your question: there are a thousand individual events in the course of every man's life by which God takes a hold of him—a thousand little doors by which he enters, however little the man may realize it. But in addition, there is one universal and unchanging grasp that God keeps on the race, no matter how men may ignore him all their lives long and ignore these thousand ways he would enter and give them his life. And that grasp is death and its shroud of mystery. Imagine a man who is about to die in absolute loneliness and cannot tell where he will go—to whom, I say, can such a man go for refuge? Where can he take the doubts and fears that assail him, but to the Father of his being?"

"But," objected Drew, "I cannot see what harm would come of letting us know a little—enough at least to assure us that there is *something* on the other side."

"Just this," returned Polwarth, "—their fears relieved, their hopes encouraged from any lower quarter—men would, as usual, turn away from the fountain to the cistern of life. They would not turn to the ever-fresh, original, creative Love to sustain them, but would rely on their knowledge instead. Satisfy people's desire to know this and what have they gained? A little comfort perhaps—but not a comfort from the highest source, and possibly gained too soon for their well-being. Does it bring them any nearer to God than they were before? Is he filling one more cranny of their hearts in consequence? Their assurance of immortality has not come from knowing him in their hearts, and without that it is a worthless knowledge. Little would be gained, and possibly much would be lost—and that is the need to trust him beyond what our minds can see. Trust is born in love, and our need is to *love* God, not apprehend facts concerning him. Remember Jesus' words: 'If they do not listen to Moses and the prophets, neither would they listen or would they be persuaded though one rose from the dead.' He does not say they would not believe in a future state though one rose from the dead—though most likely they would soon persuade themselves it had been nothing more than an illusion—but they would not be persuaded to repent, to turn to God, to love and trust and believe in him with their whole hearts. And without love for God, what does it matter whether someone believes in a future state or not? It would only be worse for him if he did. No, Mr. Drew! I repeat, it is not a belief in immortality that will deliver a man from the woes and pains and sins of humanity, but faith in the God of life, the Father of lights, the God of all consolation and comfort."

Polwarth paused, then said, "Witness our friend Lingard. His knowledge of God's love and forgiveness *in his heart*—not in his intellect—brought peace to his troubled soul. He knows of the afterlife now, because he is in it, with his Lord who loved him in the midst of his guilt. But what good would that mere *knowledge* have done him before, without the cleansing power of the Savior's love to wash the bloodstains from his hands and make his heart once again white as snow? Believing in the Father of Jesus, a man can leave his friends, his family, and his guilt-ridden past, with utter confidence in his hands. It is in *trusting* him that we move into higher regions of life, not in knowing *about* him. Until we have his life in us, we shall never be at peace. The living God dwelling in the heart he has made, and glorifying it by inner communion with himself—that is life, assurance, and safety. Nothing less can ever give true life."

The gatekeeper was silent, and so were they all. At length Rachel rose softly, wiping the tears from her eyes, and left the room. She went to the closet to check on Helen, but she found no one. Helen was already hastening across the park, weeping as she went.

36   The Curate's Resolve

The next day was Sunday.

It had not yet been a year since the beginning events of my narrative took place. The change which had passed upon the opinions in the heart and mind and very being of the curate were far beyond his imaginings. He could not have had the faintest, most shadowy conception of his transformation at the time. It had been a time of great trouble, but the gain had been infinitely greater; for at last the bonds of the finite were broken. He had burst through the shell of the mortal. The agony of the second birth was past, and he was a child again—only a child, he knew, but a child of the kingdom. And the world and all that God cared about in it was his, while the created universe lay open to him in its boundless and free-giving splendor.

At the same time, a great sorrow threatened him from a no less mysterious region. For he loved Helen with a love that was no invention or creation of his own, and if not his, then whose? Certainly this thing must also belong to the God of his being. Therefore even in his worst anxieties about Helen—I do not mean in his worst seasons of despair at the thought of never gaining her love; he had never yet regarded the winning of her as a possibility—but at those times when he most plainly saw her the submissive disciple of George Bascombe's poorest, emptiest, shabbiest theories of life—even then was he able to reason with himself: *she belongs to God, not to me; and God loves her better than I could ever love her.* And with this he succeeded in comforting himself—I do not say to contentment, but to the quieting of his soul.

And now this Sunday, Wingfold entered the pulpit, prepared at last to speak his resolve. Happily no one had yet come to him, neither the bishop, the rector, nor Mrs. Ramshorn, to suggest that he resign. Now he was prepared to tell them the decision to which the thought he had taken had conducted him.

"It is time, my hearers," he began, "to bring to a close this period of uncertainty about the continuation of our relationship together. As you are well aware, in the springtime of this year I felt compelled to think through whether I could in good faith go on as a servant of the church. For very dread of the honesty of an all-knowing God, I forced myself to break through the established conventions of the church and speak to you of my most private thoughts. I told you I was unsure of many things which are taken for granted concerning clergymen. Since then, as I have wrestled with these issues, I have tried to show you the best I saw, yet I dared not say I was sure of anything. And I have kept those of you who cared to follow my path acquainted with the progress of my mental history. And now I come to tell you the practical result at which I have arrived.

"First, I tell you that I will not forsake my curacy, still less my right and duty to teach whatever I seem to know. But I must not convey the impression that all my doubts are suddenly gone. All I now can say is that in the story of Jesus I have seen grandeur—to me altogether beyond the reach of human invention, and real hope for man. At the same time, from the attempt to obey the word recorded as his, I have experienced a great enlargement of my mind and a deepening of my moral strength and a wonderful increase of faith, hope, and love toward all men. Therefore, I now declare with the consent of my whole man—I cast my lot with the servants of the Crucified. If they be deluded, then I am content to share in their delusion, for to me it is the truth of the God of men. I will stand or fall with the story of my Lord. I speak not in irreverence, but in honesty. I will take my chance of failure or success in this life or the life to come, on the words and the will of the Lord Jesus Christ. Impressed as I am with the truth of his nature, the absolute devotion of his life, and the essential might of his being, if I yet obey him not, I shall not only deserve to perish, but in that very refusal I would draw ruin upon my own head. Before God I say it—I would rather be crucified with that man than reign with an earthly king over a kingdom of millions. On such grounds as these I hope I am justified in declaring myself a disciple of the Son of Man, and in devoting my life and the renewed energy of my being to his brothers and sisters of my race. Henceforth, I am not *in* holy orders as a professional clergyman, but *under* holy orders as the servant of Christ Jesus.

"And if any man would still say that because of my lack of absolute assurance I have no right to the sacred post, I answer, let him cast the first stone who has never been assailed by such doubts as mine. And if such doubts have never been yours, if perhaps your belief is but the shallow absence of doubt, then you must ask yourself a question. Do you love your faith so little that you have never battled a single fear lest your faith should not be true? For what are doubts but the strengthening building blocks toward summits of yet higher faith in him who always leads us into the high places? Where there are no doubts, no questions, no perplexities, there can be no growth into the regions where he would have us walk. Doubts are the only means through which he can enlarge our spiritual selves.

"You have borne with me in my trials, and I thank you. One word more to those who call themselves Christians among you but who, as I so recently did myself, present such a withered idea of Christianity that they cause the truth to hang its head rather than ride forth on a white horse to conquer the world for Jesus. You dull the luster of the truth in the eyes of men. You do not represent that which it is, but yet you call yourselves by its name. You are not the salt of the earth, but a salt that has lost its savor. I say these things not to judge you, for I was one of you such a short time ago. But I say to you simply, it is time to awake! Until you repent and believe afresh, believe in a nobler Christ, namely the Christ of history and the Christ of the Bible rather than the vague form which false interpretations of men have substituted for him—until you believe in him rightly you will continue to be the main reason why faith is so scanty on the earth. And whether you do in some sense believe or not, one fact remains—while you are not a Christian who obeys the word of the Master, *doing* the things he says rather than merely listening to them, talking about them, and holding certain opinions about them, then you will be one of those to whom he will say, 'I never knew you: go forth into the outer darkness.'

"But what unspeakable joy and contentment awaits you when you, like St. Paul, can be crucified with Christ, to live no more from your own self but to be thereafter possessed with the same faith toward the Father in which Jesus lived and did the will of the Father. Truly our destiny is a glorious one—because we have a God supremely grand, all-perfect. Unity with him alone can be the absolute bliss for which we were created. Therefore, I say to you, as I say to myself: awaken your spirits, and give your hearts and souls to him! For this you were created by him, and to this we are called—every one."

37 Helen Awake

That Sunday dinner was a very quiet meal. An old friend of Mrs. Ramshorn's, a lady-ecclesiastic like herself, dined with them. What the two may have said to each other in private, I cannot tell, but not a single remark about Mr. Wingfold or his sermon was heard at the table.

As Helen was leaving the room, Bascombe whispered to her to put on something warmer and come with him to the garden. Helen glanced at the window as if doubtful. It was cold, but the sun was shining. The weather had little to do with her doubt, however, and she took a moment to think. She pressed her lips together—and consented. George could see that she would rather not go, but he put it down to sisterly unwillingness to enjoy herself when her brother could no longer look at the sun, and such mere sentiment must not be encouraged.

When the cypress tree had come between them and the house,

he offered his arm, but Helen preferred being free. She did not refuse to go into the summerhouse with him, but she seated herself on the opposite side of the little table from him. George, however, saw no hint of approaching doom.

"I am sorry to have to change my opinion of that curate," he began as he seated himself. "There was so much in him that promised well. But the old habits and the fear of society have been too much for him, I suppose. He has succumbed at last, and I am sorry. I did think he was going to turn out to be an honest man."

"And you have come to the conclusion that he is not an honest man."

"Of course."

"Why?"

"Because he goes on teaching what he says he is not sure about."

"He professes to be sure that it is better than anything he is sure about. You teach me there is no God; are you absolutely certain there is not?"

"Yes; absolutely certain."

"On what grounds?"

"On grounds I have told you twenty times, Helen, dear," answered George a little impatiently. "But I do not want to talk about them now. I can no more believe in a god than in a dragon."

"And yet a dragon was believable to the poets that made our old ballads; and now geology reveals that some such creatures did at one time actually exist."

"Ah! You turn the tables on me there, Helen! I confess my parallel a false one."

"Perhaps a truer one than you think," challenged Helen. "That a thing should seem ridiculous to one man, or to a thousand men, does not necessarily make it ridiculous in reality. And men as clever as you, George, have all through the ages believed in a God. Only their notion of God may have been different than yours. Perhaps their notion was a believable one, while yours is not."

"By Jove, Helen! you've progressed in your logic. I feel quite flattered! Since you have had no tutor in that branch of thought but myself! You'll soon be too much for your master, by Jove!"

Helen smiled a little smile, but said seriously, "Well, George, all I have to suggest is: what if, after all your inability to believe it, things should at last prove that there *is* a God?"

"Don't trouble yourself about it, Helen," returned George, whose mind was full of something else. He was anxiously trying to clear the way for a certain more pleasant topic of conversation. "I am prepared to take my chances. All I care about is whether you will take your chances with me. Helen, I love you with my whole soul."

"Oh! you do have a soul then, George? I thought you hadn't."

"It *is* a foolish form of speech, no doubt," returned Bascombe, a little disconcerted. "But to be serious, Helen, I do love you."

"How long will you love me if I tell you I don't love you?"

"Really, Helen, I don't understand you today. If I've done something to offend you, I am sorry, but I am quite in the dark as to when or how."

"Tell me then," said Helen, paying no attention to his clear annoyance and discomfort, "how long will you love me if I *do* love you in return."

"Forever and ever."

"Another form of speech?"

"You know what I mean well enough. I shall love you as long as I live."

"George, I could never love a man who believed I was going to die forever."

"But, Helen," pleaded Bascombe, "it can't be helped, you know!"

"But you are perfectly content it should be so. You believe it willingly. You scoff at any hint of possible immortality."

"But what difference can it make between you and me?" returned George, whom the danger of losing her had rendered for the moment indifferent even to his most cherished theory. "If there should be anything afterward, of course, I should go on loving you to the very extreme of the possible."

"While you don't love me enough now to wish that I might live and not die! That seems to me a rather small love. And whim though it might be, I would like to be loved as an immortal woman, the child of a living God, and not as a helpless—a helpless bastard of Nature! I beg your pardon—I forget my manners."

That a lady would say such a word—and Helen besides! George was shocked. Coming on the heels of everything else, it absolutely bewildered him. He sat silent. Presently Helen resumed: "Are you taken aback by my terminology? St. Paul, himself, used the term when he discussed the benefits of God's discipline. You doubt me, George? Read it for yourself, then—in the Epistle to the Hebrews, I believe.

"I have given you every advantage, George, but have wronged myself in the process. You come asking me to love you while my brother lies dead in the grave. When does one need love but at the time of death, and yet you come talking to me of love with the same voice that has only recently been telling me that the grave is the end of it all and that my brother is nothing anymore. For me at least, I will not be loved with the love that can calmly accept such a fate. And I will never love any man who believes that in the end even love will be swallowed up in a bottomless abyss.

"No, Cousin George, I need a God. And if there be none, how did I come to need one? Yes, I know you think you can explain it all, but the way you account for it is just as miserable as what you would put in its place. I am not complete in myself like you. I am not able to live without a God. I will seek him until I find him, or else die in the quest. Even if there be no God, in the end I shall be no worse than you would have me now."

Helen had come awake at last! It would have suited George better had she remained a half-moveable statue, responsive only to himself. He sat speechless—his eyes fixed on her.

"You need no God," she went on, "therefore you seek none. And if you need none, I suppose you are right to seek none. But I need a God—oh, how I need him, if he is to be found! And by the same reasoning, I will give my life to search for him. Goodbye, George."

As she spoke she rose and held out her hand to him. But in the tumult of more emotions than I can name—among the rest indignation, dismay, disappointment, pride, and chagrin, he lost himself while searching in vain for words, and ignored her offered hand. She turned and walked from the summerhouse.

George sat for some minutes as she had left him. Then he broke the silence in his own ears, and snorted, "Well, I'm damned!"

And so he was—for the time—and properly too, for he required it.

38   The Abbey

The next day the curate found himself so ill at ease that he determined to take the day off. His notion of a day off was a very simple one—a day in a deep wood with a book fit for alternate reading and pocketing as he felt inclined. Lately, no volume had been his companion but his New Testament.

There was a remnant of a real old-fashioned forest on the Lythe, some distance up. He headed there by the road, the shortest way, and planned to return along the bank of the winding stream. It was a beautiful day and a great calm fell upon him. Many were the thoughts floating through his mind as he walked, but throughout all of them ever and again had dawned the face of Helen, as he had seen it in church the day before. She had sat between her aunt and her cousin, yet so unlike either. To their annoyance, she had insisted on going to church, and to hers they had refused to let her go alone. And in her face the curate had seen something he had never seen in her before—a longing look as if she were actually listening for some morsel of truth to carry home with her. In that dawn of her coming childhood, the hard contemptuous expression of Bascombe's face and the severe disapproval of Mrs. Ramshorn's were entirely oblivious to him.

All the way down the river he reflected on this change in her. When he got back into the park, he sat down again on the same stone he had sat on the day my narrative opened, and reviewed the past twelve months. This was a similar day as that. Yet what a change had come about in him! That day the New Testament had been but the book of the church—today it was a fountain of living waters to the man Thomas Wingfold. Great trouble he had had stumbling through. Now a new trouble had come, but it also was a form of life. And he would rather love and suffer than return to never knowing Helen Lingard.

The sun was down before he left the park, and the twilight was rapidly following the sun as he drew near to the abbey on his way home. Suddenly he thought he heard the faint sounds of the organ coming from the church. Never before had he heard it on a weekday. Who could it be that was now breaking the silence of the vast place with such melodious sounds?

He entered the church just as there came a pause in the music. Then, like the breaking up of a summer cloud of rainshowers, began the prelude to Handel's "Thou didst not leave his soul in hell" from the Messiah. Up toward the organ room the curate softly crept. All at once a rich full contralto voice—surely he had heard it before—came floating out into the empty abbey.

He reached the door. Very gently he opened it and looked in. He saw the face of the singer; it *was* Helen Lingard!

She started. The music stopped, folding its wings like a lark into its nest. But Helen recovered herself at once, and rose to approach the curate.

"Have I taken too great a liberty?" began Helen.

"No, not at all," he answered. "I am sorry I startled you. I wish you would come here to make such sounds oftener."

"He didn't leave my brother's soul in hell, did he, Mr. Wingfold?" she said abruptly, her eyes shining through the dusk.

"If ever a soul was taken out of hell, it was Leopold's," returned the curate. "And it lifts mine out of it too," he added, "to hear you say so."

"I behaved very badly to you. I confess my fault. Will you forgive me?" she asked.

I love you too much to be able to forgive you, were the words in the curate's heart, but a different response found its way to his lips.

"My heart is open to you, Miss Lingard," he replied. "Take what forgiveness you think you need. For what I can tell, it may be my duty to ask for forgiveness, not to grant it. If I have been harder on you than I needed to be, I ask you to forgive me. Perhaps I did not enter enough into your difficulties."

"You never said one word more than was right, or harder than

I deserved. Regrettably, I cannot ask Leopold to forgive me in this world, but I can ask you and Mr. Polwarth, who were God's angels to him. I was obstinate and proud and selfish. Oh, Mr. Wingfold, do you really believe that Leopold is somewhere, alive at this moment? Shall I *ever* see him again?"

"I do think so. I think the story is true that tells us Jesus rose from the grave."

"Will you take me for a pupil—a disciple—and teach me to believe as you do?" said Helen humbly.

How the heart of the curate beat!

"Dear Miss Lingard," he answered, "I can teach you nothing. I can but show you where I found what has changed my life from a bleak November to a sunny June. Perhaps I could help you a little if you were really determined to find Jesus, but you must determine that for yourself. It is you who must find him. Words of mine may let you know that one is near who thinks he sees him, but it is you who must search, and you who must find. If you do search, you will find, with or without any help of mine.—But it is getting dark. May I see you home?"

"Yes—please," answered Helen. "Would you perhaps stay, and take some tea with me?" she added.

"With all my heart," replied Wingfold.

As they left by the north door, the abbey was silent, and so were the lips of the curate. But in his heart, praise and thanksgiving ascended to the ear that hears every thought as he worshiped the God and Father of the Lord Jesus Christ.

Without a word Wingfold gently offered Helen his arm as they walked outside. The church was dark, but in the sky above, and in each of their hearts, many stars were shining. Slowly and silently they made their way along Pine Street, neither anxious to reach Helen's door.

————

Thomas and Helen's story is taken up again in the sequels, *The Lady's Confession* (the story of Glaston's doctor, Paul Faber) and *The Baron's Apprenticeship.*